THE LAKEHOUSE

THE LAKEHOUSE

JOE CLIFFORD

Copyright © 2020 by Joe Clifford
Cover and jacket design by Mimi Bark

ISBN: 978-1-951709-10-5
eISBN: 978-1-951709-32-7
Library of Congress Control Number: 2020937779

First hardcover edition September 2020 by Polis Books, LLC
www.PolisBooks.com
44 Brookview Lane
Aberdeen, NJ 07747

POLIS BOOKS

This book is dedicated to the BHS class of 1988, from whom I draw so much inspiration

CHAPTER ONE

SUMMER

The last thing Tracy Somerset feels like doing on Wednesday at midnight is driving two towns over to Wal-Mart in a thunderstorm. But the cramps are getting the best of her, showing no signs of surrender. Tracy checks every cabinet for pain relievers. Upstairs, downstairs, center console in the Honda CRV. Nothing. She's tried fish oil, herbal tea, Vitamin B1. The meditative techniques her psychiatrist, Dr. Bakshir, gave her aren't working. Following thirty minutes of lying in the pitch black, alternating between total sensory deprivation and the "Calming Sounds of Oceanic Friends," hot compresses and digging knuckles into her skull, Tracy gives up. She needs chemicals. Midol, Advil, a goddamn aspirin, anything to alleviate the pressure building in her abdomen and skull so she can get some relief.

Tracy knows better than to wake a sleeping toddler, it took long enough to get Logan down, but the only person to call, her best friend Diana, isn't answering. No surprise. After her nightly wine and Ambien, Diana is dead to the world.

Nothing in Covenant is open after ten o'clock, so Tracy rouses a confused Logan and sets out for the twenty-four-hour superstore in Cromwell. She prays the sudden pulsating headache isn't the onset of a stroke at thirty-two.

Tracy isn't having a stroke. But after ten minutes stalking the witching-hour aisles at Wal-Mart, weaving between gangly weirdoes and ladies in flesh-colored tights, she isn't sure she's any better off.

And she's forgotten the stroller.

Logan is slung over her shoulder, an industrial sack of mulch from the gardening section. At almost two years old, Logan is a stout, solid boy, like his father, Brett, the cheating bastard. Yeah, she got her body back after giving birth. But no amount of Zumba or spin class can prepare you for the extra twenty-two pounds strapped to your back while navigating menstrual cramps in a sea of sleepless zombies. The padded weight presses on her spine and grinds down her knees, adding pulsating fuel to the intestinal fire.

That's when she sees him.

It is the eyes that get her at first. Otherworldly blue, brilliant cobalt, teeming with life. An odd thing to notice at a time like this, but right now, the pain unbearable, exhausting, Tracy has passed socially acceptable mores, bordering on hysterical. She can't stop staring. The romantic comedies she's been binging on are cheesy, the way they tease a spotlight when that special someone appears. But she swears he shines center stage. He notices her too.

"Let me help you," he says, reaching for Logan, before retreating when she instinctively snatches back her son. "Oh my God. I'm so sorry." The man holds up his hands. "Yeah. Strange man. Wal-Mart. Give me your kid." He covers his face, turning red. Embarrassingly cute.

"No, it's okay," she says.

"You look like you are having such a hard time."

Tracy feels like crying. It is more than the cramps, the headache. Sometimes the weight of the world conspires to drag you down. Divorced single mom in a small town, Tracy knows she is never leaving Covenant. Logan is her life, she loves being a mother, but the loneliness, the lack of options, the confinement gets to her. Innocuous at first, this sensation has been squeezing tighter, a boa constrictor working its way up methodically, immobilizing the legs, squeezing the diaphragm, and now it is crushing her skull with death-grip precision.

The man holds up a finger before taking off in a brisk walk, which turns into a fast jog, in the opposite direction, his exit one of the more bizarre ways she's been ghosted. Never mind how attractive he may've been, Tracy promises herself she'll never, ever run out of Ibuprofen again.

A moment later he returns pushing a new baby stroller, price tag rippling in the breeze.

"They're having a sale in aisle forty-seven."

Tracy lays down her sleeping boy. The relief to her spine instant, immediate, like unloading grocery bags stuffed with canned goods and gallons of milk. Logan doesn't open his eyes, lost in dreamland. Enjoy it while you can, kiddo.

She thanks the stranger, takes a deep breath, arches her back, stretching her vertebrae, willing her spine to realign. "You have *no* idea how much that kid weighs."

"I can imagine."

Tracy looks him over again, trying not to be too obvious about it. Her initial assessment wasn't wrong. He *is* a handsome man. In good shape, still has his hair, rare for these parts, around her age.

What is he doing here? If anything, he is *too* good looking, over-dressed for Wal-Mart, ironed Oxford and pleated pants. A professional. Not a man you find often in Covenant or its surrounding boroughs. Her eyes drift to his naked ring finger. She catches herself, pretending to be captivated by a sale beyond his hips.

"What are you doing here?" Less sleep-deprived, fewer contractions, she'd have more tact. "That was rude. Sorry. I'm out of it right now."

"I get it. Conversation doesn't come natural in an all-night Wal-Mart. Especially after a stranger tries to grab your kid."

"You were trying to help."

He smiles, perfect teeth, and points through a wall of bicycles, out the doors and into the still-warm night. "Just moved. Been a while since I had to shop for a single man. Who knew apartments don't come with toilet paper and shampoo?"

And she laughs. Less because it's funny and more because he feels as self-conscious as she does. This is the first conversation she's had with a man since Brett. At least one she isn't paying to fix her brakes, change her oil, or take Logan's temperature. This realization makes her pause, lament she's too late. Has she missed out on it all, college, spring break, girls' trip to Aruba, a rite of passage? A time when you are supposed to go wild and have fun. She married Brett so young. And they were together long before that. Which probably causes her to make a face, because then he makes a face, and it's weird again.

She reaches past him, up on the shelf, pulling down the tub-sized jar of Aleve she's been eyeing.

"I know how hard kids can be," he says.

"Do you have any?" Tracy is already twisting the top, spilling three into her anxious palm.

"No. Planned to ... didn't work out."

Tracy stops digging around her purse for the water bottle she doesn't have, looking up, mortified. "That's none of my business. I don't know why I asked that." She jams her fingers in her eyes, pressing so hard she sees spots. "It's this headache. I don't get them often. But when I do..."

"No, it's all right," he says. "I lost my wife."

"I'm sorry."

"We wanted kids, talked about having them. I spent so much time preparing to be a dad, I guess I feel like one. Does that sound strange?"

"Not at all."

Tracy can't invent a water bottle, and she needs something to wash down the pills. Ever since she was a little girl, the thought of dry-swallowing medicine makes her gag.

The man points past her shoulder, toward the cashiers. "There's a café over there. Will you let me buy you a coffee? Or water?" His blue eyes light up. "In a totally normal, non-creeper way."

Is she really getting hit on in a Wal-Mart at one a.m.? With her sleeping son by her side?

Why not? she thinks. What's the worst that can happen?

CHAPTER TWO

Mist hovers above the water of Shallow Lake, a lazy fog that whispers of yesterday's ghosts. Detritus and debris clutter the shore. Shorn tree limbs knocked down from last night's storm, broken boat hulls, jagged stones lapped by waves, the scene tinged cadaver grey, all bloodless flesh and unearthed bones. Or maybe Covenant Chief of Police Dwayne Sobczak knows what's waiting for him at the bottom of the ravine: the first homicide victim in Covenant in twenty years.

Then again, twenty years ago, Todd Norman didn't live here.

Sobczak glares across the water. Halted mid-construction, the lakehouse remains incomplete. Batter boards and corner stakes, craters dug for the septic, plumbing pipes laid. Foundation, studs, sill plates. A work in progress. But eventually the house will be a home. And then trouble will take up permanent residence.

Sobczak climbs down the shelf, rappelling with the thick roots of a felled oak spat back from the earth.

On the beach, he kicks though leftover party favors. Beer bottles and wet matchbooks, cardboard take-out from 7-Eleven. Weeks' old trash. High school kids come to the lake to torch bonfires, drink beer, and screw around. Sobczak doesn't begrudge harmless teenage fun, but have some civic pride and clean up after yourself.

Sobczak steps over crinkled chip bags stomped in the mud, tangles of fishing line, coffee tins used as chew spittoons. He makes a mental note to call Gus Spires, who oversees community service. Tell him to bring a bum from the drunk tank, put him on litter patrol. Unsightliness rankles the chief.

The dead girl, soaked tee shirt and underpants, ribboned with frogbit, lies beside the charred, black remains of a campfire. Woman, not girl. A quick glance puts the victim in her early thirties. But it's hard to tell. Are the creases gouging her flesh the result of age or something worse? Chief Sobczak knows everyone in his town. He does not know this girl.

He crouches, inspects. If not for the blue skin, she could be asleep. Midnight swim? Dragged down by a tide pool? In the pouring rain? Despite her proximity to the water, she does not appear bloated. Rules out drowning. People in their early thirties don't drop dead, half naked, for no reason. Looming over, Sobczak notes the bruising on her inner thighs, the flecks of blood, and now he must consider the possibility of sexual assault.

A handful of department employees, most of whom are volunteers, duck between the cleanup van, squad cars, and low-hanging branches. Covenant is too small to employ a permanent staff. Only the chief is full time. Mike Armstrong hands out white placards to the crew. Yesterday, he made Sobczak's grinder at the Main Street Deli. Rick Ingalls waits with the two witnesses who found the body. Weekends, Rick tends bar at the Pine Loft Pizzeria off Route 13. Tom Kies, Chief Sobczak's deputy, rolls out the yellow ticker tape and erects a sawhorse blockade.

"Tom," Sobczak calls, pointing up the ravine wall. "Extend that perimeter to Svea Road. Once the *Herald* and *Inquirer* hear about this… I don't want anyone touching a thing until Holland gets here."

Holland County has already been called. A larger municipality, Holland will be overseeing the official investigation. Covenant lacks the resources and manpower to deal with something as serious as murder.

Sobczak's particularly proud of Tom, his young deputy. Directing traffic, toting buckets, taking charge of the situation. Sobczak can also admit another reason for the soft spot: Tom is married to Sobczak's daughter, Amanda.

For Sobczak, there is nothing strange about working with his son-in-law, Covenant one big family to the chief, who takes pride getting to know members of the community. Every day, he takes to the streets to say hi, do outreach. He makes conversation whenever he stops for gas, coffee, a sandwich. He strives to be friendly, shake the absurd Hollywood stereotype that cops are somehow the "bad guys."

A pair of Holland's finest, one woman, one man, descend the mossy banks. Sobczak made the call but he's never worked with this pair before. Then again, he hasn't needed Holland's help in a while.

"Couple kids called it in," Sobczak hollers over the gurgling sounds of tributary brooks. "Came down to fish before their shift. Found her like this."

"Detective Stephanie Ronson," the woman says. She nods at her partner. "Steve Crasnick. Kids? How old? Where do they work?"

"Young men, I should say. Everyone's a kid to me these days."

Sobczak points up the ridge, where two young men wait with Rick by the squad car. "Kelly Harwood, Rob Pandolfo. Known them my whole life. Work over at American Goods, the paper mill. Good kids. They didn't have anything to do with this."

Crasnick pops a piece of gum from its aluminum seal. "How long she been here?"

"Hard to say," says Sobczak, trying to act like he's still running the show, even though everyone knows he's not. "EMT says at least a few hours judging by the way the blood's settled. I'm guessing your examiner will be able to pinpoint a more precise time of death.

Ronson steps between the two men, squats by the dead woman. She's starting to snap on the latex gloves, when she stops, stands back up, rips them off.

"What's the deal, Steph?"

"10-18. Overdose. Check the tracks. Between the toes." Ronson sounds almost disappointed.

Like Sobczak isn't even there.

"Excuse me, detectives. There's blood on her thighs." Sobczak hasn't gotten to the juicy part: the identity of the sociopath building the lakehouse up the beach, Todd Norman. Sobczak has concerns, theories. He doesn't get a chance to share either.

"Post-mortem," Ronson says. When Sobczak doesn't move fast enough, she gives the old chief a rudimentary lesson in police work, big-city cop condescending to two-bit yokel. "Blood coagulates in a certain way." She points at the dried blood on the thighs. "That isn't from vaginal trauma. It's splatter from being cut on jagged rock. Check the backs of her legs. When they were dragging her down here, they weren't gentle."

"Who's 'they'?"

"Drug buddies."

"She's not wearing any pants."

Ronson shrugs. "Probably wasn't when she OD'd."

"We don't have a drug problem in Covenant."

"Drugs are everywhere."

"This girl isn't from town," Sobczak says.

"Then she's from out of town. In any case, she didn't die here. She was dumped."

Without a goodbye, Ronson turns, heads back up the ravine, toward the witnesses, agitated over having been woken for this.

Crasnick slaps a hand on Sobczak's shoulder. He points at the woman's feet. "Tracks between the toes are signs of a secret user, long-time abuser. When we ID her, we'll find she had a job, an apartment, kept up appearances." Crasnick opens his palms, a religious offering. "Last night, she took a hotshot, strong shit going around, dope mixed with fentanyl, junkies dropping like flies. Whoever she was with, friends, boyfriend, dealer, didn't want to be on the hook for accessory. Prosecutors have been charging anyone in the room. Serious prison time."

Sobczak points up the shore. "You know who is building that lakehouse?"

"Yes, Chief, we know all about Todd Norman."

"You don't think it's coincidental?"

"I doubt anyone checked an address first. They picked the lake because it's out of the way. A man smart enough to beat a high-profile murder rap in New York City isn't going to be stupid enough to start dumping bodies in his backyard." Crasnick pans over the crowded wooded hills. "You don't get a lot of drug-related deaths. Ronson and I cover our share. This is an overdose. Nothing more.

"We'll be in touch after the official report." Crasnick shakes

Sobczak's hand goodbye. "Trust me," he says, walking away. "We all got eyes on Todd Norman."

CHAPTER THREE

Dr. Meshulum Bakshir is running late. Not technically, since he doesn't have a patient scheduled until ten, but the doctor strives to maintain consistency. The violent winds that blew through last night knocked out power grids and bowled over street signs, leveling weaker fences and scattering twigs, leaves, refuse. Garbage cans toppled, recycled papers strewn, the neighborhood a mess. Dr. Bakshir's windows held, but a hearty tree limb has impaled Paula Rosinski's Acura. Right through the windshield. The doctor laments not having taken better precautions. Pulling out of the driveway, he observes Paula, cellphone in hand, pleasant if forced smile plastered on her plump, rosaceaed face. She waves and the doctor waves back. He doesn't feel bad for Paula, these things happen, but the misfortunate of others often highlights our own good breaks. He'd heard about the storm on the evening news, not uncommon for this time of year, Indian summer in New England, high-pressure systems smacking against cold fronts, wreaking havoc in central Connecticut. Yet he'd taken no precaution. Warned winds might broach sixty miles an hour, he'd done nothing.

On his morning drive, Dr. Bakshir finds himself questioning whether he deserves his good fate. Which may seem silly. Who cares about an insurance claim? So the tree falls twenty yards to the left and he's the one standing in the driveway on a cool, blustery September morning, on hold with an adjuster, subjected to the insufferable sounds of muzak. But this is bigger than the collateral damage of thunderstorms. The Universe and trivial inconvenience, the course of human existence, fate versus stupid, blind luck. Does success hinge on hard work and rigorous emotional honesty? Or is it one big game of chance? Celestial slot machines, a fortuitous roll of the dice.

A felled power line blocks his usual freeway entrance at Christian Lane. By the time police detour traffic around Connecticut Light and Power's cleanup crew, Dr. Bakshir is deposited halfway across town, now over an hour late and very frustrated. The morning commute from Kensington to Covenant slogs, an endless red sea of brake lights and blinkers jockeying for position. Gripped in the throes of road rage, the doctor begins thinking of times and places he'd rather not revisit.

This lack of focus might be why he doesn't see the strange car until he has already parked at his practice and walked halfway across the lot, hands full with books and briefcase, keys clamped in his teeth.

A woman wedges out from the front seat. Late fifties, early sixties, at least ten years older than he, with clipped gray hair and dressed in a pair of men's baggy jeans, she plods forward with the gruff determination of an indefatigable tugboat from a child's bedtime story. Dr. Bakshir doesn't know everyone in Covenant. In fact, he knows very few. As the lone psychiatrist in a town that cherishes its privacy, the doctor makes a concerted effort to keep a low profile. But he's gotten adept at identifying types. Everyone fits one. This woman, he is certain, is in law enforcement. Repression.

All police officers display it. And, in this case, familiarity most certainly breeds contempt.

"Morning, Doc," the woman says. "I have a word?" From the way she plants her feet, the stance she assumes, he accepts dismissing her will not be easy. Rather than fight, he will make a joke.

"Did you bring your insurance card?" Dr. Bakshir laughs. The woman returns a courtesy chuckle.

They both know she is not here for psychotherapy. New patients in small towns like Covenant don't appear often. And they call first. The doctor first started practicing psychotherapy at Green Hills in Farmington. Many years ago. Overprotective parents, court-ordered teenagers. Insurance companies fuel group sessions. The program did not last long. These days, the doctor has an independent practice. Most of his work is one-on-one with patients he's known a long time. He's never worked with a cop. Because unless mandated, cops don't do therapy.

Dr. Bakshir tries shifting his briefcase to retrieve his keys. The woman reaches over his shoulder, holding the door open for him. The gesture is both kind and manipulative.

"Thank you," he mumbles, transferring keys from lock to hand, hand to pocket.

Dr. Bakshir turns on the foyer lights. The woman follows. The space, at one point, must've been someone's home, albeit a tiny one. You find several of these small Cape Cod-style homes throughout New England, single-family, starter homes. This is the layout: entryway, short hall, boxed kitchen, which the doctor uses to make his tea. The refrigerator gave out years ago. He never saw the need to have his landlord replace it, though that is his tenant right. The doctor doesn't use it often enough to justify the effort of either party. He's taken his lunch at the same café for years. He sometimes met Wendy there. He could justify that meeting spot because they were so close to his office. But she is gone now, and thinking of her nicks pieces of his heart, like microscopic paper cuts.

The space has the two main rooms. One he uses for an office, the other for sessions. The doctor toys with the idea of bringing this woman into the latter; he doesn't appreciate unannounced visits, demands on his time when he is not given a choice. Maybe he will turn on lullabies of the rainforest, serenade the stout cop with burbling waterfalls and pan flute. The doctor ignores this childish impulse, however amusing it may be.

He pantomimes for the woman to follow him into his office.

"Please," Dr. Bakshir says, dropping his belongings, gesturing at the fabric chair in front of his desk. "How can I help you?"

The woman pulls a business card from her wallet, passes it along.

Marjorie Jessup, Investigations.

A terse smile smears her lips. "Madge is fine."

"Am I in trouble, Madge?"

"I don't know. Did you do something, Meshulum?"

The doctor reads the card aloud. "Marjorie Jessup." For her sake, not his. These techniques to establish dominance are not intentional. He is not trying to manipulate. To not use these skills would be like a bird choosing to walk instead of fly. Investigations. No police department, no division. The doctor peers over the card at the shapeless woman, who more and more resembles a gray blob without borders. "Independent?"

She nods, one bob, a woman who wastes no time. "That's right, Meshulum."

He points at the framed degree above his head, grins. "Dr. Bakshir is fine."

Madge's face twists up, an attempt to mitigate the affront. The doctor does not like this woman, this independent investigator, showing up to his practice, foisting her presence upon him. Doing so is rude, unprofessional, inconsiderate. But the doctor also tries to avoid conflict whenever possible. Classic catch-22. So the doctor laughs, lets her know he is kidding. Aside from the initial spark of such a prank, Dr. Bakshir takes no joy in seeing another suffer. Such emotions are petty, the building blocks to an unhappy life. Madge chuckles. Dr. Bakshir laughs harder.

"First names are fine," he says. "Let's keep it casual."

"Sure. Let's do that, Doc."

Dr. Bakshir removes his eyeglasses, cleaning the lenses to give his hands something to do. Without championing vanity, the doctor also knows at forty-eight he is an attractive man. Alarmingly so to some. Which can impede treatment. This woman isn't here for treatment, and the doctor is, in no way, flirting with this older, homely woman. But he admits, on some base level, he is again asserting his superiority. He does not like when he behaves like this. A psychiatrist is not exempt from keeping destructive behaviors in check.

"Don't see many female private investigators."

"Do you see many male private investigators?"

"Touché."

Madge chaws, sucks air through her teeth, as if blowing a bubble without the gum. An odd display for a woman that age.

"Used to be my husband's business," she says. "Mostly bail jumpers. He died. I took over. I take the jobs I find compelling." She checks the clock. "This is my last case."

"Retiring?"

"Something like that."

No one speaks. He doesn't like her use of silence. Not speaking is a tactic he employs with his clientele. She is playing him, which causes Dr. Bakshir to display the signs of a nervous, fidgety man. A guilty man. There is no reason for an investigator to be in his office, not now, not today.

"How can I help, Marjorie?"

"Madge."

"Apologies. Yes, of course. Madge."

"The group home you taught at. Green Hills. Farmington. Ten or so years ago?"

"I didn't teach. I was lead psychiatrist. But I'm afraid I cannot comment on that."

"I already have your patients' names. Shannon, Beiko, Wendy—"

The doctor holds up his hand, repeats, firmer this time. "Again, as I said, I am not at liberty to comment."

"Okay," Madge says. "How about Todd Norman?"

The doctor waits for more. Madge doesn't add more, eyeing the doctor, as if this prolonged lull in conversation will make him confess to something he did not do.

"I am not sure what you'd like me to say."

"Is that because you can't reveal your patients?"

"I can neither confirm nor deny. But also, I've never met a Todd Norman. I suppose it is possible, over my many years as a psychiatrist, I could've encountered a man by that name. I'd have to look through my records. But, as you know, there are limitations to what I can answer."

"This would've been recently," Madge says. "He just moved to town."

"Then, no, I can say with absolute certainty. I have never met a man named…"

"Todd Norman. He was married to April Abbott. You remember her, don't you, Doc?"

"If there is nothing else…"

Madge Jessup seems to consider this, though whether weighing his truthfulness or considering some other angle, the doctor does not know, nor does he care to pursue this interaction further.

The investigator stands, collects her things, and makes ready to leave, stopping to shake the doctor's hand and thank him for his time.

"Do me a favor," Madge says. "When Todd Norman comes to see you, give me a ring."

Dr. Bakshir doesn't respond right away, too many variables to consider. Until curiosity gets the best of him. "What makes you so certain I will encounter this Todd Norman?"

"Because," Madge Jessup says slowly, "you are the only psychiatrist in town. And Todd Norman is a sick man."

CHAPTER FOUR

Killer in town. Dead body on the shore. Sobczak doesn't care what Holland County says. That's math anyone can understand, and too much coincidence for one day. The morning drags, Sobczak tasked with cleaning up the mess. Holland will do the heavy lifting, but it's up to Covenant to clear the scene, deal with the press, comb the beach, manage the unglamorous parts, and complete the busy work.

Joe Campbell changes the lens on his Nikon as he squeezes through the sawhorse barricade, moving Sobczak's way. Joe works at the Getty station on Main Street, in the shadows of the crumbling community center, fixing breaks and changing oil for housewives. In between the spotty photography gigs, Joe also handles paperwork for the town, filing things like W-2s and speeding tickets, which keeps him plenty busy.

"What else you need, Chief?"

Sobczak, still gnashing teeth over Holland's dismissal, cranes along the upper ridge. On the shelf, a giant tree has fallen in the forest. Its deep roots peel back the earth like an old carpet. A pair of local newspapermen, Eric Serafin and Marcus DeMata, champ to get a better look. So it begins.

"Snap pictures before they get in your way."

Sobczak walks the beach, tracing the water's edge around the bend of Shallow Lake, stopping at an inlet, taking in Todd Norman's ambitious project. Quite the structure. Now that the injunction has been lifted, construction is back on track. Stacks of lumber piled high beside rented machinery covered with tarps. The walls have been plumbed, braced, roof trussed. Sub-facia boards connect the rafters. Nothing Sobczak can do about it. Makes him sick.

Tom joins his father-in-law, following Sobczak's gaze to the patchwork outline. "You look ready to blow a gasket."

"April Abbott and Amanda used to be best friends," Sobczak says. "I remember April sleeping over when she was eight. Little pink bunny jammies. Amanda used to say April was the sister she never had."

"I know."

"That SOB killed his wife, Tom. And they let him walk. And now Todd Norman is moving here. The Abbotts are still in town. They shouldn't have to see the man who killed their daughter, walking free, flaunting it in their faces."

Tom turns back toward the dead woman, now covered up, carted off. "You think Norman had something to do with this?"

Sobczak watches as they load the victim into the van and slam the doors. "No. I don't know. Holland County says the woman overdosed, not a homicide. They're the experts."

Crows scatter from branches, filling the skies, an invasion. They swoop down, en mass, repositioned like sentinels on poles and power lines, keeping watch.

Tom turns back to Norman's house. "But you don't believe that."

"I don't know what to believe. Except the guy moves to Covenant and next thing you know we got a dead girl on the beach."

Tom scratches his head. "What's Holland's theory? Our vic was doing drugs, alone, by the lake, in the middle of a storm?"

"Holland says she died somewhere else. Body dump."

"Why here?"

Sobczak can only shrug.

Tom gestures toward the unfinished lakehouse. "You talk to him since he's been back?"

"Norman? No reason. Until now."

"Place doesn't look ready to live in yet."

Sobczak turns over his shoulder, up the access road, through the thick thatch of Covenant forest. "He's renting a small apartment in town, above Lucy's Bakery." Sobczak pulls cigarettes from his coat pocket. "Don't tell Amanda," he says, lighting up.

"Won't say a word."

"Only smoke when I get stressed." Sobczak takes a drag, doesn't speak, eyes focused across the water.

"Why would he dump a body in his backyard?"

"Who knows why some men do what they do?"

"He was cleared of the charges."

"Lawyers and money, son." Sobczak drops his cigarette, quashes the ember with his heel, picks up the butt, and sticks it in his pocket to throw away later. "Lawyers and money."

Memory is a funny thing. Sobczak remembers the murder of April Abbott like it was yesterday, knows the family well. Art Abbott was a rising star in local politics until a scandal derailed his aspirations. Amanda's friendship with the girl is fuzzier. After the childhood sleepovers and birthday parties, Sobczak wasn't as involved. That was Mary's department, navigating the ins and outs of teenage relationships. Of course, Sobczak drank back then; alcohol impacts recollection. He doesn't drink anymore. Save for his single nightly beer. Watching your wife die forces a man to make changes.

"Dad?" Tom peers up, a little kid trying to get his father's attention.

Sobczak glances over.

"Sorry. I tried 'Chief' and you weren't answering."

"Thinking about something else."

"Todd Norman."

"He's guilty, Tom. Holland is gonna do what Holland is gonna do. In the meantime..." Sobczak fits his sheriff's hat in place. "I think this merits a face-to-face."

"You want company?"

"No, I need you here." Sobczak places a hand on Tom's shoulder. He doesn't know much about his son-in-law's childhood, except that Tom's own father wasn't much of a dad. Second chances in life are rare.

When the chief is halfway up the beach, Tom hollers after him. "You need to come by for dinner soon."

Sobczak knows he needs to see his daughter more often.

But sometimes it's easier to chase killers than it is to mend bridges.

CHAPTER FIVE

"Still? A year later?" Diana swirls clouds in her coffee. "Did he run out of students to fuck?" Diana has no patience or sympathy for Tracy's ex Brett Coggins.

Tracy can't answer her question though. If she couldn't figure out her ex-husband when they were married, what's the point trying now? Marriage is difficult. There were more problems than the affairs. Brett is a liar. He lies about lying, the kind of man who says he had Chinese for lunch when it was really Italian. Pointless, inconsequential. But also brilliant long-term strategy for a perpetually unfaithful man. Anytime Tracy called him on these inconsistencies, he'd say it was an oversight, dismiss her concerns as grousing, needless paranoia. So when she'd catch the big stuff, he'd be able to act indignant, get to say, "Oh, not this again." This technique, Dr. Bakshir has taught her, is manipulation, fueling efforts to discredit and undermine, a form of gaslighting.

When Tracy got back from Wal-Mart last night, the email from her ex-husband was waiting for her. It seemed, on the surface, harmless, tender, flattering, even. But read more into it. More excuses, games, passive-aggressive baiting. He started out all fond remembrance, uncharacteristically sensitive. Brett's message was so open and unguarded Tracy suspected alcohol might be to blame. After spouting the profoundly obvious epiphanies that come with drinking alone after midnight, he got to his point: he wanted to give it another go. Reconciliation. For Logan's sake. At least think about it. Any other time, Tracy maybe falls prey. Loneliness is a horrible thing. But last night she'd had a date. Sort of. Over coffee, they'd talked about life, love, those parts of the human heart that truly matter in this maddening world. It felt like something real.

Tracy spirits around the living room, collecting the destruction only a twenty-month-old can produce, a toddler who is now, thankfully, at one of his two days a week in daycare. Two days doesn't seem like much, but Tracy needs the respite. Since Brett moved out, Tracy has been on her own. Besides Diana, she has no outside help. Brett's parents live in Massachusetts, where Brett teaches, and despite how much she loves her ex-in-laws, marriage is a package deal. Lose the husband, lose your new mom and dad. Tracy's own parents haven't been around for a while, so the loss of replacements hits extra hard. Tracy hasn't worked since the divorce, which means she could keep Logan home every day, but trips to the doctor and DMV are much easier without having to worry about disrupting naptime. Being a mother is what Tracy was meant to do. But it's a full-time job, twenty-four seven, no vacations. She'll take any break she can catch.

"That divorce was the best thing to happen to you," Diana says, hands wrapped around her coffee, sitting at Tracy's kitchen table. "I never liked him."

"You've made that clear." Tracy tosses robots and stuffies into the toy box.

"No, I'm serious. You're lucky."

"I'm lucky walking in on him having sex with that girl in our house?"

"A house you get to keep. And I know what that jerk has to pay you. So, yeah. Lucky." Diana gazes out the long window, over the deck and swimming pool, closed for the season. "Sorry about last night. Must've had the ringer off."

Through the woods, a long meadow of white snakeroot, baneberry, and dryer's greenweed leads to the shores of Shallow Lake, the large body of water smack dab in the middle of Covenant. Takes up half the town.

"What's going on over there?"

Tracy looks through the window, across the water to the opposite shore, where it appears construction is back on track. It is hard to see from this distance. "God, they're starting that up again?"

"Who moves to Covenant?"

"Someone started building that thing five years ago. I figured they'd given up." She thinks about last night and can't stop smiling.

Diana studies her friend, face pinched, quizzical. "What are you so giddy about?"

"I'm hardly giddy. I'm exhausted. I need a job, and if I get one, what do I do with Logan? Life goes on, alimony or not." Tracy rearranges the pillows on the sofa, a strategic pattern that is too neat, too orderly. A little too … OCD. Something else to discuss this morning with Dr. Bakshir.

Diana spins back around. "No, you've been acting weird since I got here."

Finished with her morning pick up, Tracy reheats cold coffee in the microwave. "I'm in a decent mood for a change. Is that a crime?"

"In your case? No. It's a miracle. There's something you're not telling me." Diana squinches an eye, intensifying her stare, as if to peer into Tracy's heart's deepest desire. "Please tell me you're not seriously considering taking that cheating asshole back."

Coffee in hand, Tracy joins her friend at the table. "Why would you say that?"

"You're swooning like you did in high school when you were crushing on some boy."

"I was with Brett in high school."

"When you weren't on one of your infamous breaks." Of all her high school girlfriends, Diana was the one who always stuck by her side. Lisa, Judi, Marlene, each got fed up with the Tracy-and-Brett drama. Diana did too. But she never shut Tracy out.

Across the lake, Tracy studies the outline of construction. An odd location for a home. Or not. Hidden by thatch and thorn, you'd have your privacy. At least from the road.

Then, a few hundred yards up shore, through heavier cover, swirling lights. Tracy points, Diana follows. "Looks like the cops." Tracy squints. "Is that an ambulance?"

"What are they doing down there?"

"No clue." Tracy repositions the fake fruit centerpiece, an arrangement that mirrors her childhood home, same plastic purple grapes snaking waxed maroon apples. Weird how repetition of the mundane can elicit such comfort. But it also makes her think of her mom and dad, and she relives the orphaning all over again.

"I know what you're thinking," Diana says. "That you'll never meet anyone in this town. You'll be stuck here, get older, lose your looks—which, by the way, will *never* happen because you are, and will always be, effing gorgeous. You'll be this single, old mom. But, honey, any man would be lucky—"

"I met someone."

Diana exaggerates the jaw drop.

"Knock it off."

"And you were planning on telling me this…?"

"Last night."

"I thought you said you were stuck at Wal-Mart in Cromwell?"

"I was."

"You met someone … at Wal-Mart?"

"Yes. We had coffee."

"At Wal-Mart?"

"Yes!" Tracy says, unable to stop giggling. God, it feels good to laugh. Something as frivolous as flirting, a crush. Nothing will come of it, this isn't high school, but it's a nice feeling nevertheless.

"Okay," Diana says, leaning in, wiggling fingers. "From the top, girl."

Tracy sighs like it's an inconvenience, but truth is she's happy to talk about it, anxious to do so, even. "He helped me out with a … situation."

"What kind of situation?"

Tracy tells her about the cramps and headache and carrying a passed-out Logan; about his coming to her rescue with a stroller.

"Knight in shining armor. Romantic. Old fashioned. I like it."

"Then he bought me a coffee. Out of the cooler. The café was closed."

"Because it was one in the morning."

"He was sweet."

"I'm happy for you. You deserve this."

"He lost his wife a few years ago." Tracy returns to the window, stares at the police lights. What is going on down there?

"You get his number?"

"He got mine."

"Ooh, this is like that movie we saw. How every great love story begins. Who is it? Do I know him? Where's he live?" Diana strains to think. "I know every single guy in this town worth a damn."

"He just moved here."

"What's he do?"

"I don't know. I didn't have him fill out a questionnaire." Tracy checks the clock on the microwave. "Shit. I'm late." She scoops up her purse and keys. "Besides, crazy as my life is right now, I don't have time for more than coffee anyway."

"Coffee's good. Maybe next time he can take you out during waking hours."

"I'm sure." Tracy snags her jacket, pointing at the mugful Diana is still drinking, feet up on the adjacent chair. "Feel free to hang around."

"Oh, honey, I plan to." Diana is fixated on the fracas down by the water. "This is the most excitement this town'll see all year. I'm not giving up a front row seat."

"Call me later."

"You know I will."

"Hey," Diana says as Tracy opens the door. "So I can do a Google search and make sure he's not some weirdo, what's this sexy stranger's name?"

"Todd," Tracy says. "Todd Norman."

CHAPTER SIX

The loud knock on the window doesn't startle Todd Norman. In fact, he doesn't even look over right away. Sobczak is not surprised. Norman's been answering this call for five years. He'll be answering it for the rest of his life.

Norman's beat-up red pickup truck is parked at Covenant Commons, the town shopping plaza. Given their proximity to the Home Depot, the chief guesses Norman is here to pick up construction supplies for his lakehouse. He followed him from his apartment, hoping for a more sinister destination. No luck. For the past ten minutes, Norman has sat idle in his truck, staring through the glass at nothing at all.

Todd Norman unrolls the window. "In or out, Officer?"

Sobczak glances at the filthy passenger seat, ruptured upholstery, tuffs of white insulation sprouting through cigarette burns in the pleather from generations of previous owners. The truck is clearly used, the kind bought at rock bottom prices in Darian. A long way from penthouse living.

Sobczak introduces himself, points to his left, at an adjacent Dunkin' Donuts. "Coffee's on me."

"Do I have a choice?"

"We all have choices, Mr. Norman. You have the choice of saying no. I have the choice of taking you down to the station and making this more official." The chief carves a smile. "I prefer cordial, don't you?" He waits patiently for a response. "Think of me as the town welcoming committee."

"Where's my fruit basket?"

Sobczak loses his smile.

Inside the Dunkin' Donuts, Sobczak orders a coffee, black with sugar, no cream. Over grinding beans, he asks Norman for his order, but Norman says he already had his morning cup.

Todd Norman follows Sobczak, who brings his coffee with him outside, to the little bench by the storefront. The chief sits. Casual. September retains the heat of summer but you can feel the change coming. Soon it will be cold enough to see your breath. In this part of New England, change can happen overnight. Sobczak wants to enjoy being outside while he can.

"Why don't you take a seat?" Though both men know Sobczak is not asking.

Sobczak pans over the parking lot, at the glut of cars and minivans arriving, the young mothers pushing small children in buggies. Besides the Home Depot and Big Y supermarket, the plaza comprises mostly niche baby boutiques. Mommy and Me. Little Sailors. Princess and the Pea. Sobczak wonders when Amanda and Tom will give him a grandbaby.

He pulls his cigarettes, holds them up. Norman says no thank you. Sobczak didn't expect the tight-buttoned banker man to say yes. Still, he likes to be polite. "I'm quitting again tomorrow," the chief says, laughing at his own joke.

Todd Norman does not laugh. Murder charges aside, Sobczak

wonders what any woman would see in the guy. Besides the money, which, judging by the sad state of his truck, he doesn't seem to have much of these days. Sure, he's good looking enough, but so are most men that age. Overall, Todd Norman seems joyless, devoid of charm, dead-eyed, a real wet blanket.

Neither speaks for a spell.

Norman cracks first. "What do you want, Chief?"

Good. Let him feel the urgency.

The big cop flicks a contemptuous finger, across the buzzing highway, over the tops of still-green trees, toward the lake. "You still planning on building that house of yours?"

"Yes." There is no pause before Norman answers. No hesitation. No shame. The expediency irks the chief.

"You think that's a smart move?"

"Not sure how to answer that."

Sobczak flirts with notions of sympathy, how difficult life would be for a truly innocent man. Except Norman is guilty, certain as Sobczak is still alive and breathing. What they are engaged in now is quintessential cat and mouse, a game of show and tell.

Okay, Mr. Norman, we'll play your game.

"What do you expect from your investment?" Perhaps speaking Norman's language will help.

"In terms of real estate value? Very little. Property doesn't appreciate much in these parts."

Norman is toying with the chief, and Sobczak does not like it.

"You worked in finance back in New York, right? Investment banking. Not exactly a lifestyle upgrade."

"The position is not as glamorous as TV would have you believe."

"Long hours?"

"Among other things."

Sobczak cracks the lid on his cup to let the steam escape. "We know about you."

"Am I supposed to be hiding something?"

This makes Sobczak chuckle. "Can I be frank, Mr. Norman?"

"It's all the same to me."

"We don't think it's smart for you to move to Covenant."

"We?"

"We're a small town. Covenant. A community. Everyone knew April Abbott. My daughter knew April Abbott. Several ex-class-mates still live in town." Sobczak takes aim into the ether. "Her parents still live in this town."

"I'm well award." Voice calm, composure collected. No indication of nervousness. His hands never shake.

"Suppose someone lets it leak," Sobczak says. "Suspected murderer Todd Norman has moved to Covenant, hometown of his alleged slain victim. Papers pick up on it. Becomes the talk of the town." He points through the forest. "That's his house right there, on the banks of Shallow Lake, middle of nowhere. Works alone every day. Here's the address. Go say hi."

"If there's nothing else," Norman says, getting to his feet. "I need to pick up lumber—"

"Actually, there is," Sobczak says, pushing himself up, which takes more effort than he'd like. "You have an alibi for last night?"

"Alibi?"

"Someone who can vouch for your whereabouts. Between one and three a.m."

"Isn't that when most people are sleeping?"

"Most people."

"This is harassment."

"Don't think a judge would agree." Sobczak again gestures through the dense Covenant woods, toward the lakehouse. "Found a dead woman this morning. Right on the beach. Not far from your place. Either you give me an alibi, or looks like you're gonna spend whatever savings you got left fighting another murder rap." Sobczak drops his hands by his cuffs, leaves them there, lets them linger.

"Yes, I have an alibi."

Sobczak pulls back. He'd been waiting to bring up the body, wanting to get a read, a handle. He'd come to shake down Norman, suss out a few things. Rattle his cage, smoke him out of the hole. But Todd Norman does not disturb easy.

Or maybe the man is one stone-cold killer.

"An alibi, eh?" Sobczak says. "Okay. Name and number."

CHAPTER SEVEN

For the three years she's been in therapy—the two before the divorce and this past one repairing the damage—Tracy can't remember walking into Dr. Bakshir's office feeling this hopeful. It's more than a chance encounter at a midnight Wal-Mart. Tracy is old enough, smart enough, to know nothing will come of it. At thirty-two, she's more grounded than ever. Okay, that's not true. She still gets the sads, can feel lost and alone. Without Diana and Logan, she *is* alone. But she was meant to be a mother. Which makes it hard to outright hate Brett. Without Brett, there is no Logan. Get rid of her demons, the angels might leave too.

But that doesn't mean she has to spend the rest of her life feeling lonely, either. This is bigger than Todd, a man she spoke with for less than two hours. The experience has shaken Tracy out of her rut—the ludicrous notion that her life will forever be a staid series of mind-numbing twenty-four-hour loops and brain-dead interactions punctuated by Hollywood-manufactured stereotypes of romance, buoyed by mid-priced wines and lowered expectations. Sometimes it happens like that. Song comes on the radio at the right moment. Smell a sprig of lavender at a certain time of year.

Wind blows along the shore and you taste cotton candy and the salt in the air, suntan oils, lime, and like that you are young again. We get locked into patterns. We don't notice another year has gone by. And then another, and another, faster and faster. And, no, she hasn't been miserable, or even unhappy. Not exactly. But this is also her reminder: she can be something bigger.

Yes, this is what Tracy will talk about with Dr. Bakshir today. She likes to prepare for her sessions, mentally outline subjects, develop topics, instead of staring mindlessly at her phone in the waiting room. Therapy is work, on both ends.

But before she can hit the buzzer, Dr. Bakshir jerks open the door. He does not look well. Clichés aside, the first thought that pops into Tracy's brain: like he's seen a ghost. Eyes plagued with concern, system overload, the sole witness to a horrific accident. A deer flattened on a country road, a doe about to give birth. The baby didn't make it. It's that kind of look.

"Is everything okay?" A stupid question. But that is what we do in these moments, isn't it? Like when someone's sister has cancer. Is there anything I can do? Of course not. Nature is in charge, not you.

"I'm sorry, Tracy," the doctor says. "Something has come up. I have to cancel today's session."

She double-checks her phone. Five minutes till ten.

"I apologize I didn't call sooner. Of course, you won't be charged."

"Oh, sure. No problem." Tracy shoulders her bag. "Hope, um, you feel better." Tracy has cancelled sessions, several times. When Logan's been sick or Diana's planned an impromptu day at the beach. But when the doctor cancels, it feels like rejection.

Tracy wants to say something more but can't think of what;

Dr. Bakshir is already ushering her out the door. "I'm sure it's just a head cold," he says, agreeing with her premature assessment of illness for convenience sake.

They don't even reach the door before Dr. Bakshir peels off, returning to his office and computer. From afar, Tracy spies a newspaper article on the monitor. A grainy photograph of a body on the beach, a headline she can't make out. The doctor spins around, smiles, and slams his door shut.

Was it something she said?

As she makes her way into the small parking lot, the police car is turning in. Chief Sobczak, Covenant's police force. Like everyone in town, Tracy knows the chief. Though mostly she remembers him as Amanda Sobczak's father. Tracy wasn't friends with Amanda in high school. Two grades below, Amanda was part of the too-cool-for-school crew, Regina George of the Plastics. Which isn't fair. But the movie had just come out, the comparison an easy one to make. Truth is, Amanda was always nice to her. It was a numbers game. Amanda, April, Amber Coit, four is a crowd. Everyone called them "the A-holes" when they weren't around. Tracy can admit envy played a role in the nickname. Amanda, April, and Amber, pretty, popular, and perfect. You either wanted to be them or be with them.

Why are the cops at Dr. Bakshir's? Has something happened? She turns back to the office. Is that what had the doctor so distraught? Tracy knows little about the doctor's personal life. Married? Father? Divorced? Has a loved one been in an accident?

Don't be one of these annoying, nosy suburban housewives, Tracy tells herself. Housewife? She's not married anymore. She continues to her car, expecting the chief to blow past, but Sobczak cuts her off.

"Do you have a second, Tracy?"

Tracy stows her keys, slow to process why the chief of police would want to speak with her.

The big, old cop rocks back on his heels. He reminds Tracy of an old Western. A man's man from a forgotten yesterday, like a discount John Wayne. Not that he resembles a movie star. Big nose, less hair, pear-shaped body. It's the hitched-up gate, the slow, serious manner in which he moves, his presence expansive, like his entire being would fill the screen. And he's a man of few words. In all the time Tracy's lived in Covenant, which is her entire life, she hasn't exchanged more than a handful with the guy.

"Hello, Chief," Tracy says. "How are you?" It's been a while since she's talked to him. So long in fact it's hard not to think of him as Amanda's dad, Mr. Sobczak.

"Fine, Tracy. Just fine. Sorry to bother you." He motions toward the doctor's practice. "I didn't mean to invade your privacy."

Coming to her therapist's office *is* weird, now that she thinks about it. Dr. Bakshir's place is off the beaten path, the only thing nearby, a tiny deli no one in Covenant goes to.

"I stopped by your house," the chief says. "Your friend told me I'd find you here." He nods over the hedgerow buffering the street. "I was waiting till you finished."

He was watching her?

"What did you need?"

The chief hooks thumbs behind his buckle, brow clipped, all business. "Last night. Around one o'clock a.m. Would you mind telling me where you were?"

Tracy's first thought is, Good news travels fast! She immediately feels stupid for thinking this. Why would the town sheriff care about her emotional journey?

"What's this about?"

"If you could just tell me where you were around one a.m., I'll be on my way and you can get on with your day."

"Um," Tracy stammers, trying to understand why he cares. "Wal-Mart. I had a bad ... headache ... and was out of aspirin. I couldn't sleep." He doesn't need to know about her menstrual cramps. "Logan and I drove to Cromwell."

"Were you alone?"

"No, I just told you. I had Logan with me."

"Did you speak with anyone else while you were there?"

"Yes. A man helped me. Logan was getting heavy and he grabbed a stroller—"

"Did you happen to get his name?"

"Todd. Todd Norman."

"And how long were you with Mr. Norman?"

"I wasn't *with* Todd." Tracy resents the implication, even if she's not sure what's being implied. "He helped me get some Ibuprofen."

"That's it?"

"What else do you think happened?"

"When did you leave Mr. Norman?"

"I don't know. After a while?"

"I need to account for Norman's whereabouts."

"Why?"

"Please, Tracy. Just tell me how long you were with Todd."

"Again, I wasn't *with* Todd. We had coffee, talked. Is that a crime?" Tracy will later feel stupid for taking so long to get up to speed. If she isn't at the therapist, maybe her head is in a different space, maybe she's not thinking about life paths and failed marriages, worried about dating again in a small town where everyone loved her ex-husband, thought he was a swell guy, a real catch, because that's what last night really opened up. Maybe *she's* the catch. Her whole life she's been a girlfriend, a wife, now a mom. Last night reminded her, above all, she's still a woman. She has hopes, dreams, desires, wants that extend beyond these stifling, convenient definitions.

"There is nothing wrong with a single woman—which I am—talking to a man. Even in Covenant. Jesus. This town…"

"From one a.m. till?"

"I don't know. Three?"

"Two hours? You had coffee and … talked … for two hours?"

"I don't know what you are suggesting." Tracy is still fighting that part of her that feels judged, shamed. Hester Prynne and scarlet letters were born here.

Tracy turns to get in her car, irate. The questions irritate, yes, but something deeper has been touched.

"Listen to me," Chief Sobczak says. "Todd Norman is a bad man. Stay away from him."

CHAPTER EIGHT

Dr. Bakshir sits at his computer, scrolling through the online edition of the *Journal Inquirer*. After Madge Jessup left, he'd sat down to read up on Todd Norman.

He didn't get far. Another story caught his eye first.

They found her.

The doctor re-reads the short article. It doesn't seem real.

Body Found At Shallow Lake Identified
By Eric Serafin, *Journal Inquirer* Staff Writer

The body found this morning on the shores of Shallow Lake has been identified as Wendy Mortensen, 30, former resident of Covenant, Connecticut. Mortensen had been living for the past several years in Meriden. Cause of death is being listed as heroin overdose…

Wendy Mortensen was a former patient of Dr. Bakshir. He met her twelve years ago when he was at Green Hills. The doctor had arrived with an impressive pedigree. His work was considered cutting edge, blending cognitive and behavioral therapies in a unique way, making his services highly sought after. Idealistic, Dr. Bakshir thought he could do the most good at Green Hills, which targeted teens, cutting a wide swath across socio-economic backgrounds.

The summer he began sticks in his memory, vivid, fresh, fragrant, pungent as the pollen-saturated air that invades New England each June. The distinct scent fills his nostrils again, brings him back to a special place, a special time. Though barely a decade's passed, the doctor laments a lifetime lost.

Like everyone in Covenant, the doctor is aware of the fate that befell April Abbott. The generic name Todd Norman, however, never entered his consciousness.

But that isn't what plagues Dr. Bakshir most.

It's not what he knows about them. It's what the rest of them know about him.

He stares at the grainy photograph. Black and white, pixelated, shot taken too far away, zoomed in on afterward, the hallmark of shoddy, amateurish work. The doctor closes the browser. He needs to get that picture of Wendy, shrouded in a sheet, out of his head.

He walks to the window and sees the police car, an officer standing alone, in his parking lot. This is both a surprise and not totally unexpected. He's been preparing for this conversation, but he is not ready to have it yet. Dr. Bakshir's heart seizes, anxiety gripping. The events are out of order. Dr. Bakshir is a brilliant therapist with a deft grasp on the human psyche. Although he suffers one fatal flaw: disruption of order can leave him unhinged, unsettled, less than precise. If events transpire as they should, cogent, cohesive, orderly, the doctor remains composed, is able to answer reasonably, adequately, professionally. But they are here too soon. Their presence is invasive, inconsiderate, rude.

The big cop glances back at the doctor's window. Their eyes lock.

Then the cop turns, climbs in his car, and drives off.

Dr. Bakshir releases his breath, alarmed to find he's been holding it so long.

***

By the time Tracy Somerset gets home, she is worked up. She knows Brett is well loved throughout this town. Played in that stupid horn band with his brothers for years. Great guys. Ask anyone.

But that's not why the cops needed Tracy to verify an alibi. Cops don't visit your therapist's office to check up on the aftermath of an ugly divorce. When she throws her purse across the counter and the contents tumble out, it feels like her insides are spilling as well. When the lipstick hits the floor, she stops fuming long enough to realize she's let it get personal, assuming intentions, something Dr. Bakshir has often warned her about, instead of hearing what Chief Sobczak was actually saying.

Todd Norman is a bad person.

Of course he's bad news, Trace. You like him.

Tracy logs in and pulls up a search engine. She doesn't have to search far. Chief Sobczak wasn't trying to scare her, and this has nothing to do with Brett.

April Abbott's murder in New York City five years ago was big news in Covenant. But the name of her accused killer never registered. Todd Norman. Such a simple, common name. Non-descript, ordinary, unmemorable. The more she reads, the more snippets and details creep in. Investment banker, insurance scam, the plot of a dozen bad books and countless movies. No one ever gets away with it. Except, apparently, Todd Norman.

She'd just supplied an alibi. For a killer. She'd let him near her son. She'd given him her number, which also means he can get her address. She could be his next victim!

The more she reads, however, the harder it becomes reconciling portraits of a psycho killer with the kind man from last night. Then that little voice: all those crazies are charming. Richard Ramirez. Ted Bundy. Jeffrey Dahmer. No one ever describes sociopaths as lacking charisma. How off is Tracy's moral compass that she couldn't pick up on that?

Against better judgment, she keeps reading about the murder, getting reacquainted with particulars, beating herself up along the way. Of course Todd Norman denied the charges. Said he'd been out getting flowers. The prosecutor maintained the alibi was too tidy, convenient, orchestrated to provide amble cover for a hired assassin. The defense argued against motive. Todd Norman was already a wealthy man; he didn't need the insurance money. The prosecution painted the portrait of a greedy man unhappy in his marriage who wanted more. The jury sided with Norman: not guilty on all counts. Afterward, his ex-in-laws, the Abbotts, slapped an injunction to stop him from building on their property. He beat that rap too.

That is *his* lakehouse across the water.

This is why Todd Norman has moved to Covenant.

And now a dead woman has been found on the beach, a few hundred yards from his door. Mere hours after she'd been talking to him. That's why the police were down there this morning.

Tracy jumps up and checks to make sure the door is bolted, a pointless precaution. This isn't a horror movie, and if someone wants in her house, a single-latch lock isn't keeping them out.

Tracy waits for the heart rate to spike, the anxiety to flood. Why isn't she panicking? Something about the story doesn't feel right.

That whole production in Wal-Mart to establish an alibi?

She researches the dead woman on the beach. Wendy Mortensen. Heroin overdose. No foul play suspected. April died from blunt force trauma to the head, beaten to death with a landline telephone. The article says Mortensen, a drug addict, died somewhere else and fellow junkies tossed the body.

How does that add up?

After Tracy gets Logan from daycare, she is visiting the Covenant precinct to get some answers.

CHAPTER NINE

Fat raindrops fall and the temperature drops by several degrees. Sobczak starts the slog to the precinct. This day is not going the way he'd hoped. Corpse at dawn. Drugs and riff-raff infiltrating his community. Psycho killer on the loose.

But a psycho killer with an alibi.

This rankles the chief, like a chunk of gamey chicken in the stew clogging his esophagus. He has no reason to believe Tracy Somerset is lying. He is still waiting on official word from Holland. A quick visual is all well and good, but until he hears it from the medical examiner, Sobczak isn't willing to chalk up location and timing to happenstance. How cold-blooded can a man be? Help a woman with her toddler in the middle of the night, buy her coffee, have a pleasant two-hour chat, and then immediately go out, pick up another, and kill her? Sobczak does not like Todd Norman, and he sure does not appreciate this scam artist being in his town. But Sobczak is, above all, a cop. Facts before prejudice. He goes by the book because that book has stood the test of time and, more often than not, that book is proven correct. Right now, that book appears to be offering conflicting reports.

An identity of the victim would help.

Sobczak pushes through the front door.

"Nice work, Chief," Ron Lamontagne, one of the town's maintenance workers, says.

"Huh?"

Tom enters from the copy room. "Body was ID'd. Wendy Mortensen. Thirty. Meriden."

The name sounds familiar but the chief's not sure why.

Tom waves Sobczak past Ron and the smattering of phones that seldom ring, toward a corner. By the water cooler, Tom fills a cup, passes it to the chief. "*Journal Recorder* already has it online. Originally from Covenant. Parents divorced. Mom and brother moved out of state."

"I don't remember any Mortensens."

"Might've been before your time. Hard as that is to believe." Tom jabs the chief's shoulder to let him know he's kidding.

"Did you go to school with anyone by that name?"

"Don't think so. But, hey, we got a positive ID. That's good, right?"

"Be nice if someone would've let me know."

"Tried calling."

Sobczak checks his phone. No missed calls. Nothing came over the radio. No big deal. This isn't on Tom.

"Holland got all this?"

Tom nods. "Talked with a Detective Ronson half hour ago. Medical examiner confirmed. Overdosed elsewhere, body transported. Also got a TOD." Time of death. "Harder to pin down because it's an OD. They think she injected the drugs around midnight. Might've even still been alive when whoever dumped the body. Guess Wendy was working part time as a medical coder for some temp agency."

"Where was she living?"

"Meriden. Had her own apartment."

"They had that big fentanyl bust a few months back. Don't you have a buddy on the force over there? Play golf together?"

"Pat Foster. Used to hit the links at Timberlin." Tom checks past Sobczak's shoulder to make sure Ron's not listening. "Why dump a body from Meriden at Shallow Lake? So close to Norman's place?"

Tom has a point. The Connecticut River, the vast woods along Interstate 84 or 91, an alley in the city, one of the myriad quarries in the state. There are plenty of places to dispose of a body. Riskier to be driving around, middle of the country, in a strange car at three a.m. Asking to be pulled over. Then again, who ever accused drug addicts of being smart?

"Maybe they knew her?" Sobczak says. "Wanted to bring her home?"

"Norman off the hook?"

"For now. Has an alibi anyway."

"You think he's lying?"

"I don't know what to think."

The front doors blow open. A woman swinging a car seat marches in. Tracy Somerset.

"Where's Chief Sobczak?"

"Over here," Sobczak says affably. First rule of policing: defuse when possible, keep everyone calm. The woman has murder in her eyes. Sobczak, as always, puts himself in position to play peacemaker.

The boy fusses in his seat. She unlatches the car carrier, and her son wriggles free, tottering off to explore the precinct, reaching for cords and plugs, the assorted bright colors of tangled telephone wires. She tries to corral him. But he's off, a running back slipping tackles, challenging gravity.

"It's okay," Tom says, moving toward the boy. "I was just telling the boss here how much my wife and I want kids. This'll give me hands-on training. What's his name?"

"Logan," Tracy says.

Tom crouches eye-to-eye with Logan, greets him with a beaming smile. "Want to see some of our toys?"

"We have toys?" Sobczak says.

"Park and rec next door."

"We have a park and rec?"

"Good one, Chief."

The boy jumps at the promise of playtime. Tracy appears calmed down, if only by degrees. Sobczak hopes she's changed her tune about Todd Norman. By now she's researched the man, read up on his past. Sobczak will use any ammunition he can get to force the SOB out of town.

The chief waves Tracy into his office, the only one with a door at the Covenant precinct. Sobczak lowers the blinds halfway. You want transparency. But with the door closed, Sobczak becomes aware of how foul the room smells, the ripe odor of a fifty-six-year-old man's trapped quarters. When Mary was alive, she made sure everything was laundered, would tell him when he could use a spritz of Febreze. All these little things the chief can't do for himself.

Sobczak walks around his desk, drops in his chair, less because he is tired and more because he wants to put distance between them. He understands being a tall man is intimidating. "What's on your mind, Tracy?"

"What was that earlier? Coming to my doctor's, bombarding me with questions?"

"I needed to verify the whereabouts of someone."

"Todd."

"Yes, Todd Norman."

"The same Todd Norman who was accused of *murdering* his wife in New York City five years ago? You didn't think to, maybe, tell me that?"

"I told you he was a bad man and to stay away from him. I didn't know he would be shopping at Wal-Mart the other night or I'd have told you sooner."

"This isn't funny. I have a son. He has my number. And what's this about a ... dead body ... by the lake? Did he have something to do with that?

"Please, sit down."

"I'd rather stand. Thank you."

Sobczak would love to hang the Mortensen rap on Norman. But he is not going to fabricate evidence and needlessly scare residents. "Far as we can tell," he says, "Todd Norman didn't have anything to do with the woman by the water."

"Didn't you find her near his house?"

"Few hundred yards down the shore, yes. Reports indicate the young lady had a drug problem, overdosed. Norman isn't living at the lakehouse. He's renting a small apartment in town until he finishes it."

"How do you know he didn't inject her?"

"No evidence supports it." Though the possibility always exists of a deliberate hotshot. Who'd want to kill a junkie? "There doesn't seem to be any pattern, no MO." Sobczak stops, leans across his desk, fighting frustration. Damned if you do, damned if you don't. "Tracy, *you* provided his alibi."

"That was before I knew I was talking to a possible murderer."

"If you weren't with him last night, now's the time to tell me."

"I was with him. I'm not lying. We had coffee, from one till maybe three. Maybe two-fifty?" Tracy takes a calming, collective breath. "Did he do it? In New York? Did that man really kill his wife? I remember April."

Yes, the chief thinks, he killed her. But she isn't asking his opinion. Facts. Stick to the facts. "Todd Norman was cleared by a court of law. I have faith in our justice system. The courts get it right more often than not."

"I'm sure O.J. would agree." Tracy tilts back her head, grinds her jaw, as if she wants to scream; instead, she chokes out a stilted laugh.

Sobczak pushes himself out of his chair, comes around to her side. As the chief of police in this small town, he has more than one job. It pains Sobczak to say these things since he *does* believe Norman is guilty. But he has no more proof of that than the NYC prosecutor's office.

He takes Tracy's hand, a concerned dad. "I know this is a scary situation."

Tracy peers up, momentarily soothed.

"When we talked last night," she says, "he seemed like a nice guy. A good guy. More than helping me with Logan or the coffee afterward. He *was* a good guy. At least I thought so. And if I was wrong about that…" She doesn't have to finish the sentence.

"You worry about being a mom. Let me handle the law. We will be keeping an eye on Todd Norman. In the meantime, stay away from the internet. Don't answer numbers you don't recognize. If you see something suspicious, call." Sobczak walks Tracy to the door. "There's nothing we can do legally to stop him moving here. But we won't make it easy."

After she leaves, Sobczak reflects on what it must be like for Tracy, single mother, the humiliation of having been cheated on, the whole town knowing her business. Tracy is not a stupid woman. The onus of her ex-husband's infidelity doesn't fall on her. Brett Coggins lied to her, pretended to be something he wasn't. How can you defend yourself against that kind of duplicity? Against someone who chooses to live their life behind a mask?

Tracy sits in the Covenant PD parking lot, boiling inside but working to keep it together. Logan doesn't need to see his mother losing it. Tracy is grateful to officer Tom Kies for keeping her son entertained. Tracy remembers going to school with Tom, or rather being in school with him at the same time. Not the most attractive guy in town—not the worst either—but in Covenant, pickings are slim. She recalls a quiet kid, neither athlete nor artist. More of a wallflower. Surprising he'd marry a social darling like Amanda Sobczak, on whom the spotlight naturally shines. But high school is a weird time. And post-graduation in a small town only gets weirder. Marriage becomes a game of musical chairs. Tracy might've picked her seat too fast, but at least she had somewhere to sit, everyone else left scrambling to beat the music. Look at Diana. Not a worthwhile eligible bachelor remaining. Todd Norman is the best catch in town, and he might be a killer.

Driving home, Logan gibberishing to himself in the backseat, Tracy thinks about high school, a time she doesn't often revisit. Outside of Diana, Tracy doesn't see much of her other friends.

She's stayed in contact with Lisa, Marlene, and Judi on social media. Instagram. Pinterest. These aren't close friendships. Who has that many intimate friendships at thirty-two? Maintaining friendships requires time and effort. Tracy doesn't have much to spare of either.

Late-day traffic clogs Route 49, all the songs on the radio lie, and Tracy can't stop thinking about pom-poms and keggers. First kisses and crushes, the slow dances. In between Brett and the breakups, she remembers the flutters and tiny heartaches, the furtive little feelings, how good it felt to fall for someone new.

Tracy isn't taking any calls from Todd Norman. Cleared or not, a murder charge is a deal-breaker for any sane woman. She's watched enough *Dateline* to know the danger of predators lurking in small-town USA. But no matter how hard she tries, she can't reconcile fantasy with reality. A couple enjoyable hours over coffee shouldn't be able to erase the severity of manslaughter, acquittal or not. She hates considering the other possibility: maybe she doesn't care because she disliked his dead wife so much.

Tracy's initial reaction to learning April Abbott was dead: so what? God, that makes her a terrible person, she knows. No one deserves that fate. But the scars of middle and high school cut deep. Amanda, April, and Amber really were assholes. Tracy remembers the day the three girls slathered their hands in silver nitrate, which they'd stolen from the chemistry lab, slapping Brenda Prescott in the face, leaving palm-sized imprints on her flesh. What was that about? Tracy can't recall. Brenda making out with some boy? Fuzzy. Still, such a severe, violent response. Who does that? Brenda wore that scarlet palm print for a month. Everyone knew who did it, but no one, including Brenda, would tell.

What is Tracy doing? Sitting in her driveway, car idling, reminiscing about the "best years of her life," which were anything but. A murderer in town, a dead woman on the beach, and she's developed a crush on the killer.

"Sorry, Logan," she says, climbing out and unbuckling his car seat. "Mommy needs a nap. You want to take a nap?"

"No."

"That'll change when you get older, believe me."

Because everything changes when you get older. Who knows? Maybe Amanda, April, and Amber changed. Tracy can't talk to April, and Amber left town ages ago. Maybe Tracy can send Amber Sobczak—Amanda Kies now—a direct message or something. Grudges are stupid, and holding on to resentment is a waste of time. She'll reach out and see if Amanda is free for coffee or lunch one of these days.

CHAPTER TEN

Dr. Bakshir cancels his week's appointments. A short form email to each patient, explaining that a personal matter has come up. In case of emergencies, he advises calling 911.

Inside his Kensington home, several towns over from Covenant, lights off, only the day's gray guiding the way, he prepares his tea. Dr. Bakshir hasn't been able to stop thinking about her, about what he did. Sometimes the doctor feels like he is split in two. He understands where this division comes from. His life is dedicated to treating problems, locating the source, eradicating malignant thought processes, which, yes, left unchecked can metastasize, no different than tumors. Doing so prescribes to a school of study. Though he implements aspects of cognitive therapy, the doctor is, for the most part, a behaviorist. This philosophy dictates actions are governed by conditioning, in relationship to our environment. For instance, drug addiction stems from negative experiences rather than a genetic predisposition. Other factors play into it—nothing is that cut and dry—but, in the doctor's experience, these negative experiences occur early on. Adverse Childhood Experiences, or

ACE, yield a greater likelihood, worsen odds, not predetermine fate. Within these schools, there can still be disagreements. The doctor isn't interested in debating academic minutia. At least not today. Thinking about Wendy, he reflects on his role in the Green Hills group. The secrets he learned then. How he handled this information. The secrets he knows now.

We've all done things we're ashamed of. Skeletons in closets, scandals we try to bury. Big city versus small town does not make a difference when we are talking about human make-up. We are composites, not compendiums. In that regard, a doctor is no different than a construction worker or fisherman. The worse the humiliation, the more vicious the guilt and shame we carry, the more we compartmentalize. It's how fetishes are born. We all do it. It's the only way to survive a mad, mad world. Dr. Bakshir is both a doctor and a man, split in two. Analysis of others, that's the easy part.

During a session last week, a patient posed a simple question. After confessing a litany of wrongdoings, unburdening regrets, avowing subsequent neuroses and insecurities, the man asked, "Do you think I'm insane?"

"Of course," Dr. Bakshir replied. "You are human."

The doctor is human. Sometimes he compartmentalizes, separates himself, convinces himself that he is different than the patients he treats. They are sick people. He is the professional. He offers them treatments. Never cures. No promises. Treatments. And in doing so, he maintains that slight elevation. The one-eyed man in the land of the blind. But, no, Dr. Bakshir is human, too. The doctor is just as sick, just as insane.

Sitting at his kitchen table, tea warming, he opens his laptop and reads the paper. The *Journal Inquirer* has expanded its initial small write-up.

In the years leading up to her death, Wendy Mortenson didn't have much contact with her family. This is not a surprise. The doctor knows all about her family dynamic. Her struggles with drugs and alcohol are also highlighted. Wendy's depression as well, which, of course, was no secret to the doctor. He'd treated her for it. Treated, not cured. And he'd made good progress.

When the doctor met Wendy, she was, like most girls at Green Hills, not fully matured. Seventeen, the average age of patients, some a couple years younger than that. The program targeted the teen years because that was where directors felt they could do the most good, the liminal state between child- and adulthood. He immediately took an interest in her case. Patients like Wendy were why Dr. Bakshir entered the field in the first place.

After Green Hills pulled the plug on the program, Dr. Bakshir continued to see Wendy. While many of her high school friends headed off to area colleges, Kent, UConn, Amherst, Wendy stayed behind. A bright, funny, smart, attractive girl, Wendy was slow to join the ranks of growing up. Upbringing played a huge role, as it usually does. Parents divorced at a young age, father not around. When Wendy's mother Carolyn remarried, Wendy's younger brother Mikey, with whom she was quite close, was invited into the new family. Wendy was not. That was Wendy's interpretation anyway. Later, she went to live with her biological father Donald, and that experience did not go well. Caught with narcotics, Wendy, a first-time offender, was remanded to Green Hills.

And this is when the doctor's own sickness began manifesting itself.

The house has long gone dark, the change over from gray to gloaming, from black to nothing. He's sat here most of the morning, afternoon, evening, watching, waiting, ruminating, night bleeding daylight dry.

Dr. Bakshir's entire career has been built around the concept of learning to let go. Stop holding on to the past, surrender behaviors that are counterproductive to your goals; do not be your own worst enemy.

Watching moonlight carve long shadows from crooked trees, Dr. Bakshir is haunted by what happened at Green Hills. Ironic how having such a firm grasp on the difference between right and wrong can make choosing the correct path more difficult sometimes. He feels like he is cracking up, like he needs to see a therapist.

He returns to his computer. The police are still calling it an overdose. There will be no inquiry. This is good, right?

Except ... Todd Norman.

Before that investigator Marjorie Jessup visited him, he hadn't put the two together. April Abbott had also been in that group with Wendy. He was fond of April. A doctor does not forget his patients.

Dr. Bakshir now knows Todd Norman is living in Covenant, building a lakehouse next door to where Wendy's body was found. If foul play was suspected, Norman would be the first person they'd question. Unless the media is being used...

Why was that cop at his office?

When the Green Hills program ended, Dr. Bakshir confiscated all files. There were four girls in that group. Wendy, April, Beiko Talo, and Shannon O'Connor. Poring over notes, Dr. Bakshir, so thorough, so detailed, argues with himself.

Will talking to the others do more harm than good? Who is he trying to protect? These are tough questions.

Dr. Bakshir has never been one for chance. And the connection to Todd Norman is too alarming to overlook.

There is only one way to know for sure.

He must hunt down the remaining Green Hills girls.

CHAPTER ELEVEN

The night is coal black, a hard bite to the air, the kind of chill that chews through bone, gnaws on the marrow. It is late and Beiko Talo doesn't feel like going home yet. Home? What home? The one she shares with her mom is a house; it's not a home. A rotating cast of loser boyfriends, deadbeats who move in and out, eating all their food. One week this guy, the next that, sometimes so fast they don't bother with introductions. Beiko's partying isn't the same thing as a divorced mom at forty-seven. It's pathetic, desperate, the way her mother Rhonda lets these men do whatever they want. Makes Beiko sick. Sometimes Beiko walks through the door and *two* different guys will be living there. Beiko doesn't know if there is some kind of arrangement, monetary or otherwise, doesn't care, the apartment a perpetual cloud of acidic smoke. No place for a kid. Not that Beiko is a kid anymore.

At twenty-seven, Beiko is several years removed from high school, a time she spent skating by, which is easy to do in public school, in a big city where they stamp diplomas on rolls. Process the next one as soon as they age out. In a state best known for insurance and a hockey team that no longer exists, no one cares if a girl like Beiko skips class. Eighteen turns twenty-two, twenty-two twenty-five, and now here she is, almost thirty, drifting, party to party, club to club. Technically, she lives with her mother. But her mom doesn't keep tabs, doesn't care. Beiko hasn't been home in three weeks.

Sometimes she crashes with her half-brother Scott at his place in Wellington. Almost six years older, Scott escaped, broke the cycle. He has a college degree, good job, condo; and maybe because of this he acts like he is her dad. In a way, it's sweet he cares so much. But if Beiko wanted a lecture, she'd have gone to class. Truth is, Beiko is lost. She knows it. She's screwing up. She knows that too.

She can see the party ending. And not just the one tonight at Little Sarah's. But the *party* party. The bigger picture one. The one that says it's time to pack up, get your shit together, go to bed before midnight, wake up before noon. These degrees of separation grow harder to explain to friends, a group that dwindles by the day. Sometimes she thinks her last real friends were at the group home. Green Hills. Wendy, April, Shannon, the closest thing to a family she's ever known.

And here comes that sinking feeling, like she's going to drown. Sucked deeper down the whirlpool, part dream sprawling backward, part lucid, vivid, conscious hell. She has this sensation often, awake or asleep. Teeth dreams. Sometimes she can't tell the difference between the two.

Back when she was a patient at Green Hills, the shrink would ask questions, trying to undercover root causes. He used corny terms like "reparenting" and "inner child." She'd laugh. But at least he gave a shit. Which is more than she can say for her mother. The best thing—the *only* thing—Rhonda ever did for her was committing her to Green Hills. Meant as punishment, it offered salvation, however fleeting.

But that was a long time ago.

Beiko first started getting loaded in the seventh grade. Kara and Jamie, her besties. Other stuff followed, the pills pinched from medicine cabinets, the prescription pads swiped from assorted doctors, the powders of unknown origins. Good times.

Kara and Jamie are gone now. Wasted, Kara wandered into traffic at sixteen, got hit by a bus. Jamie ended up where she was always going to end up. Living in Los Angeles with her "producer" boyfriend, pretty much code for doing porn.

This year has been a hard one for Beiko. Not sure why twenty-seven is any rougher than twenty-six. But she feels abandoned. She watches friends come and go, new ones she meets at the bar or clubs, girls in college who start taking studies seriously, applying for graduate school(!). Like that had been the plan all along. (Why hadn't anyone told her?)

Two a.m., Prospect Avenue is dead. A light rain starts to fall. Little Sarah said she had a friend coming over. Code for Beiko to get lost, party for two. Which is messed up. Because who knows? Maybe Beiko finds the guy cute and they could *all* have some fun.

Fine. She'll sleep at her brother's. But he isn't picking up, and then there is the little matter of getting from West Hartford, where Little Sarah lives, all the way to Wellington. Scott is sous chef at a seafood restaurant, and sometimes he works well after closing, cleaning up. He's given her a key but she doesn't have the money to catch multiple buses. Which leaves Mom's. Now it starts to rain, a cold, late-night city rain. Nothing left for Beiko to do. So she starts walking up the hill, through Elizabeth Park, past the roses, beginning the long schlep to Rhonda's. The only other option is the church, and that's too far out in the sticks.

She left her jacket at Little Sarah's. Freezing, teeth chattering, Beiko isn't a quarter way through the park when she says screw this. Just because all her friends are lame there's no reason why she can't have some fun. Beiko still has a couple Molly in her pocket, which she's been saving for when they'll do the most good, but who knows when that'll be? She pops them, washing them back with rainwater that tastes like gasoline.

Downtown, the Meteorite blazes bright. Always among the last to close, the bar is as close to a nightclub as this city gets. Beiko has started to go numb. That's how she knows it's working. She scratches the side of her nose, and when she can't feel her face anymore, she knows she's high.

The bar splits in two. Up above, the visible section, a tiny tin dinette serves greasy comfort foods to sop up late-night drunks. Fries, pulled pork, burgers, breakfast all day. In the back, where the restrooms are, a staircase leads downstairs. A basement, really. But Beiko prefers to imagine the space as a catacomb. Like one of those romantic cities, Paris, Rome, Budapest, a subterranean labyrinth with candle-lit walls and piles of skulls; one of those cities Beiko will never visit.

House and trip-hop bleed up the well, the techno fusion and world-beat soul that has invaded every club, European DJ'd bands like Wigglefish and Smokey Boy. Reared on mainstream classic rock, Beiko used to hate the stuff, but she's grown to tolerate it, like it, even.

Not too many people for a Tuesday night. But more people than you'd expect on a Tuesday night around here. Rows of alcohol bottles glow kaleidoscopic behind the bar, neon violets and roses, chartreuse, vermillion, crimson, other dazzling gradations and variations that Beiko retains from the art classes she used to love, back when she thought being an artist yielded a future, before she recognized the futility of trying.

She's been coming to the Meteorite since she was fifteen. Beiko had no trouble getting served. You could be twelve down here, and as long as you were pretty and painted up, you'd get served. Isn't an issue these days. She won't be buying her own drinks anyway. Never does. Who can afford to get drunk if you have to pay for your own alcohol? Some guy will come, sooner than later, chatting her up. Then all she has to do is flirt enough to get his money before she slips off, waits for the next guy's dick to pry open his wallet. It's an art. And it pays a helluva lot better than painting stupid birds.

"What're you drinking?"

Right as rain.

"Vodka and soda."

She hears him scoff, like she doesn't know her alcohol.

"Grey Goose," she adds. Yeah, Beiko drinks her share of cheap beer like any hard-up twenty-something, but she isn't getting felt up over a Keystone Light. He waves the bartender over, a bleached-out blonde well past her prime. In fact, when Beiko checks him out, he appears on the wrong side of thirty, too.

Drink in hand, he gestures to a booth in the far corner. They wriggle through the drunk girls dancing in pairs, writhing against each other.

The booth, like the rest of the downstairs Meteorite, is slathered in black. Fluorescent graffiti shares unwanted phone numbers and snippets of bad poetry. Neon sharpies rest on the tabletop; the Meteorite encourages the vandalism.

"Do I know you?" Beiko asks. "You look familiar." Beiko is so high right now, vision fuzzy, everything bathed in soft white light, she can't make out the face. But she knows he's cute.

"Hold old are you?" she says, relieving him of his drink.

"Maybe I should be asking you that question."

"Old enough to know better."

"Better than what?"

Beiko shrugs. She often gets mistaken for being younger than she is. Not a bad thing. And she couldn't care less how old he is. She'll take the drink and ghost. Or maybe not. Because she likes the way he looks, likes the way he's looking at her. Maybe it's the Molly, maybe she doesn't feel like gambling it gets any better tonight. Men, women, boys, girls, Beiko isn't too discerning in that department.

"I know you," Beiko says again. "I've seen you before."

"I've never been here."

"What's your name?" she asks.

Maybe he answers, maybe he ignores the question, maybe the music is too loud; Beiko doesn't care what his name is.

"What are you doing out so late on a school night?"

"Wouldn't you like to know?" She twirls a finger through her hair. If he gets off thinking she's jailbait, she'll play along.

A new song kicks in, rolling ocean waves, ethereal and sublime, before the bass-heavy beat drops, swells with the urgent, surging synth, then that smooth-as-sin voice. God, she loves this band. She closes her eyes, swaying to the words about love for one night.

"You want to dance?"

"So you can grind up on me?" Not that she would mind so much, the drugs and drink, the music hitting her right where it matters.

"It's gotta be rough."

"What's that?"

"Being so much smarter than everyone else your age. Quicker, funnier, weirder, sexier. Hotter." He waits. "All around better."

He slides out of the booth, grabbing her by the hand. She goes without a fight.

"Where we going?" she asks, not carrying much about the answer.

"Trust me," he says.

CHAPTER TWELVE

"Murder?"

At the word, the waitress stops warming their coffee mid-stream. Tracy forces a smile. Logan coughs in his sleep, tossing in his car seat.

"Netflix," Diana tells the waitress before taking another bite of her breakfast, one egg, spinach, no bread.

It is ten a.m., new day smeared with buttery light. Outside Josie's Corner, the seasons tease switching over. Almost October and cooler, the sun seems to burn extra bright, a parting reminder. See you again next year.

Tracy waits till the waitress has walked far away, fetching more muffins and large coffees for townies in faded flannels. "Cleared," Tracy says. "He was cleared of charges."

"But he *was* charged."

"There was a trial, if that's what you mean." Tracy takes a bite of her scrambled bacon bagel. "Not guilty."

"I can't believe you didn't tell me sooner."

"I found out a couple weeks ago. We haven't talked a lot since then."

"But we *have* talked."

"You had that thing at work—"

"It's so much easier when they let me work from home—"

"—and I didn't want to worry you."

"You gave him your number. Aren't you scared?"

Tracy knows it doesn't make sense. But, no, not really. At first, sure. She could explain bursting into the Covenant police department that afternoon, her freak out, double-locking every door and window. But the next day it was back to normal. The woman on the beach turned out to be a dead junkie from out of town. Unrelated. Some mornings she can see him out there, hammering away, building that lakehouse across the water.

"You remember the news?" Tracy asks.

"About April Abbott?" Diana wrinkles her bunny nose. "Of course. We were a few years older. But those girls…"

"What?"

"You know." Diana raises her eyebrows, miming so she won't have to say it. Tracy shrugs, even though she knows the answer. "They were all assholes. Isn't that what everyone called them?"

"The A-holes, yeah. But it doesn't mean she deserved to die."

"I didn't say she did." Diana sips her coffee. "I thought it was a mugging, robbery. Stuff that happens in New York. None of my business. Plus, I never liked April. I didn't care she was dead." Diana covers her mouth. "Does that make me a bad person?"

"No," Tracy says, not wanting to admit she'd had the same reaction.

"Those girls—Amanda, April, Amber—they were … weird. You know Liz Tadeshi says she caught them in bed together."

"Bullshit."

"Some party. Dick Barbagallo's or Jon Dempsey's. Walked in.

And there they were, all three of them naked, going to town."

"Jesus, I'm so glad to be out of high school. Liz Tadeshi used to smoke cinnamon sticks to get high."

"Just telling you the rumor I heard."

"Exactly. Rumor. People in this town are so fucked up."

"You should be more worried about dating a possible serial killer."

"He's not a serial killer. And I'm not dating him. We had coffee. Once."

"Why do you seem so unfazed by this?"

"I'm not unfazed. Couple weeks ago, I was a wreck."

"And today?"

Tracy stirs cream and sugar.

"Leave it to you. The first guy you're into since the divorce has a murder rap."

Tracy knows she's trying to lighten the moment. This is what Diana does. Take nothing too serious, treat everything as a joke. A lot of times it's the right note. Sometimes, however, Tracy feels trivialized.

Outside the café window, speeding tires spray road water from last night's passing storm, droplets rainbowed through sunshine. How much has this town changed over the years? Not much. The Quiznos is new. Used to be an Arby's. The Mobil station has been renovated, Shell station now a mini-mart. There's a Big Y, finally a bona fide supermarket in town. Up the Turnpike, Stew Leonard's, with a Starbucks right next door. They even have a movie theater. Discount. Two films at a time. Never the new releases.

"Tracy?"

"I've had time to calm down. And now it's not—"

"What? Such a big deal?"

"I read up on the case." Tracy takes a moment, gathers confidence for what she wants to say next. Rolling the words around in her head, they sound nonsensical. But she says them anyway. "Maybe it's not so cut and dry."

Diana stares, deadpan, emotionless, which conveys a whole lot of emotion.

"He won his case. He had an alibi. The prosecution couldn't show any transfer of funds. No blood on his clothing. And, I don't know ... maybe…"

"Has he called?"

"No."

"Is that good or bad news?"

When Tracy doesn't answer, Diana shakes her head and pouts, but not in a cruel or judgmental way. Diana hops up and comes to Tracy's side, hugging her around the waist. Diana is an inch or two shorter than most women, Tracy a few inches taller, the difference netting a solid half-foot gap.

"Stop it," Tracy says, half pushing Diana away, the other half grateful she has such a constant, positive force in her life.

"Sorry your first post-divorce crush turned out to be a possible psychopath. But, hey, at least he's an improvement over Brett." Diana laughs. Tracy does too, pulling away, but not hard enough to break free from Diana, who squeezes extra tight.

"Come on," Diana says, looking down at her bird-pecked plate. "Let's go to the mall. All the cute unemployed guys are at the Cinnabon this time of day.

For all her annoying quirks, Diana never fails to remind Tracy not to take life so damned seriously.

CHAPTER THIRTEEN

"Hi, Dad." The greeting carries all the enthusiasm of a bored, overworked dollar-store cashier at the end of a mandatory holiday weekend.

Sobczak pans around the inside of his daughter's modest home, the one he helped buy, contributing to the down payment. He laments the lack of presence in his only child's life. She keeps a picture of her mother on the foyer table. Several of them, in fact. There is none of him. Lord knows he's tried. For whatever reason, Amanda's erected a wall. That's not true. He knows the reason. Mary's death.

Amanda has never been rude or cruel, done nothing overt, but she makes it painfully obvious: if Sobczak didn't seek her out, call, try to insert himself into her life, she'd never make the effort. In some ways, this hurts worse than if she outright hated him. He's inconsequential. This pangs Sobczak's heart. He knows being a parent is learning to let go. She isn't his little girl anymore. Doesn't make it hurt any less.

"Tom's not here," Amanda says.

"Actually, I came to see you."

Amanda doesn't hide the inconvenience. Sobczak is forced to note both how beautiful his daughter is, the spitting image of Mary, and how dramatic she can be.

"Mind if I come in?"

"The house is such a mess right now..." Amanda drops her haunches, steps aside to clear the way. "Sorry. Of course." She reaches over to hug him. Despite the perfunctory effort, the press of her skin unleashes a painful wave of nostalgia only a father can understand, a lifetime relived in seconds.

Sobczak peers around her, into the well-maintained living room, the U-shaped navy couches and glass end tables, the throw rugs. Immaculate. Nothing out of place. The home looks staged. Like Amanda's room as a child.

Amanda breaks the embrace, walks away, water bottle in hand, toward the kitchen. Briefly, Sobczak flashes on the time he caught her with a vodka-filled Dasani at the football game, a silly thought. She is a grown woman, who, far as he can tell, has developed into a well-adjusted, responsible woman, certainly not the type to be drinking hard liquor midday. He's proud of her. He wishes he could tell her these things. Every time he tries, the words come out condescending or backhanded. Sobczak has never been good at expressing himself.

Amanda opens the refrigerator, which is stocked with leafy greens and red, bloody meats wrapped in tight plastic. She scans the shelves, past the almond milk and yogurts, takes nothing, closes the door. She seems distracted. Restless. Something on her mind? She hops up and sits on the counter beneath the cupboard, an oddly playful move for a twenty-nine-year-old woman. Or maybe not. Today's world is different than the one Sobczak grew up in.

"So good to see you," Amanda says, before adding an extra sweet, "Dad."

Amanda hasn't offered a seat, but Sobczak takes one at the kitchen table anyway. "I wanted to talk to you about April Abbott."

Hearing the name, Amanda closes her eyes tight, swaying side to side, a tilt-a-whirl motion. Sobczak wants to tell her to knock it off, the theatrics.

"You have *got* to be kidding me," she says.

"I'm guessing you've heard the news about her husband."

"Ex. *Ex*-husband. And yeah. I'm married to your deputy. What do you think? I was April's best friend. The asshole is moving to town. What do you want me to do about it? Isn't that your job?"

A sudden, random thought strikes Sobczak. "Did you attend their wedding?"

"What?"

"Todd Norman and April Abbott. I don't remember you going. Just curious. If you were, like, the maid of honor, a bridesmaid?"

Amanda jumps down, snares a mug. "They didn't have a wedding. Justice of the peace, civil ceremony. No one was invited. April cut us all off after she met that psycho."

"I didn't mean to upset you."

"I'm not upset." Amanda pours a healthy glassful from her water bottle, tossing it back like she's just finished a marathon. "You drop in and start asking questions about my dead best friend. I'm feeling *terrific*."

Sobczak sidesteps his daughter's snarky reply. "Todd Norman is already here. He's building a house by the lake." He stops to let his daughter think about what he's said. "Are you okay with that?"

"No! I'm not *okay* with that. Are you?" Amanda seethes. "Guy killed his wife, buys his way out of prison, and now he's living down the street from me? Of course I'm not okay with it!"

78

No one talks. Amanda drinks her water, watches out the window.

Seeing how upset she is, Sobczak changes the topic. "How is everything with Tom?"

"Why? Did he say something?"

This is going all wrong. Sobczak wanted to stop by and talk to his daughter about Norman moving to town, keep lines of communication open. He didn't mean to aggravate her. As usual, everything he says makes the situation worse.

"You work with the guy. You're the one who gave Tom that friggin' job—"

"I'm trying to make conversation."

Amanda crosses the floor, each step angrier than the last. Then she stops, peels a stick of chewing gum. And, like that, her entire mood swings, an understanding twinkle in her eyes, all batting lashes and sweet-as-pie smiles. "Sorry, Dad. Rough morning."

"Anything I can help with?"

"No." She shakes her head, laughing it off, rambling about some side enterprise. Cosmetic and pampering products. Mail order. "The last thing you care about, I know. But I get bored. Tom is *always* gone. I have nothing to do. Thought it would be fun. Selling avocado peels and mud masks online. Turning into one giant headache."

"You know," Sobczak says, trying to keep things light. "I wouldn't mind a grandbaby."

"I know, Dad. You mention it *every* time I see you." Amanda reaches up and takes her father by the shoulders, looks him in the eye. "I'll see what I can do." She kisses him on the cheek, the smell sweet as cinnamon.

Sobczak says goodbye to his daughter, and heads out into the brisk air.

Driving away, Sobczak admits he isn't sure of the purpose of his visit. He was looking for more than his daughter's feelings about Norman's arrival. Assurance? Information? Clues? Even though Sobczak doesn't know what that specific question is, he leaves feeling like he's somehow gotten an answer.

CHAPTER FOURTEEN

FALL

The doctor closes his practice till the New Year. The time off is not a vacation. Dr. Bakshir wouldn't know what to do with a vacation if it was court-ordered. A man most comfortable working, he is not wired to relax. Unlike many, Dr. Bakshir does not dread the workweek, nor does he look forward to an all-too-short weekend. In fact, his life is the exact opposite of everyone else: his weekdays are his weekends. He loves his job, the human mind an endlessly fascinating puzzle. Some consider psychological maladies a fault, a failure of evolution. Not Dr. Bakshir. Each roadblock is a potential path to the ultimate freedom: self-actualization.

When the doctor is not working—when he has no puzzles to uncover or pieces to reassemble—he is left alone with his thoughts, his own being. Due to his desire to reach an unattainable perfection, Dr. Bakshir, invariably, ends up disappointing himself.

He has no choice. He is not in the right headspace to treat patients.

Each morning he scours the papers for any new information, but we are going on a couple months now and the police have not come for him. How likely is it authorities will reopen a case like Wendy's? Aimless, addicted, alone. No, the doctor should be free, clear. But this does not make him feel better, forced to consider how Wendy died, how she spent her last moments. He is haunted by the tragedy.

First, he had to grieve. Which he did. For the first few weeks after he closed his practice, he mourned. A professional in the field, Dr. Bakshir tackled Kübler-Ross in record time. Afterward, he tried distracting himself with day trips, revisiting old haunts, bed-and-breakfasts, sugarbushes. Nostalgia. Up to Plymouth Rock, the Cape, Sturbridge Village, better days. Fall in New England is a lovely time of year. The cascade of changing colors, a metamorphosis. Until he realized he was in denial, no better than an addict, wishing salvation through diversionary tactics.

He can't shed Wendy or Green Hills like trees do their leaves.

Now the real work has begun.

The others gone, his attention has turned to finding Shannon O'Connor.

Which is proving problematic.

Part of the doctor thinks, leave well enough alone. There is no one left to tell. And Shannon, God bless her soul, the poor girl has always been a little off. Who would believe a word she says?

Dr. Bakshir has never been one for half measures.

Shannon's parents died six months to the day of one another. Her mother contracted scleroderma, an autoimmune disorder. Her father died of a heart attack. Random and unrelated. This was when Shannon was young, before she was sent to live with her aunt. That experience did not go well and, like Beiko Talo, Shannon O'Connor ended up on the streets.

If finding Beiko promised a headache, tracking down Shannon won't be any easier.

What other choice does he have? Until he finds her, the doctor will forever be looking over his shoulder.

Pushing a sleepy Logan through the Big Y, Tracy tries to remember everything she has to pick up at the store. Thanksgiving shopping. Not much cause for celebration these days. Tracy has received a few invitations, but she always feels these invites are out of sympathy. And when she accepts one, she ends up feeling lonelier than had she stayed home alone. It'll be better if she pretends it's not a holiday, thinks of it as just another Thursday. Diana will stop by. They can roast a chicken, drink wine, maybe bake a pie.

Tracy has gotten in the habit of not writing a shopping list, her reason suspect. Before he died, Tracy's father developed Alzheimer's. During one of her visits to the nursing home, his doctor mentioned how the brain, like any other muscle, needs exercise, to be challenged, tested, or it fails. Since then, Tracy has stopped writing little notes to herself, has given up the to-do lists; if it is important enough to do, she'll remember it. Her theory was put to the test the first time she visited her father's grave and forgot to bring flowers.

The movement of the shopping cart keeps Logan calm. He's a good boy, has her temperament and not, thank God, Brett's. Tracy is picking out spinach in the frozen food section when she bumps into him. The first thought that comes to mind isn't murder but that old Dan Fogelberg song her father liked so much, the one where old lovers meet in a grocery store and drink beer in the parking lot because no bars are open, before the snow turns into rain.

Todd Norman doesn't say anything. What can he say? He gave the police her name as an alibi. He must know she's found out by now. Tracy isn't quite sure how to describe the look on his face. It isn't outright embarrassment or shame. More regret. But not for what was. For what could've been.

"What are you doing here?" she asks. An odd question but that's what comes out. What's he supposed to do? Spend the rest of his life as the Elephant Man, canvas bag draped over his head, sequestered indoors, screaming he's not an animal?

"I need to eat?" He says it like a question, but he's being polite.

The frozen food section of the Big Y is well lit with plenty of customers; Tracy isn't scared or nervous. Standing two feet from him she feels what she felt that first night. Electricity, a charge. His smile warm, his eyes—those brilliant cobalt blue eyes—knife her heart. They are not the eyes of a sociopath—could her instincts be that far off?

At first, Tracy had been worked up, livid, fearful for her safety—for *her child's* safety. Who wouldn't be? The guy had been charged with murdering his wife! Except now all that rage feels contrived. The man standing in front of her, Todd—the same man Tracy laughed with over coffee at an all-night Wal-Mart a couple months ago—doesn't project arrogance or narcissism or any of the other colorful descriptions the papers used to paint the portrait of a psycho killer. In his Barbour Devon jacket, dark jeans, and Wolverine boots, he looks like he's stepped out of a *Huckberry* catalog.

The silence carries out comically long as Tracy tries to summon the outrage, the injustice of having been wronged.

Before becoming a mom, Tracy was prone to gullible mistakes.

Stupid, silly ones. Buying jewelry from a phony website in China, duped by panhandlers in the city, sob stories about having run out of gas. Little things. Not like she fell prey to Nigerian princes or IRS scams with Indian accents. But after Logan, her senses have sharpened. A mom now, evolutionary upgrades have kicked in, preservation of the species, she sniffs out danger, a feral beast, the mother bear protecting her cub. Tracy knows which side of the street not to walk down, which deal is too good to be true. These new superpowers are what led her to uncover Brett's affair (with one of his students, a nineteen-year-old named Kylee, two Es). To-day, she takes different routes on instinct, goes the long way when she anticipates trouble. Why isn't she feeling any of this trepidation with Todd? Is he that good? Can a mask so skillfully hide true in-tentions? Guess so. Because next thing Tracy knows, she's ponder-ing a different set of questions. Like, what if he didn't kill his wife, was falsely accused, destined to forever search for the one-armed man, no one believing him, that poor guy...

While she is thinking all this, still no one is talking, Todd watching her, fascinated. She knows her face is twisting up, betray-ing a hundred different emotions. Tracy is desperate to pull off one that conveys admonishment, a stern lashing without using words. She is failing miserably.

He *is* that good.

"I'm sorry I didn't call," he finally says.

Tracy stops rocking Logan. "I think we both know why you didn't."

Todd drops the basket he is carrying, a bachelor's shopping supplies. Cold cuts, milk, bread, mustard. His black hair, neat and combed, musses, a rogue lock falling across his forehead. And maybe it's the mother in her, but it takes all her self-control not to lick a thumb and slick it back in place.

This is why you are in therapy, Trace.

He starts to open his mouth, like he wants to say something, explain, but abandons the effort.

Logan stirs. Tracy rocks the wheels. "What I don't understand ... you had to know I'd find out."

"Yeah," he says. "I knew."

"So you wanted to play with my head for a night? Saw a lonely, single mom and thought, 'This'll be fun.'"

"No, that wasn't it."

Tracy leans in, whispering, a big scandal in the frozen food section of the Big Y. "You were flirting with me ... hitting on me." She waits, like he's supposed to refute this.

Instead, he says, "Yes. I was."

Tracy shakes her head, grabs the shopping cart handle, and starts to back up. She can't stop shaking her head. She also doesn't have anything to add. She's hoping this facsimile of a pissed-off woman will get her point across.

He picks up his shopping basket, makes to leave. "Tracy?"

She stops.

"I'm sorry."

"If you didn't think you could explain, why would you—"

"Have coffee with a pretty woman I liked? If I knew it couldn't lead anywhere?"

"Yes." This is the question she's wanted to ask since she first saw him tonight: why bother with a lost cause?

"I was being selfish." He half shrugs, which doesn't exactly exude regret. "What else do I have to look forward to? Flirting with a pretty woman, the occasional conversation where I can forget, pretend I have my life back." He catches her eye, before breaking into a grin. "I liked you."

And, like that, she feels that old familiar pain.

Logan starts to stir, restless at the extended stop. She bends to soothe him. He's hungry. She needs to get home and make dinner. Tracy fishes out the sucker from the spilled Cheerios and cheddar bun-buns in his seat, but she can't get a good grasp, and it slips again. She digs it out, wipes it off, sticks it in his mouth, hardly sanitary.

When she looks up, Todd is gone.

Tracy has just talked to a man arrested for murdering his wife. Why isn't her skin crawling? Why is she feeling that same strange tingle of excitement? Because he called her pretty and said he liked her? What is this, seventh grade? Is she that far out of it? So removed, lonely, and desperate she's willing to overlook one little murder charge because a guy is cute? No, she isn't that careless, reckless, stupid.

Tracy can't know for sure what really happened in that Manhattan townhouse five years ago, but Mama Bear isn't sensing danger. She prays her instincts are more honed this time around.

Because, goddamn, she's crushing.

CHAPTER FIFTEEN

Sobczak overlooks the choppy waters of Shallow Lake, where Todd Norman cuts wood on a band saw. The ample maple-colored foliage of the ridge shrouds his intrusion. Sobczak can sit here for hours. Strange as it sounds, these are the most peaceful moments of his day. New England is loveliest in the fall. More than the changing of the leaves or the cooling temperatures, there's a sense of growth, a state of transition, which only a native New Englander can understand. Time is, granted, an arbitrary marker. Sobczak understands this. The cyclical rhythm to what we, as human beings do, is wedded to a clock, a calendar, a made-up human construct to note the passage of time. But the change from summer to autumn is bigger than bulky sweaters, more than pumpkin patches and county fairs and apple orchards. Fall arrives with the reminder that nothing gold can stay. This is not depressing for Sobczak, who is reminded of Mary and poems from school days. He will see her again.

During these times observing Norman, Sobczak does not see a murderer; he sees a man busting his hump. Never would've pegged that stuffed suit for such a hard worker. Norman isn't afraid to get his hands dirty. Twelve-hour days, dark to darker.

Regardless of Holland's confirmation that Wendy Mortensen died of a drug overdose, Sobczak's old-school gut keeps telling him there is more to this case. And if not Norman, then who? He wants to let it go—why invite the extra work? What confounds Sobczak most, however—more than the body on the shore—is why the man is building this lakehouse in the first place. Norman can't expect to find peace in their insular town. With each passing day, the rumor mill grinds: whispers at the Big Y, innuendo at the Dunkin' Donuts, construction workers tying one on at Dino's, pitchfork talk turning to "setting shit on fire." Sobczak hears everything in this town. No secrets can be kept. And now that they know April Abbott's killer is here, in their town, putting their wives, children, and livelihood at stake, the vigilante tough guy talk has begun to escalate.

Sobczak could bust Norman for failure to secure all his permits. Chances are he's forgotten something, no matter how meticulous the guy is (someone always forgets something). But Sobczak won't do this. He doesn't want to bring down Al Capone for income tax evasion. Still, if he's being honest with himself, he's developing a begrudging respect for the man's work ethic.

Down below, the man takes a pickaxe to shale.

The workday ends and Sobczak drives back to his house. This is when life gets more complicated. As these dreary November days become the norm, chill turning cold, cold turning raw, Sobczak finds his normally steady outlook tested. Sobczak is not a man easily shaken. He sees an order to things. Some might call this rigidity, inflexibility. Mary once called him ... immoveable. Sobczak takes comfort in patterns, logic, reason, its rules and regularities. Since Mary died, he has settled into single life. He shops meals for one, seldom cooks more than pasta, cube steak, turkey burgers, meatloaf, which is followed by a single beer. If there's a ballgame on, he'll catch an inning, quarter, or half. He is calmed by consistency and routine. They are reaffirming, safe.

For a long time, this philosophy has served Sobczak well, a confirmation of the natural order of things, like the changing of the seasons. Life. Death. Rebirth. Sometimes we lose loved ones too soon. Loss and grief are the price of loving. With family, no one is really gone. We keep them alive in our hearts and memory; and even if that sentiment is shared on overpriced greeting cards, it doesn't make it any less true.

Except Todd Norman's return has highlighted a flaw in this belief system. Surviving isn't living.

It wasn't always like this. Sobczak recalls seeing Amanda at the Dairy Queen, her friends April and Amber stuck like glue. He'd cruise by and wave from his patrol car; sometimes, if the mood struck, he'd hit the lights and siren, just to watch Amanda act embarrassed. But he'd see her giggle. She used to like him. Used to respect him. Until Mary died.

Didn't happen right away, the divide. For a while, it felt like Mary's passing brought them closer. Or maybe he'd missed the warning signs. He had a lot on his plate. Sobczak was grieving, attending to family matters, the bureaucracy of death, paperwork to switch over accounts and settle credit card debts, pick out the perfect casket and headstone, a plot with a view.

Everything fell apart at once, right around graduation. Amanda withdrew from her friends, isolating, refusing to talk. Sobczak didn't know how to handle an emotional teenage girl, didn't have the first clue. Seemed like next thing he knew, years had passed,

April Abbott was dead, and the chasm between them had grown unbridgeable.

There was no official falling out, their relationship never "estranged." Sobczak gave Amanda away at her wedding. He hired Tom, good job security for a young family, helped pay for their house. Father and daughter see each other often, occasional Sunday dinners, the major holidays, but since Mary died, things haven't been the same.

Tonight, Sobczak sits at his kitchen table alone, reheating meatloaf that was reheated to begin with.

In his empty home, Sobczak observes the leftovers of a life. Pictures of his family together. At the Berlin Fair, Oakdale, Old Saybrook. Amanda as a baby. Amanda in pigtails. Amanda as a laughing, joyful teenager. Before she morphs into unrecognizable stranger.

Sobczak finishes up the meatloaf, which tastes like a sad brick, and washes the single plate, fork, and glass he'd used for his milk, setting each to dry in the rack.

He grabs his nightly beer, a Heineken, and moves to the living room to see who's playing, when his cell phone buzzes.

"Chief Sobczak?"

"Speaking."

"This is Detective Stephanie Ronson. We met a couple months ago."

"I remember, Detective."

"Are you familiar with a nightclub called the Meteorite?"

"I'm aware of its existence, yes." Sobczak recalls Amanda and her friends sneaking into the Hartford hotspot years ago. Even got a call one night. Had to put the foot down, give a good, stern talking to. "Didn't know it was still open for business."

"Very much so. Can you meet me there?"

"When?"

"I was hoping now. I know it's a little late in the work day."

Sobczak checks the clock on his stove—6:47. The sky is dark but the day is far from over.

"Sure," Sobczak says, gathering his belt and keys. "Mind telling me what this is about?"

"A woman is missing. She was last seen at the club."

"The Meteorite? That's Hartford County."

"We have reason to believe Todd Norman is involved."

CHAPTER SIXTEEN

The holidays evoke nostalgia for Tracy. After she puts Logan down for the night, Tracy digs in the cubby, fetching her old high school yearbook. Sitting on the couch with a glass of wine, she flips through the pages, trying not to cringe every time she sees a photo of herself with the same Jennifer Aniston haircut every girl seems to have.

Even though they all went to the same small high school and most have stuck around town, Tracy seldom sees her ex-classmates. Besides Diana. Which is why after her third glass of wine, Tracy does something she rarely does these days: makes a phone call, talking instead of texting.

The lunch at the Chili's on Stanley Circle turns out to be an unofficial class reunion. Even though Tracy has known Lisa Blake, Judi Drake, and Marlene Carlson since grade school, they drifted out of her daily life following graduation. Tracy's marriage to Brett sucked up all her time.

Over frozen midday margaritas, Tracy sees no one harbors resentment; no one blames her for the failed marriage—which they make clear before the first corn chip hits guac. They call Brett a dog, a cradle robber, and, her favorite, a man whore. No one gives her a hard time for shutting them out. They were a close-knit crew back in high school. Tracy had forgotten just how close.

"This is fun," Lisa says. "We should do it more often."

The four rehash the past couple years, trying to remember the last time they were all together, no one able to agree whether it was Melissa Cote's wedding or Caroline Revis's divorce when they bumped into one another at Slider's, the townie bar no one wants to admit going to.

Out of nowhere, Tracy says, "Do you guys remember April Abbott?" Why she's asking this exactly, Tracy isn't sure. Since bumping into Todd at the Big Y, she's been thinking about him often. And it is hard to think about Todd Norman without thinking about what happened to April Abbott.

"I remember when April slapped Brenda Prescott in the face with that crap they stole from the science department."

"The A-holes," Lisa says.

"Were they that bad?" Tracy asks. "Amanda, April, Amber?"

"Are you kidding? All three were *bee-atches*."

Two pitchers of frozen margaritas have loosened tongues, laughter growing raucous, housewife hair coming down.

"That poor girl," Lisa says, unable to suppress the grin. "Brenda had that hand print on her face for class pictures."

Now Lisa laughs. Marlene and Judi do too. Even though the act was cruel, there's an odd gallows humor that highlights the perverse savagery of high school.

"You know I work for her dad, right?" Judi says.

"Whose dad?" Tracy asks.

"Amanda Sobczak—Kies. Her father Dwayne is the chief of police."

Tracy had forgotten that when she stormed down to the police station back in September. She wonders if Judi heard about her outburst. If she had, she would've brought it up it by now.

"You're still working part time at the town hall?" Marlene asks. "I thought you were quitting to go full time at Kevin's." Judi's husband Kevin owns two used car dealerships on the Parkway; his beaming cue-ball head stares down from numerous roadside billboards around town.

"That's still the plan," Judi says, "but right now we can use the extra income. Derek and Devin are both playing soccer and I swear the cost of two boys and their sports, the travel, the uniforms, the camps—it drains a bank account."

"Tell me about it," adds Lisa, who has two girls of her own. "Cheerleading isn't any cheaper."

All the women at the table have children in middle school. Only Tracy has such a young one to raise. After graduation, everyone in Covenant gets married and starts families. Except Diana, who is still wild. Tracy wonders if Diana will ever settle down with anyone. She is too spunky, too independent. Then again, Covenant isn't crawling with intriguing single men. Men? What does Tracy know about men? Her first and only real relationship was with a cheating jerk. She's never fallen hard for anyone else. And now she finds herself thinking about Todd.

On cue: "I know she was a bitch," Lisa says, "but what happened to April…" Lisa doesn't need to add any more. Everyone in town knows the story, even if they don't know the whole story, glomming on to the sensational parts. Murder for hire. Cold-blooded banker. Insurance scam.

"You know he's in town?" Judi says. "Moved here this past summer." When no one responds, she adds, "Don't you read the paper?"

"You mean our trailblazing *Journal Inquirer*?" Lisa laughs.

"Wait," Marlene says. "Who moved here?"

"The man who killed her. The man who killed April Abbott."

Lisa and Marlene look stunned. Tracy tries to show shock but the manufactured effort feels insincere. Because, of course, it is.

Judi waves for the waitress, who holds up a finger. The Chili's lunch-hour rush is no joke. The Stanley Circle location splits the difference between bigger towns and the factory outlet malls, so you get a lot of traffic certain times of day.

"A murderer? Living *here*?" Marlene says. "In Covenant. You're kidding me."

"Nope. Building a house on Shallow Lake."

"That's *him*?"

"Actually," Tracy says. "Todd was acquitted of the charges."

"Who's Todd?" Marlene asks.

"The guy who killed April. Todd Norman. The one building the lakehouse."

"Don't you remember they found that woman on the beach?" Judi says. "Two, three months ago?"

"I thought some drug addict overdosed in, like, Middletown, and her friends left her there?"

"*There* being Norman's doorstep."

"He didn't have anything to do with that," Tracy says. "According to the police."

"Then he must have the worst luck in the world. Talk about wrong place, wrong time."

"I'll tell you this." Judi scoops a shovelful of guacamole. "Chief

Sobczak doesn't think he's innocent. They've got people watching him night and day."

"Why haven't they arrested him?"

"He's loaded. Got a high-powered lawyer on retainer." Judi snaps her fingers. "He'd be out next morning."

"Whoa," Marlene says. "That is seriously effed up."

The harried waitress hurries over, apologizing for the delay in a desperate bid to save her tip. It doesn't take long to place orders. Three salads with dressing on the side. Tracy orders a cheeseburger. This is why she works her butt off in the gym. Real butter, real sugar. The occasional burger won't kill anyone.

"Let's talk about something else," Tracy says after the waitress races off.

"A murderer?" Marlene repeats. "In Covenant? I cannot believe it."

"I'll tell you something else," says Judi, happy her dull part-time job for the town is finally paying dividends in the gossip department. She puts a hand over her heart. "Chief Sobczak and Amanda..." She stops there.

"What?"

"All I know," Judi says. "Poor Tom is stuck in the middle."

"Amanda and April were best friends," Lisa says.

Judi slurps her frozen margarita.

"Can't imagine she's happy that Norman guy is living here."

"I didn't know you were friends with them," Tracy says.

"God, now I feel bad talking shit."

"I wasn't *not* friends with them," Lisa says. "We went to the same parties, football games. You couldn't escape the A-holes. You had to be friends with them."

"And hope you didn't piss them off like Brenda did."

"Does anyone know what happened to Amber Coit?"

"I heard she married some rocker, follows him everywhere. Tours the world."

"I heard they got divorced."

"Someone said she's in Arizona."

"Amber got married?"

"That's the story I heard," Lisa says. "Left the fall after graduation. You know she was always crazy. Who gets that drunk in the ninth grade?"

"Amanda and April had to sneak her out and carry her home."

"The A-holes were like a gang," Marlene says.

"Yeah, a gang of nymphos."

"That was some *Heavenly Creatures* shit."

"What are you talking about?"

A couple of the others roll their eyes, stifling laughs.

"Come on, Trace," Lisa says. "Bobby Bradley's party? Senior year?"

Tracy has no idea what she is talking about.

"Mrs. Bradley walked in on them? In the backyard pool house?"

"Walked in on them? Doing what?"

The women laugh harder.

"Oh, that was a rumor," Marlene says, defending Tracy's ignorance.

"I wasn't into parties." Tracy doesn't want to mention Brett didn't like her going to parties without him, and that weekend, which she remembers well—Bobby Bradley's party was a big deal—Brett was off scoping colleges.

"Rumor?" Lisa laughs, then gives a thumbs-up.

"What happened?"

Lisa leans in, glancing around to make sure no one can over-hear the salacious knowledge she is about to drop in the middle of a Chili's on a Tuesday afternoon.

The others, including Tracy, lean in too. Tracy hates still get-ting caught up in this drama. A thirty-two-year-old mom. She pulls back and pours herself another drink.

"Mrs. Bradley caught them having sex. All three of them. With each other."

"I'm still not sure I believe it," Marlene says.

Lisa nods knowingly. Tracy checks with Judi, who shrugs, un-willing—or unable—to deny it.

"Yep," Lisa says. "Amber had gotten her hands on a bunch of ecstasy. Of course she shared it with her two besties. And the three of them were rolling so hard, they snuck off to the pool house, and…" Lisa falls back, the rest of the tawdry tale self-evident.

"Who told you this?" Tracy asks. The story sounds like a fan-tasy invented by some oversexed teenage boy.

"Bobby Bradley. His mother was *furious*."

"A pervy high school boy." Like Tracy thought.

"I remember the party ending—" Judi snaps her fingers "—like *that*."

"That was because Mrs. Bradley said she was calling the po-lice."

"Amanda's dad," Judi says. "Oh, I would've loved to see that."

"Sounds like a high school rumor."

"I believe it. Those three were always close. A little *too* close."

Tracy promises herself next time she is waxing nostalgic she'll watch reruns of *Buffy the Vampire Slayer* instead.

"You could ask them, I suppose," Lisa says. "Except Amber is a rock 'n' roll groupie. And April is dead. Invite Amanda out for coffee. Something tells me the daughter of the town sheriff—who's married to the town deputy—won't be forthcoming about her *Girls Gone Wild* years." Lisa finishes the rest of the pitcher. She slaps Tracy's arm, clearly buzzed. "Don't look so serious!"

Tracy stares at the wall. Is there a whole world she knew nothing about? How sheltered was she?

"Now," Lisa says, "let's see some pictures of that adorable boy of yours."

CHAPTER SEVENTEEN

Since his meeting with Ronson at the Meteorite two weeks ago, Sobczak has been in frequent contact with the Holland detective. It had taken almost a month for Beiko Talo to be reported missing. The woman split her time between her alcoholic mother Rhonda's, her half-brother Scott's, and the streets. In short, she was the sort of person who could go missing and not be missed.

When the call first came in to Hartford PD, no one took much notice. With a history of drug abuse and homelessness, Beiko was a prime candidate to go MIA. There was little reason to put out an APB. It was only at Scott's insistence that Hartford got off its butt and was able to track down Beiko's last-known whereabouts to the Meteorite, where eyewitnesses reported seeing her leave with a man in a truck.

The bartender got the best look, but her physical description was too generic to yield traction. She couldn't even be sure of the race, the bar so dark. The suspect paid cash, left no credit card receipts. Hartford had no other leads. Since Scott, a resident of Holland County, filed the report, the case was handed over. By the time it was passed along to Detectives Ronson and Crasnick, efforts to find Talo had dwindled to perfunctory. That all changed when Ronson made a startling discovery.

Twelve years ago, Beiko Talo and April Abbott were enrolled in the same residential treatment facility. Green Hills in Farmington. The program targeted unruly teens, first-time offenders caught with marijuana, pills, powders, DUIs, wild children worrying their parents. Green Hills has long since closed, no one left to talk to, information hard to come by. Given Norman's recent relocation, this unsettling connection between Talo and the banker-man's dead ex-wife has sparked renewed interest in the case.

Because no one can prove Norman was ever in Hartford, let alone at the Meteorite, he has yet to be charged or even questioned. But the Holland detectives are working hard to fix that, and want Sobczak to ramp up his observations. No more a few hours here and there—the chief is now on permanent patrol, every day, driving to the bluff overlooking Shallow Lake. The job isn't a complicated one, and Sobczak could assign any of his charges, Tom, Joe, even Ron. But Sobczak has to admit there is a strange thrill being on active patrol.

From his car overlooking the lakehouse, Chief Sobczak talks to Detective Ronson on the phone. They've been doing this briefing daily, discussing how to proceed.

"Maybe it's time we talk to April's father," Ronson suggests. It is the same suggestion she makes most days, and Sobczak offers a variation on his usual rebuttal.

"Art Abbott is a big man in this town. I'm not saying we can't talk to him. But going to him right now, asking why his daughter was in a crisis program for troubled girls in Farmington? Given his feeling toward authorities? I can tell you how he's going to respond. He's gonna rail into you. And me. He'll demand to know why Todd Norman is being allowed to build that lakehouse. Art is a private, protective man who doesn't let go of something once he gets his teeth in it." Sobczak pulls out the binoculars. "Then we'll have his attorneys to deal with."

"Helping us helps him."

"It runs deeper than that. Art's still bitter about the DOT scandal. He won't be anxious to help the same police who he thinks screwed him over and then let his daughter's killer go free."

"Those are two separate cases."

"Not to Art. Tell me more about Green Hills. What makes the place so special?"

"Besides it being a hospital for troublemakers? Usually with substance abuse issues?"

"I never heard about April having a drug problem." Sobczak gazes down the ravine. "Covenant is not that kind of town."

"Drugs are everywhere, Dwayne. Green Hills took both private and state insurance. Not many higher-end hospitals do that. Means you got a mix of clientele. Some with money like April. Some street kids like Talo. And everywhere in between."

"April was friends with my daughter. She was over the house a lot. They were teenagers and I'm sure they snuck beers. But you're talking about a residential rehab for the hard stuff."

"I've told you everything I know. Hearsay. Records are sealed. We can't get access without a court order, and we don't have enough to go before a judge. We'd get laughed out of chambers."

"Do you have a theory?"

"Nothing that isn't fantastic and far-fetched."

Down below, Sobczak watches Todd Norman stack slats of lumber. Despite the cold, nothing slows him down. The man is a machine. Clockwork. Even his trips to the john after his morning coffee and Danish—he's had a port-o-potty installed on site—regular as spring showers.

"Right now," Sobczak says, "I'll take far-fetched."

"If the two girls were in a program together, maybe April said something to Talo."

"Such as?"

"Something people don't want getting out. When we were searching Talo's belongings at her brother's, we found correspondence between the two girls."

"Saying what?"

"They're the kind of letters teenage girls write to one another."

"I was never a teenage girl, Detective."

"Secretive, serious, emotional. Nothing specific. More a tone. But there are references to 'keeping mouths shut' and 'not telling anyone,' things like that. Piques curiosity. Girls that age can be dramatic. April was dating Norman by then. Two girls linked to the same bad man. One dead, another missing. One is chance. Two is a pattern that hasn't been discovered yet."

Along the shore, Todd Norman pounds, slaves, hammers and hauls. In the past couple weeks alone, the man has made considerable progress. The exterior is still unpainted but the windows and doors are up. This early December morning, temps have dipped well below freezing. Even in his car with the heater full blast, Sobczak can see his breath crystalize. Sobczak's spied the rolls of insulation. Soon as Norman gets heat, the SOB can move in whenever he wants.

"Maybe you're right," he says. "About Art Abbott." Sobczak checks the time. "Let me talk to him. We have a history. I think he'll be more receptive if I handle it."

"I realize how sticky this is for you," Ronson says. "I have one more avenue to explore. Long shot. A friend with ties to the Bureau of Rehabilitation Services. He's trying to get me the name of the Green Hills group facilitator."

"What about confidentiality laws?"

"I'm hoping that because the program was terminated, we won't be stymied."

Sobczak and Ronson end their call with the promise to talk again after Sobczak meets with Art. Setting his cell in its dashboard holder, Sobczak rubs his hands for heat till they feel red, chaffed, prickly. He puts on his leather gloves while that lunatic Norman hoists a pick ax over his head. Wrenching his back with considerable torque, Todd Norman drives the blade into the hard dirt over and over and over.

Sobczak pulls his secret pack of Pall Malls from the glove compartment, lights one. His stomach rumbles. Needs food. He'll call Art, set up a meeting. But he's stopping off for a sandwich and coffee first. Norman isn't going anywhere. Maybe it's not hunger that's giving his gut fits. Sobczak's nerves are acting up. Dealing with Art Abbott promises to be an ordeal.

The chief reverses on the bluff, k-turns, heads back up the hillside access road, disappearing over the crest.

Down below, a Honda CRV slowly pulls in the drive.

CHAPTER EIGHTEEN

Tracy didn't plan on coming here when she asked Diana to babysit this morning. At least she tells herself that. Tracy needed to run errands. Gym, grocery store, pharmacy. Nothing about William Sonoma on the agenda. No housewarming present. No intention of seeing him. Tracy needs for this to be true because if it isn't, if she intended to end up here, what does that say about her? Not just as a mother but as a human being?

Yet here she sits in the Honda CRV, engine idling, gift in hand, watching a man she barely knows as he brings a sledgehammer over his head, thundering down on shale, cracking open the hard surface. It's a violent, unforgiving motion. Why does she feel drawn to him? How have two brief encounters burrowed into her brain like this? Is something seriously wrong with her?

Tracy isn't the type to vet prospective boyfriends. Even after her ex. But Todd is a special case. Not many crushes are accused of homicide. In order for her to be sitting in this driveway, Tracy has come to accept a couple truths: one, yes, she is attracted to Todd, no point lying to herself anymore; and, two—and this is the more important one—she doesn't believe he did it. She has spent many late-night hours reading up on the trial, articles from the library and online. Not one shred of evidence says Todd did it. No DNA, no history of violence, no real motive. All the prosecution had was conjecture: the life insurance policy, taken out shortly before April was murdered. Only Todd didn't need the money; the man went broke fighting the charges. In the end, why should it be up to him to prove his innocence? Isn't it supposed to be the other way around? Why is it so hard to believe what Todd said during the trial? He wasn't there. Credit card receipts, surveillance cameras confirm this. A nutcase, some desperate junkie, lifelong petty criminal broke in looking for cash, got startled, panicked, and killed his wife. What if prosecutors hadn't been able to get the conviction, not due to any legal loopholes or slick lawyering, but because they were wrong?

You're not planning on marrying the man, Tracy tells herself. And who says he feels the same way? Maybe he was just a guy trying to be helpful at a store. Except, no. Tracy may've been out of the dating game a while, but some parts remain primal. Flirting is flirting, and he hadn't been subtle. He admitted as much at the Big Y during their Fogelberg moment before Thanksgiving.

Todd takes notice. Took him long enough. Tracy has been sitting here, watching him work, running through the myriad contingencies and rotating reasons why she isn't crazy for the past ten minutes. He's been so focused on the task before him, dedicated, unrelenting, oblivious to her presence. But now he drops the sledgehammer, slides his winter coat over the long-sleeved thermal. Tracy's dashboard reads seventeen degrees. He's been out there in nothing but long-john top and jeans, hat and gloves. The man must be freezing, working up a sweat... Oh my God, Trace, you're cracking.

He doesn't walk toward her, not at first, face twisted in a peculiar expression. He's probably wondering the same thing she is: what is she doing there?

The wind lashes ice. As cold as it is outside, Tracy isn't so careless as to invite the man inside her car. They are in the middle of the woods, no one watching. No one knows she is here. Diana might've been able to deduce something was up, but that doesn't put Tracy at the lakehouse. Then again, knowing Diana, she can picture her friend in the kitchen with a pair of binoculars and bowl of popcorn cradled in her lap, watching Tracy act like a schoolgirl.

Tracy's heart races, rams, pinballs around her rib cage. But not from fear. It's exhilaration, the rush of doing something dangerous. Is this what thrill-junkies experience? A reckless dance with death. Tracy admonishes herself for being so dramatic. Deep breath, head up, project as much confidence as you can.

She's parked a good fifty yards away. Todd isn't rushing, more observing, head tilted, curious, an animal poking its snout out the cave, determining its next move.

Grabbing the large ivory gift bag, Tracy jams her other hand in her pocket, the one with the keys, slipping a pair between her knuckles, trying not to laugh. Nervousness? Feeling stupid for being so frivolous? Leaving her warm cab, Tracy knows she isn't any safer in the wild.

Todd studies her face, which no doubt twitches and switches emotive response like an actress warming up before a play.

"Hi," she says when he's within earshot.

A stronger-than-usual wind races over the lake, rustling birch branches. Rough waves slap railroad-tie barriers.

"Hello," he says, nodding at her purchase. "What's in the bag?"

Tracy takes a step forward, places the bag at his feet, two steps back, like ordering lobster bisque from the Soup Nazi.

"What's this?"

"Housewarming present."

Todd crouches down and extracts the long, thin metal stake with the praying mantis head. He glances up.

"It's for gardening," she says. "A weathervane." And she wants to retreat inside her coat for bringing such a random, silly gift. But that's not why she's here, and they both know it. The gift's a pretense. She spent six minutes picking it out.

He turns the stake upside down, grim mouth threatening to break into a grin. He presses his finger against the tip. "Sharp," he says.

She tries not to laugh. Nerves. Tracy nods at the house. "So this is the lakehouse." Way to lead with the profoundly obviously, Trace.

"It is." Todd turns toward the large structure, which now features four walls and a roof. Unpainted, still a lot of work to do, but getting there.

"Thank you." He holds up the gardening stake. "Might surprise you, but this is the first housewarming present I've received."

Tracy turns around and starts walking back to her car. After a few feet, she glances over her shoulder at Todd standing there, lumberjack stance, and those alien blue eyes, praying mantis gardening stake still in hand. The sensible part of her says to forget she came here, chalk up a stupid idea to folly. Leave it at bizarre housewarming gift. The memory will fade with the rest of life's embarrassments, another clunky object in an unflattering cupboard you don't bother opening or sifting through.

Instead she tosses her hair and waves him along.

Tracy keeps walking, not waiting for Todd's response. Inside the car, she turns the motor over and buries her face in her hands. When he knocks on the window, she jumps and he laughs, but not in a mean way, more to say it's just as weird for him.

She unlocks the door and lets him in.

Blasting the heat, Tracy places her frozen fingers against the vents like she's fire-roasting marshmallows. "I can't feel my toes."

"Figured you'd be use to this weather by now. It gets cold in the city, but nothing like this. I think my internal organs are calcifying."

"Did you do it?"

She hadn't, of course, planned on asking that. Completely lacking in tact. But it comes out, subconscious overriding sensibility.

On the stony shore, the gardening stake stands tall, praying mantis head staring out of the ivory gift bag.

"Thanks for the housewarming present," he says. "But if you are still on the fence about whether I'm guilty, might not want to go with a gift so ... stab-y."

"I'm sorry. I don't know why I asked that."

Out the window, a murder of crows flocks from the trees. Wide black wings spread, swooping down, grazing the water, before figure-eighting back to the branches.

"Did you know," Todd says, "every other part of the country, crows migrate south for the winter? Not Connecticut. No one knows why. They gut it out." When Tracy has no response to the random, avian trivia, he adds, "Does it matter what I say?"

"A bit, yeah."

"I tell you no, what then? We can still be friends?"

Tracy wants to tell him here's his chance to earn an ally in town. She brought him a housewarming present, didn't she? Welcome committee, peace offering. She doesn't think he's a bad guy. She *wants* to believe. She understands how someone can get caught up in a messy situation; can be saddled with an undeserving, lousy reputation; become the victim of circumstance. But it's hard to find the right words.

He helps her out. "There is no right answer. No, I did not do it." Todd pans over. "But what would you expect me to say if I did? I won a protracted court battle, which stripped every asset I had to my name, but now, sitting on the banks of the choppy water, I'm going to confess? Because that's what you'll think later, no matter what I say, when it's two in the morning and you can't sleep, or next Friday when you're standing in line, getting your coffee, picking up light bulbs at the hardware store, whatever. I gave up trying to convince anyone. People are going to believe what they believe."

"If you want to be left alone, why move to Covenant? If you couldn't escape this mess in New York, you have to know it'll be ten thousand times worse here."

"I made a promise to someone."

"People are already talking about it. Central Connecticut has a bunch of good ol' boys who like to think they're rednecks. Take pride in it, in fact. Drive around with Confederate flag decals on their trucks, listening to shitty country music, chawing tobacco. One night, a few too many beers, a bunch will drive their 'Merican four-by-fours down here, playing tough."

"Not sure the response you're looking for."

"You'll be a hermit, forced to live behind a fence like that guy up on Gores Highway."

"Sorry. I'm not familiar with local lore."

"There's a house up on Gores Highway, by the orchard, got fifteen-foot-high walls. Old colonial. Rumor has it guy who built the fence was on the Titanic, dressed up like a woman to get on a lifeboat. When people in town found out what he'd done, they'd drive by and pelt his house with rotten tomatoes. So he built the wall."

"Is it true?

Tracy flusters. "I don't know. It's a story everyone around here knows."

"What was his name?"

"I don't know."

"Never bothered to fact check whether the story was true?"

"This's from when I was a kid. We didn't have internet access like today."

"You do now."

"It's just a story."

"Right. A story."

Tracy wants him out of the car. He's too hard a nut to crack, like a lot of men she's known. Rigid, tightens up, gives what he feels like when he feels like giving it and nothing more. She's offering him a chance to tell his side of the story, willing to be open-minded, hear him out. Which is a better deal than he'll get from anyone else in this town. He's not even trying to convince her. They could've had this conversation the first night and been done with it.

"You're right," he says. "I could head west, south, out of the country. I have the money to do that. Get a condo on the beach in the Cayman Islands, eat fresh Mahi-Mahi, crack coconuts. But I made a promise. Anyone who knows me, which I'll admit is a dwindling number, knows what my word means."

It's an impassioned speech, a closing note and final say on a matter. But he doesn't exit the car.

"You want to get dinner sometime?" he asks.

"Excuse me?"

"Dinner. You and me. Like a restaurant? Put on nice clothes. We'll order food, wine. Talk."

"Are you ... asking me out?"

"I'm doing my best." He smiles.

Tracy feels her stomach flutter.

But she is *not* saying yes.

He holds the pose a few. Tracy can't even respond, incredulous, the proposal outlandish. When he accepts that being cute won't be enough, that charm only goes so far, Todd reaches for the handle. A part of him had to know it wouldn't work. High hopes?

"Thank you for the gift," he says, climbing out of the CRV. He strips off the bulky winter coat, athletic build on display, winks. "You know where to find me if you change your mind."

He walks back to his tools, selects the one that'll do the most damage, and rages against the rock.

CHAPTER NINETEEN

The Abbotts live in the deep, dark wood of Metacomet Circle. Art Abbott, who once owned an insurance company in town, has retired. For a while, Art dabbled in politics, running the DOT, Department of Transportation, until he was accused of nepotism and forced to step down before he ever got a leg up. A minor scandal, but his reputation took a hit, legacy tarnished. It is a slight Art has never forgotten. His bank accounts and investments survived fine. He's made enough money to retire early. He and his wife, Beverly, do not lack. Small-town rich. Big house, bigger yard, a lot of time on their hands. They never moved past their daughter's death. How could they? They've always hated Todd Norman, never trusted him, always thought he was a con artist. That's the official version, and Art Abbott is nothing if not stubborn.

Though their children grew up together and both men enjoy positions of stature in Covenant—the chief likes to believe they share equal footing—Sobczak and Art were never friends. That was before. And now Sobczak is part of the same system that failed the Abbotts. Sobczak tries to see it from Art's point of view and not take it personally. Sobczak can't imagine how he'd respond if it were his daughter.

Sobczak agrees that the evidence against the Abbott's former son-in-law is staggering. Sobczak has done a fair amount of digging. Not hard in a town like Covenant. Everyone knows everyone. Everyone has a story. Once upon a time, the Abbotts very much loved their son-in-law, enough to hand over valuable lakefront property to Todd and April as a wedding present. Art's hatred for the man came later, after their daughter's death, intensifying after he beat the charges. They sought an injunction to stop him from building the lakehouse. He beat that too. Why Norman would choose to move to his dead wife's hometown, Sobczak can't hazard a guess.

The image Todd Norman portrayed during court proceedings, which Sobczak has relived via transcripts, paints a dull picture. Hard-working, loving, loyal husband. If anything, Norman was *too* hard working, *too* loving. *Too* loyal. That alone makes Sobczak suspicious. Todd Norman, handsome man in high finance who wheeled and dealed in the swankiest parts of New York, a playground for a man of means, has no skeletons. Not so much as a single delinquent credit card payment, parking ticket, nothing. Everyone interviewed expressed the same shock and surprise—"He seemed like such a nice man!" "They seemed so in love!"

That's New York. This is Covenant, where people don't worry about political correctness. The man is guilty. Twists only come at the end of movies. Like Ronson said on the phone this morning: "A dead wife? Wake me when it's *not* the husband."

Punching his squad car in park, Sobczak hops down, feels his heft when he lands, the weight adding dignity, evidence he exists.

Art Abbott is already waiting at the door, worked up, frantic, checking his watch. Art is quintessential Type A, a very high-strung man, fastidious, meticulous in his diction, unwavering in his expectations.

"It's almost twelve o'clock." He stands at the top of his stairs, arms akimbo, an admonishing dad, even if he and Sobczak are the same age. Growing up with the man must've been a joy.

Sobczak observes the topiary choices in the hedgerow that frame the manicured lawn. Like a presentation at the state fair. Circus animals on parade. How often do the gardeners have to come out here and trim these elephants?

"Noon," Art repeats, pointing at his watch. "You said you'd be here at eleven-thirty, Dwayne."

As if Sobczak can't tell time. He decides to forgo the handshake, establish authority. Sobczak is the cop after all, the one in charge. You can't let a man like Art think he's running the show. Gotta put him in his place from the start. This isn't a reunion, and as unpleasant as this might be for Art, the chief has a job to do.

Sobczak bulls past the gaunt, former insurance broker, the disgraced DOT commish, inside the opulent home. Who needs a place this big? Too many empty rooms. Even the paintings hang overtly resplendent, gaudy, trying too hard, not one the teensiest bit askew.

"I thought you said you'd be here half hour ago?" Art Abbott says, belaboring the tardiness. "I understand circumstances change, unforeseen events come up, but a simple phone call—"

"Where's your wife?" Sobczak asks. He knows Beverley is home. Poor thing never leaves, sequestered.

"Lying down. She's not feeling well. It has been a very difficult week. Month. Year. Nothing has been easy since that night."

Sobczak can't imagine the pain of losing a daughter, one's own child, and he doesn't wish to make light of another's pain. Still, hearing Art complain about hardships feels out of place, like salt in coffee. There is an air of theater when he speaks. Rich people can hurt, too. Maybe Sobczak is a class warrior after all.

"I'd like to talk to you both, if that's possible."

Art glances up the long, winding staircase, seeming to consider the request, dismissing the possibility before he's finished shaking his head. "Anything you tell me, I will relay."

With Beverley, Art will be less hostile. The questions Sobczak needs to ask are not easy ones. Like, why was your daughter in a group home for drug addicts? What kind of drugs? How long was she using? When did she stop—*did* she stop? Most importantly: what about these friends she kept after the program? Asking about precipitating events makes it sound as though Sobczak is questioning Art's parenting, placing some of the blame at Art's feet, and that is not his intention. But he needs to differentiate between what was warranted and what was overreaction. Green Hills is now a lead, a veritable starting point, and Sobczak must build a case from the ground up. He never gets the chance to develop a strategy.

"I read in the paper that the girl they found was some junkie?"

Takes Sobczak a moment to come around on the conversation. Of course Art is up on current events.

"From Meriden? 'No suspicion of foul play,'" Art quotes verbatim from the newspaper.

"Yes. A mixed-up young lady. Where they found the body seems to be a coincidence."

"Convenient," he says.

"Not sure for who. We've already visited Norman. He has an alibi."

"We?" Abbott spits out the word. "Your staff barely qualifies as police. One of them made me a sandwich the other day. Another changes my brake pads."

"Not enough crime in town to employee a full staff."

"What's our next move?"

"I'm not sure what you mean, Art—" Sobczak now sees the error in his approach. If Sobczak had wanted to talk to anyone else, more than likely he just shows up, unannounced, catches them off guard. With Art, he called first, as a courtesy. All he said on the phone was that he needed to talk to him about the case. Makes sense Art would assume this involves April's death. The cops call and want to talk, it's going to be about solving April's murder, nothing else.

"You're supposed to be the professional. Find something!"

"Can't find what isn't there."

"Wait," Art Abbott says. "That's it? A dead woman shows up on that son of a bitch's doorstep and you're going to lie down? Like a dog?" Art resumes his agitated pacing. "If you're not going to help catch Norman, what the hell did you want to talk to me about? Why are you here?"

"I have to ask you some questions."

"About what?"

Sobczak checks the ceiling. "I think Beverley should be present—"

"I already told you. She isn't well. What is this about, Dwayne?"

"Green Hills."

Art Abbott's face gathers fury. He stabs a bony finger out the window. "That monster killed my daughter! Got our money. Took our land. Now he's here, murdering again, rubbing our noses in it. And you want to talk about my slain daughter's emotional hardships when she was seventeen?" Art Abbott grips the sides of his slick head, fingers furrowing for hairs that no longer exist.

"I need to ask you some questions—"

At his maple desk, Art plucks a card, hands it to Sobczak. "That is the number for my attorney. Any questions you have can go through him. Do not bother me again." Art Abbott walks to the door. "I thought you came here with answers, Dwayne. I can't believe I was foolish enough to pin hopes on you. I should've known better. You're not a cop; you're a glorified meter maid." He opens the door, stands to the side, and won't condescend to look until the big, old cop lumbers past, showing himself out.

CHAPTER TWENTY

Although he's cancelled all appointments through the New Year, the doctor likes to maintain his schedule, keep up appearances of regularity. He is still a practicing psychiatrist after all, and when he resumes seeing patients, Dr. Bakshir won't be able to withstand the tarnished reputation of a man sleeping till noon, seen driving through city center disheveled and unkempt.

The doctor wakes at six every morning, goes for a run, and picks up his morning paper. The local convenience store is attached to the Mobil station. He makes small talk with the cashier. He could have a paper delivered, but Dr. Bakshir enjoys the fresh air, getting out of the house, the conversation. Since the news about Wendy, he's been inclined to isolate, not a healthy coping mechanism when mourning.

Dr. Bakshir sits at his computer, reads the *Courant*, and scours the online sites. The Green Hills files rest by his feet in case he needs to cross-reference.

He begins today, as always, by looking for further details about Wendy. These are cursory glances. We are going on several months now. The chances of police reopening the overdose of a junkie rests somewhere between the odds of an intravenous opiate addict getting sober and true political reform, that is zero and non-existent. This perfunctory checking for additional information has become a tic, an obsessive-compulsive tendency, the same malady afflicting some of his patients. And just as he advises them, he could fight the urge—simply not do it, don't feed the beast—but sometimes it is easier to acquiesce, requires less effort to play along with our mind's games.

With no one and nothing left to chase after, he's grown bored. The doctor considers reopening the practice earlier than he intended. New Year's has always been a symbolic target date. He anticipated needing more time to deal with fallout from the Wendy situation.

He has begun composing a welcome-back message to his clients, informing them that he is, again, open for business, ready to resume the hard work of unwavering self-analysis. As he mentally formulates phrasing and syntax, he stumbles upon an article in this morning's paper that gives him great pause, forcing him to reconsider those plans.

Beiko Talo, former Green Hills' client, has been reported missing.

With great interest, he reads on. The police blotter does not offer much. Few details. Last seen at a Hartford nightclub. "Persons of interest," no suspects, generic description, man of a certain age with whom she was seen speaking; they don't even have a definitive race or composite sketch. No one is calling it a kidnapping or, heaven forbid, something worse. A troubled young woman without a home, Beiko hasn't been seen in well over a month. An investigation is under way, and anyone with possible information is asked to please contact police. The doctor is now glad he did not leave his name when he called her half-brother Scott. Sometimes the doctor thinks his subconscious is smarter than he is.

Then again ... phone records.

How hard are the police going to search for another homeless drug addict?

They are interested enough to print her disappearance in the paper.

And given his connection to the Green Hills girls, the fates of April, Wendy, and now the uncertain status of Beiko—how soon before the police start asking questions?

There is only one girl left.

He had a difficult time locating Shannon O'Connor that first time around, the lack of leads forcing him to abandon efforts. How hard had he tried? Not hard enough. And now stakes have been raised.

Dr. Bakshir lifts the milk crate containing the Green Hills files onto his kitchen table. Then he gets a cold glass of whole milk. The doctor hasn't eaten breakfast. He's been having a hard time keeping down solid food of late. Nerves. Milk, despite its having fallen out of favor with the mainstream, is an ideal complete protein. It's why we feed it to infants. If the doctor had to pick one perfect foodstuff, the most efficient delivery of nutrients and vitamins, he'd be hard pressed to find something better than whole cow's milk.

The doctor knows he is not thinking well.

He sifts through the reports on Shannon, searching for any small detail he might've missed, but gets stuck on Wendy. He shouldn't revisit Wendy's case. *Not now.* He knows this will not help. But he cannot help himself.

Scouring these files, he feels his heart break all over again.

God, so much potential, wasted. He wonders if Wendy ever appreciated his faith in her.

As her treating therapist, Dr. Bakshir had been aware of the psychological problems, the depression, the self-harm, the history of substance abuse. He didn't learn about the sexual trauma until it was too late.

A doctor never stops being a doctor. Random get together, birthday party, holiday bash, someone eventually uncovers his true identity, and then the self-conscious jokes begin.

"Better watch what you say. He's a psychiatrist. He's probably analyzing you!"

Then they all have a good laugh. Dr. Bakshir always plays along.

"Of course not," he'll say. "Even psychiatrists take breaks."

In truth, he *is* analyzing. Everyone. Each word. All the time. He is unable to turn that switch off.

With Wendy, he got as much of the story from what she didn't say as from what she did. With her self-harm behaviors, Dr. Bakshir would've guessed it eventually. The numbers backed him up. Close to one in three women are sexually abused at some point in their lives. Factor in the behaviors Wendy demonstrated—the drugs, promiscuity, and cutting—she was textbook. But at the time, Dr. Bakshir was new, inexperienced, optimistic. Necessity made Wendy a loner. Like so many victims of sexual abuse, she excelled at rehearsed responses, excuses, and cover-ups.

Dr. Bakshir finishes his milk.

This is not going away. Regardless of what the police discover about Beiko, until Dr. Bakshir finds the last girl, nothing is going to change. He'd been lucky with April, the case so sensational, his role relegated to afterthought. Wendy, a classic case of misdirection.

No, Dr. Bakshir will not be reopening his practice early after all. He will not close his eyes and hope for the best. When it comes to luck, Dr. Bakshir believes in making his own.

The only working number he has for Shannon, her Aunt Laura's, yielded nothing that first attempt. During their brief, contentious phone conversation, Dr. Bakshir learned little, except Shannon is not welcome at her house any more. No addresses for friends. No telephone numbers. No names. Before the phone was abruptly hung up.

Telephones and computers are no longer viable research methods. If he is to find Shannon, if the doctor is to close this book for good, he will need to be far more proactive.

The doctor powers down his computer, brings his teacup to the sink. He does not wash it. He does not set it to dry on the rack.

He snares the notepad with name and address, yanks his winter coat from the rack, and flicks off the lights.

The doctor has a new mission.

CHAPTER TWENTY-ONE

"You did what?" Diana drinks her wine at the bar, making Tracy repeat what she heard her say the first time. These are the little games that Diana plays. Innocuous usually. This evening, they annoy.

"I went to his lakehouse." Tracy thinks about ordering something stronger than wine, maybe get good and drunk for a change. But she's not twenty anymore. Tracy can't remember the last time she got hammered.

Tonight is the start of Brett's weekend. He came to get Logan earlier. He never made mention of that earlier email, the one where he hinted, none-to-subtle, about getting back together. Which cements Tracy's initial belief that it had been sent at the end of a long, liquored, lonely night.

"I brought him a housewarming present."

"You are *crazy*." Diana's eyes betray a touch of admiration. There is so little to do in Covenant that brief exchanges with possible psycho killers feel exotic.

The bar, Slider's, is a sports bar on the outskirts of Covenant.

Too bright. Too many TVs. Too many overweight, past-their-prime, balding ex-jocks, drinking their sad American beers. But nightlife options in Covenant are limited. There's this, the Station Café by the old, defunct train tracks, built long ago when trains had a reason to stop in towns like Covenant, or TGI Fridays by the mall. If Tracy felt like heading into the city, there's the Meteorite, if it's even still open. Tracy is too old for places like the Meteorite. Even if she, like every other kid in Covenant, snuck down to the nightclub at some point in high school.

The bartender, a young girl with a nose ring who looks half Tracy's age, asks what they're having. Everyone seems half Tracy's age these days.

"House red," Tracy says.

The bartender points across the way at two men who look familiar. Both are losing their hair with tired, old eyes. "First round is on them." One of the men smiles.

Tracy recognizes Dave Mancini and John Bynum, Class of I Can't Believe We Graduated the Same Year. Tracy winces a smile, lifting her hand, as Diana grips her knee, nails like talons digging into her flesh. But what's she going to do? They all share this small space, and Dave and John were both nice guys in high school. Not the type Tracy dated, but she's not going to be rude.

"Tracy Somerset," Dave says.

"Dave Mancini," Tracy says.

John settles next to Diana, who shifts in her seat.

"Still want that house red?" the bartender asks as if she can read minds, but Tracy sticks to the plan.

"Haven't seen you in here before," Dave says.

"Come here often?" Tracy says, but no one gets the joke.

"Every Friday." Dave nods toward a dartboard sandwiched between a pair of old-school pinball machines, one of which is out of order. "Dart league." He pauses a second, tries to catch John's eyes. "Finals tonight."

"How'd you do?"

"You know what they say. No such thing as second place." Dave grabs his sad American beer. "Just first loser."

Diana wriggles free from John, who hasn't done anything but sit down near her, and comes around to Tracy's side.

"So what have you been doing for the last—when was graduation? Thirteen years?"

"Fourteen."

Diana catches the sparkly bartender's eye for another glass of wine.

"Well, you look great," Dave says.

"You too."

Dave drops deadpan. "I'm bald, Tracy."

The joke eases the tension. Dave isn't here to try to pick up anyone. He's an old classmate saying hi. Diana recognizes this as well, and takes her old seat next to John.

They rehash the good ol' days that weren't so good the first time around: the classes they had together; teachers who were nice; the ones who weren't. Tracy, Diana, and Dave rehash. John drinks his beer and watches sports highlights. It doesn't take long for conversation to steer to April Abbott. Her murder is the biggest thing to happen to this town, and with Todd Norman in Covenant, the subject is back in the news.

"You want to know what's crazier?" Dave says. "I heard the guy who did her, her psycho ex? Rich bastard who bought his way off? He's building a house on Shallow Lake."

"You're shitting me?" Beyond the casual "What's up?", this is the first thing John Bynum has said.

"I didn't tell you about it?"

"Rich asshole." John returns to his beer and TV.

Diana nudges Tracy to keep her mouth shut. She knows her friend. Tracy Somerset, forever defending the wounded birds of the world.

"I wouldn't worry about it," Dave says. "You know Covenant. No *way* someone doesn't take a hatchet to the place."

"What's the guy's name?" John asks, eyes still glued on football replays.

"I don't remember."

Tracy bites her tongue.

"Although," Dave says, "if we're being honest? Between April and Amber, you figured one of them would get mixed up in something bad."

"You're forgetting Amanda," John says.

"The town cop's daughter?"

"The A-holes," John says.

"Oh, I remember. Inseparable. The hot girls every guy wanted." Dave checks with Tracy and Diana, trying to work out how to say they were pretty too. Tracy taps his thigh to let him know he can stop thinking so hard. Dave lets go an audible sigh. "I mean, Amanda, she had her head on right. Those other two… That's why they got sent away."

"Sent away?" Tracy says.

"Right after high school."

"During high school," John says.

"I don't remember that."

"No offense, Trace. But you were with Brett Coggins, like, twenty-four seven. Plus, they were, what? Two grades below us?"

"What ever happened to Amber Coit?" Tracy asks.

"Heard she met some rocker guy. Drummer, I think. Pretty big band. Can't remember the name. Went off with him, never came back."

Tracy starts to take a sip of wine, stops, thinks. "You said they were sent away. April and Amber. Sent away where?"

"April's father shipped her off to some psych hospital. Think she got caught breaking in to the old Railroad Salvage, drunk."

"Smoking pot," John says.

"All I remember is her and Amber got in trouble."

"So they got locked up in a hospital?" Tracy had graduated by that point, had started making plans for her wedding, which left less time for high school gossip.

"Part of their sentencing? I don't know. But it wasn't both. Just April. End of their senior year. Amber found Jesus."

"Thought you said she ran off with a rock star?"

"You know Amber Coit. Girl was *crazy*. Drugs, religion, same difference. She was always chasing. She smoked cinnamon sticks trying to get high."

"Dried banana peels," John says, before sipping his beer.

"Something weird." Dave waves over the bartender. "Shot of Jameson." He turns to Tracy and Diana, who shake him off. "And a Bud Light."

"Amber was living with the Abbotts, wasn't she?" Diana says.

"Senior year anyway. She was an orphan."

This part Tracy remembers, Amber not having parents. Such a sad story. Maybe because Tracy lost her parents young too. Amber's mother died of cancer, like half the people in Covenant, and then a year later her father died of a different type of cancer. One day someone will do a study about the abnormal number of cancer cases in Covenant. Like the entire town was built atop a radioactive burial ground.

"A lot of families took her in," Dave says.

"Covenant's like that."

And they all nod, because, say what you want about Covenant, but it takes care of its own. Which also makes it a town that doesn't take kindly to strangers.

Dave says he needs to get back to the wife before she tears him a new one, and he and John make ready to leave. Dave says they'll keep in touch; he'll look her up on Facebook. Tracy says great. Tracy doesn't use Facebook.

"Glory days," Diana says after they are gone. "Yay." She shakes her little fists. "Back to Todd. How was your date?" Tracy bristles when Diana squeezes her shoulder. "No, seriously, what was it like? Where did you talk to him?"

"In my car."

"Alone? In your car? In the middle of the woods? Living on the edge, girl."

"It's possible he didn't do it."

"And it's possible he did. I don't care how good looking, no *way* I get in the car with a man like that."

"You don't even know what he's like."

"You do? I read the stories. Rich banker, under water, kills wife and collects the insurance money. That is, like, every Lifetime movie ever made."

"That's not even what happened."

"Suddenly you're an expert on the Banker Butcher?"

"Banker Butcher?"

"I read the nickname somewhere. I think a reporter was hoping it would stick." Diana pouts. "It didn't."

"That's because it's stupid."

Diana's next wine arrives. The bartender checks with Tracy, who shakes her off. Two glasses is her limit if she's driving. Diana, on at least number five, isn't getting behind the wheel anytime soon.

Neither woman speaks for a while.

Then Tracy turns to her friend. She is desperate to have someone understand, or at least listen so Tracy can make sense of what's going on, verbally process this inextricable pull she feels. Like a color you don't have a word for, a sensation under the skin whose point of origin cannot be pinpointed but the itch torments insatiable nevertheless.

Empathy fills Diana's big eyes. "I know you feel like you missed out." She shakes Tracy's shoulders. "Brett is an asshole. Best thing you did was leave his cheating ass. I'm glad you're reconnecting with our graduating class. But you didn't miss anything while you were gone." She nods toward the door. "Dave Mancini and what's-his-name are nice enough. But face it. They are boring as hell. Dart league?" Diana squares up Tracy, as if to impart important wisdom. Instead, all she says: "Nothing happens in this town."

"April Abbott?"

"Well, there's that."

"What if the jury got it right? That means the guy lost his wife *and* now has to endure a lifetime of scorn. Everyone hates him—"

"Not everyone." Diana smirks.

"It's rubbing me the wrong way. I've spent time with the man."

"You had coffee once. Then bumped into him at the Big Y. And now you let him sit in your car, where he, I'm guessing, professed his innocence."

"He didn't say he was innocent."

"Even worse!"

"No, that's not what I mean. Todd didn't go off about how he'd been railroaded or framed or talk about it as one big injustice. He responded the way someone would if he *didn't* do it."

"And how's that?"

"Like life can just squeeze you sometimes for no reason. Bad luck. Bad hand. Because there is nothing Todd can ever do to change perception. For the rest of his life he will be viewed as a murderer."

"Which might be fitting."

"Or it might not." Tracy stops. "When we were in high school, I was in a park, taking a nap."

"Taking a nap in a park? What are you, a bum?"

"My parents had caught me coming home drunk a few weeks earlier. It was during that stretch junior year where Brett and I broke up."

"Can you narrow it down?"

"Thanks. I was partying all the time, drinking more than I should. I was a wreck."

"Breakups suck."

"That's not what I'm saying. My mom and dad were pissed. They came down hard."

"And?"

"I needed to get away from them. I snuck out, and was taking a nap in a park."

"Which park?"

"The one with all that old leftover playground equipment McDonald's donated. It was a nice summer day. I could smell the new mown grass. Sun shining. And I was lying there thinking, wondering what I was doing with my life, staring at the clouds. I'd just started to feel like everything might be all right. All of a sudden, I feel this tremendous pain in my neck, fire shooting up my skull, burning my brain."

"Headache?"

"This was before the headaches. Someone hit me in the neck with a rock."

"A rock? Who?

"Some kids."

"What kids?"

"I don't know. Just some kids, hiding in the woods, throwing rocks."

"Why would anyone throw a rock at you?"

"No clue. But I took off after them. They were young, elementary, middle-schoolers? They had bikes, and booked it down the trail, laughing. Gone, by the water."

"That's so random."

"When I got home, I had this big welt on my neck. My parents asked what happened. I told them some kids hit me with a rock while I was napping in the park. They thought I was lying. That I'd gone out, gotten drunk, and fallen, had a fight. They wouldn't believe me. No matter what I said."

"What did your mom and dad do?"

"Grounded me longer? I can't remember."

"What are you trying to say, Trace?"

"Weird shit happens, shit that looks like total bullshit to the outside world. And no matter what you say, no one's going to believe you, even if it's the truth. But sometimes you really *do* get hit in the neck with a rock while taking a nap in the park."

CHAPTER TWENTY-TWO

Dr. Bakshir sits in his parked car outside the residence of Shannon O'Connor. Or the closest thing she has to one. Dr. Bakshir is here after a face-to-face with Shannon's Aunt Laura. The plump, dour woman was not happy to see him. When he made it clear he was not leaving without answers, she supplied this address, saying Shannon sometimes slept here. Before she told him to get lost and slammed the door in his face. The doctor did not grow angry, did not entertain fantasies of karmic payback. Malcontents that miserable already endure a never-ending hell of their own making.

The old, yellow depository sits back from a lost highway, on the edge of a forgotten town, off an exit few take. In short, not a place people live. Dr. Bakshir must've passed this way before—the road more travelled before the new interstate—but he does not recall seeing this building. Not a building, he thinks, a warehouse. Maybe an old packing plant. Either way, it has seen better days. Strips of paint peel from the exterior, the weed-filled yard littered with junk—discarded furniture, chairs with missing or fractured legs, rusted bicycles with flat tires abandoned in the rain for too many seasons, the hollow casing of an old refrigerator. The place bears all the hallmarks of a hoarder home.

Several cars are parked, haphazard, off to the side. By all indications, these are not working cars. The collection resembles an automotive graveyard.

No other houses are visible in either direction. Deciduous trees, choke cherry, black ash, and sweetgum, expand dense and thick, blanketing views. A short stonewall meant to shield traffic noises fails to serve a purpose. The wall is missing stones and the traffic is too far away to matter.

Mangy field cats roam the tall, brown grasses. Dr. Bakshir starts doubting anyone is inside at all. If not for the cars, he'd have lost all faith, which is already wavering. When Green Hills closed its doors, who could've guessed the fate that would befall these girls?

Dr. Bakshir hasn't stepped five feet onto the property when the front door pushes open, and a tall, lanky man steps out. Older. Sixties, with shaggy, white-blond hair and a Sam Elliot mustache that overpowers his lip. Dressed like a farmer in a pair of dungaree overalls, he lopes forward with a long, uneven gait.

"You lost?" the man says, mouth full of crooked, country-yellow teeth.

Dr. Bakshir double-checks the address he's written down, the one he got from a curmudgeonly aunt who kicked her own niece to the curb.

"I don't think so," the doctor says.

"Oh, we're all lost, in one way or another, aren't we?" The tall man extends a hand. "Robert Tompkins." He thumbs over his shoulder. "This is my church."

Church? This doesn't look like any church Dr. Bakshir has ever seen.

"Pastor Tompkins, I am looking for Shannon O'Connor. I was told—"

"Friends call me Uncle Bob."

"—that she lives here."

The man steps forward, age stamped on a timeworn visage. In the light, he appears closer to seventy.

"No one lives here. Just told you, son. This is a church."

Strange to be called "son" at his age. Dr. Bakshir scopes the cars peppering the drive. Some must work. "No one else is inside?"

Uncle Bob breezes past the doctor, craning his neck up the long country road that leads back to the highway, looking for what, Dr. Bakshir does not know. In any event, he seems satisfied with what he sees, or doesn't see.

"I didn't say that," Uncle Bob says. "It's a place of worship. People come to celebrate the Lord. Some stay longer than others. This is all impermanent, brother, Earth but a temporary address. To dust we shall return." He clasps his hands together. "We live in the Lord."

"I need to speak to Shannon. It's important."

Uncle Bob studies the doctor, as if weighing whether he is worthy. "You got a number or something?"

Dr. Bakshir extracts a business card from his wallet. The doctor stares at the card, which has both his work and home numbers, as well as address, which he's written out in big, block letters on the back. The doctor debates whether to leave personal information with this preacher man.

Before Dr. Bakshir can decide, the pastor reaches over and plucks the card from his fingers.

"Head-shrinker, eh?"

"Psychiatrist."

"Them's just labels. Don't matter what we call it. We're all searching, aren't we, Dr. Bake-shear?" The pastor pauses. "Indian, eh? You're light-skinned for an Indian."

The doctor remains silent.

"We're both salesmen," the pastor says.

"I don't consider what I do selling—"

"Everyone claims to have the solution, the answer, how to solve the big riddle." Pastor Uncle Bob glances up at the sky, pointing a bony finger. "Do you know why people seek out these things? Psychology, astronomy, pills and chemicals, yoga and whatever else is trending this week?" The pastor seems proud to know the term "trending."

"I think it is a natural—"

"Because they live in a godless world. Without Him, there are no answers, just more questions. Will drive you mad, make you do terrible, terrible things."

Every person Dr. Bakshir meets, he can size up, address, solve, like a puzzle. The picture isn't always pretty, but it comes together one way or the other. If they operate along a broad spectrum of quantifiable human behaviors, even granted wide berths. Men like this Uncle Bob Tompkins cannot be reached. The man believes in magic, in an invisible, all-knowing father in the clouds. How many thousands of gods throughout the history of the world, and yet each believer, regardless his or her faith, is certain theirs is the correct one.

"That leaves the non-believer two choices," the pastor continues. "The fruitless search. Or you give up. You either run like a wild dog, snapping at everything in sight, seeking, yearning for that peak experience, which cannot last. So you're on to the next place, aching to feel a little more. Until you realize you are a dog all right, chasing your own tail. Then tired, exhausted, spent, you settle for the best deal left on the table. A wife, a job, house. Don't need to find love in these things. This is the better of the two options, sure. But it isn't thriving. It is surviving, at the most basic level."

Dr. Bakshir considers this man a charlatan, but Uncle Bob is right about one thing: he *is* a salesman, and like all good salesman, he isn't letting the doctor leave without his best pitch.

"I can offer you more—more than an abyss where you will never find satisfaction. The human mind is not a coloring book. We are more than crude outlines." He gestures over Dr. Bakshir's fit physique, which the doctor takes pride in—the dedicated result of running, calisthenics, eating right—dressing down that effort, as if it were a bad thing, weakness, a sign of vanity. "We are more than shells housing a soul. We are a soul capable of so much more."

CHAPTER TWENTY-THREE

Three police cars pull up the driveway on Savage Hill Road, an outermost district in northernmost Covenant. Farmhouses are interspersed across the surrounding hillside. The squad cars are parked in front of one of these houses. Two of them, actually. There's this bigger one up front. And a smaller one out back. An in-law unit or carriage house. The buildings belong to a man named Jeffrey Franklin. Or rather they belonged. Franklin is deceased, the homes unoccupied. Have been for almost nine months. Late-afternoon winds spin the weathervane, the day heavy, gray, cold. A dusting of new snow covers the field.

With everyone in position, Detectives Stephanie Ronson and Steve Crasnick give the order, waving Holland officers from their patrol cars.

Entry is swift, sudden, efficient. A quick announcement of "Police!" is followed by the sounds of doors being kicked in, battered with rams, brittle woods and locks splintered, smashed. This process carries out, room to room. Until someone shouts, "Secure!"

Nothing. No one. Both dwellings are empty.

The police are looking for Beiko Talo. A pair of witnesses interviewed at the Meteorite claim they saw Talo leave in a truck. Dark green, newish. The truck, both witnesses agree, had a large dent in the fender.

The first thing Sobczak did was re-check Todd Norman's truck, which is red, old, and without dents in its fenders.

This information went on Holland PD's website, and was sent out with mass mailings and electronic community bulletins. Someone called in, reporting seeing a green truck with a dented fender. Fortunately for Sobczak, this came in time to overshadow his ill-fated meeting with Art Abbott, which the chief downplayed to Ronson, painting his performance in a better light, saving face and dignity. Unfortunately, the witnesses who reported seeing the green truck waited two weeks before coming forward, leaving scant hope of finding Beiko Talo. Still, Sobczak wants to be optimistic. When he told his deputy Tom about the raid earlier this morning, he went so far as to say he had a good feeling about it. That good feeling is now gone, replaced by Sobczak's old-school bloodhound sense telling him something is wrong. He wanders the grounds.

The carriage house can't be more than five, six hundred square feet. The main room sports an old couch, stained upholstery, ripped cushions, which sits atop an older, filthier rug, threadbare and worn in spots. Off that area, a smaller room, encased by glass. The first image that comes to Sobczak's mind is of an insolation booth, as if, at one time, the space had been used to record music. Though why a recording studio would be this far out in the sticks, he hasn't a clue.

Sobczak walks room to room. Doesn't take long. Other than

refuse, there is little to see. Articles of dirty clothing lie strewn across the floor, old Converse shoe, flannel, blue jeans. Kit-Kat and Butterfinger wrappers. Flattened Bud boxes. The carriage house retains a strange odor, a tang that permeates the air, urine perhaps. Ammonia. Feral cats. Or maybe evidence of the burgeoning homeless population, which Sobczak had no idea existed. Makes as much sense as anything else these days.

A small bathroom, big enough to fit a toilet, no sink, is the only space left to explore, and too small to be harboring ... what? Fugitives? Sexual deviants? Wayward musicians? Chief Sobczak holsters his firearm. He begins questioning where Holland got its information, because a kidnapper using Savage Hill as a stash house is as likely as Todd Norman being innocent.

Sobczak steps to the window above the toilet, overlooking the back of the property. Long fields of milkweed, withered from recent frost, poke through the snow, dotting the horizon where great mounds of canary grass rise. Knolls, now browned and thinned, will be lush again come spring.

His eyes follow the grand countryside, dipping in gullies and rising over crowns, spanning the sedge fields, to the thick forests that define Covenant, most of the small town swallowed by impenetrable wood.

Movement catches his attention, tree branches rustling out of the corner of his eye. Thoughts of an animal, deer, even a bear. Then he sees the arm. Human. Ducking into the woods, slapping at crooked branches, making a getaway.

Sobczak runs from the carriage house, gun at the ready, toward the woods, shouting back to Holland police, who mill by their cars far up the drive in front of the main house.

"Movement!" Sobczak hollers. "We have movement!"

But he can't wait for backup, and the big cop hoofs into the forest alone.

Though stripped of its leaves and cover, the red maples and white pines of Covenant provide a huge advantage for whoever is fleeing. Sobczak yells, "Stop! Police!" But it is pointless. Too much scenery flies by. He thinks he sees a figure moving, a man, hands, arms, legs. He can't be sure, everything whipping past too fast. Trunks, knots, branches, long, slender limbs, the low winter sun throwing shade against a day's dying light.

Sobczak checks behind him, left, right, spinning around to the front, waiting for help. None is coming.

Twigs snap, sharp bark slicing his hands and face as he burrows deeper into the jungle, barren blackberry bushes wielding thorns like spike strips and barbed wire. Dodging boulders, Sobczak gives pursuit, hopping trickling streams, missing his mark more often than not, boots stuck in the sludge. He is familiar with the terrain, as much as anyone in Covenant can be, but this wilderness is vast, impossible to track; the deeper you go, the more treacherous it becomes.

He is losing distance, ground, sight. Until, out of breath, the big cop drops to a knee. He sees nothing, hears nothing, just the thumping of his old heart.

Trudging out of the forest, pant legs caked in mud, he bumps into a pair of Holland officers, followed by Ronson and Crasnick.

In the clearing, Sobczak sits on a felled log, wiping the cold sweat from his brow, as Ronson fires questions about what he'd seen. Reflecting, Sobczak wonders what he saw, if it was even a man. Or had his mind been playing tricks? He hadn't gotten a good look, not one stopped frame, just flashes of light and speed and slashes of sound.

"What did you see?" Ronson asks again.

"A man," Sobczak says. "I think it was a man."

"You ... think?"

Fifty-six is not that old. But Sobczak is wheezing, out of shape. He needs to give up the cigarettes for good, lungs like a dumpster fire.

"Dwayne? What did you see?"

Sobczak glances up at Ronson, shaking his head. "I'm not sure."

When Sobczak returns to the office, of course no one is there. Today is Saturday. No one shows up on Saturday. Sobczak makes for the precinct bathroom and the first aid kit behind the mirror. He dabs salves and balms on his wounds, which are mostly superficial. The one by his eye is nastier, flesh flayed, a butterfly cut of raw chicken, peeled about an eighth of an inch, from where that one birch branch snapped and thwapped him good. He applies the antibiotic, and covers the gash with a band-aid. Closing the mirror door, he stares longer than he wants to. Behind the abrasions, the thinning hair, the start of an extra chin, the dark circles under his eyes, a young man lurks. He doesn't have the time to find him right now.

"Chief?"

Sobczak turns around to see Tom walking in the back door, red-faced, big bag slung over his shoulder.

"What are you doing here?"

Tom smiles, drops the bag, radar gun poking out. "I was bored. Sat on Deming for a while with the gun. Why not, right? Nothing else to do. Amanda's shopping." He extracts a sheaf of yellow speeding receipts. "Caught a bunch. Like pulling pike out of the pond. Nice drop in the bucket, eh?"

"Put them in Joe Campbell's box," Sobczak says, pulling shut the bathroom door. "Then get out of here. It's late. Go home."

Sobczak walks from the bathroom to his office, every muscle aching.

"You okay? You don't look so good."

Sobczak drops into his chair. The chief isn't much of a talker, doesn't go for the touchy-feely stuff. Mary had been like that. Always wanting to discuss her day, the trivialities, the inconsequential trips to the store, the stories of whose marriage in town was crumbling, whose son was off to college. Mary would talk while Sobczak ate in silence, nodding, occasionally asking questions so Mary would know he was listening. And he was listening. He just didn't care. He liked the sound of her voice. He dismissed Mary's ramblings as insignificant, immaterial, irrelevant. He'd do just about anything to hear her voice again.

Tom pokes his head around the edge of the door. "What happened to your face?"

"That raid I told you about. Savage Hill Road."

"Right. How'd it go?"

"Thought I saw someone running away. Gave chase through the woods. Think it might've been a deer."

Tom points at the bandage. "How bad you cut yourself?"

Sobczak shakes his head but without clear indication of what he's shaking it for.

Tom leaves, returning with gauze and tape, scissors and antibiotic. He holds them up for Sobczak to see. "Let me redress that."

The old chief nods. Tom dresses the wound. Careful in his motions, deliberate. Yes, Tom is his son-in-law, family, but he's also a cop, a man, and there aren't many tender moments like this. Someone taking care of him, in a small way, nothing he couldn't do for himself. This is something Mary would've handled. The intimacy brings the big, old cop to tears.

"Did I rub the cut?"

Sobczak stands, securing the tape and gauze in place. "No, it's fine. Just tired."

"Maybe you want to come over for dinner tonight? Amanda would love it."

The chief doubts his daughter would be happy to see him. "Another time."

Tom bobs like he understands but looks heartbroken. Sobczak feels like a broken-down old man. And worse? He is doubting the things he is sure of. God have mercy.

"Go home, take care of my daughter. She doesn't want to see me right now."

Tom doesn't move, crestfallen. It's more than disappointment over missing dinner. A hard stare from Sobczak, and Tom breaks character, returns a knowing grin, cat with canary.

"What is it, son?" Sobczak asks the question but he's already started to suspect the answer. His gut tells him it's true. He doesn't want to get his hopes up.

Tom's face contorts, grin surrendering to uncontrollable smile, until he can't contain it any longer. "Amanda is going to kill me."

Sobczak waits for the official confirmation.

"Nursery goes up in the spring."

And like that, the old chief's dark outlook suddenly turns bright. "When did you find out?"

"Yesterday. I was *supposed* to invite you over for dinner, on the sly, so *she* could tell you." Tom closes his eyes. "Man, I am going to be in serious trouble. That was the whole point of coming down here this afternoon."

Sobczak shakes his head, fighting his own case of the giggle fits.

What a day.

Dwayne Sobczak is going to be grandpa.

CHAPTER TWENTY-FOUR

WINTER

As the start of winter slides in, Beiko Talo is still missing, a story that Dr. Bakshir follows with obvious interest. She is never found. December passes, Christmastime, almost to the New Year. Not as much snow as usual. In fact, no significant accumulation yet, odd for central Connecticut, particularly the country hills, but not unheard of.

Shannon O'Connor never got in touch. Dr. Bakshir is not surprised. He did not like that pastor, Uncle Bob. The doctor can't be certain his message was passed along. Every other stone he kicked yielded nothing. He can't wait any longer to get back to work. A therapist without patients goes mad.

The doctor has sent out an e-mail informing clients he is ready to restart their therapy. Of course, having been set up with other therapists while he was on sabbatical, the patients have the choice whether to continue with their temporary provider or come back to him. The doctor is not worried. He has worked with most of these people for years, has cultivated relationships; they've developed bonds. Dr. Carson, Dr. Walker, and Dr. Ajay are all fine psychiatrists. This is not a knock on their collective skills, nor is the doctor overinflating his own prowess. He just has the utmost faith in his abilities.

Dr. Bakshir places his leftovers in the oven to reheat for dinner. The doctor has a microwave but prefers the old-fashioned method. He has nothing against technological advancement or time-saving measures, and he isn't one of the many misguided types who believe their food is being saturated with radioactive particles. Despite the added time, Dr. Bakshir, a lifelong vegetarian, has found fruits and vegetables better retain their original flavor in an oven. And he has the time to spare. These past weeks, months have dragged. The grieving went quickly. The thirst for revenge has been harder to satiate. He's entertained notions of confronting Donald, Wendy's father, but Dr. Bakshir is not a violent man.

Sitting at the kitchen table with his bharta and milk, the doctor unfurls today's paper that he has yet to read. The knock at the door comes as a surprise. Although the doctor gets the occasional solicitor, mostly college students canvasing for politicians or trying to sell him on the benefits of solar, they do not come this late.

The woman standing at the door looks familiar, but not in a way the doctor can grasp. Dirty blonde, pretty in a simple, modest fashion. But older than her years, worn down by time, experience. He puts her at about Wendy's age. For a brief second, he feels the presence of Wendy. But then the moment passes, a trick of the brain.

"Dr. Bakshir?"

"Yes?"

"It's me, Shannon." The girl, woman, pulls a card, *his* business card. "I got this at the Crossroads. Uncle Bob, Pastor Tompkins, said you wanted to talk to me?"

He hasn't forgotten about Shannon O'Connor. He has switched gears, was moving back into work mode. The displacement takes a moment to overcome. The doctor must readjust, reconfigure, re-acclimatize.

"Yes, of course, Shannon. It's good seeing you after so long. Please, come in." He glances at his phone, wondering if he missed a message. "Did you try to call first?"

She shakes her head. No explanation. Shannon has always been this way, peculiar, a very specific girl.

"I was about to have dinner," the doctor says. "Can I get you a plate?"

Even though they are no longer doctor and patient, personal contact with clients is discouraged, frowned upon as unprofessional. Such offers, however, are generally met with a polite, "No, thank you." They are a courtesy, an empty gesture, goodwill, something we all say, like offering to pick up a check we already know someone else is getting.

To his surprise, Shannon nods. "Yes. Thank you."

No question of what the food is. The enthusiastic acceptance tells the doctor that Shannon does not have the luxury of turning down a free meal.

The doctor sets out another plate, and collects the bowl of eggplant leftovers from the refrigerator. He ladles out a healthy scoop and places the plate in the microwave. Waiting for the bell to ding, neither speaks. But he does observe. It is impossible for him not to.

A doctor never stops being a doctor.

What he saw at the door—a pretty young woman—proves deceptive. Shannon is not old, and beauty still resides, but her missing years have been hard, unhappy ones.

Dr. Bakshir slides the plate in front of her. The act feels fatherly, nurturing, the difference in age supports that, but this simple, humane act of offering sustenance to another so helpless also stings. Shannon is lost. Those who are lost project their condition; and it's a condition every bit as valid as schizophrenia or borderline personality disorder or ADHD. Being lost isn't as easy to qualify, categorize, remedy. The AMA recommends no medications to treat it. That doesn't mean medications aren't available. They just tend to be of the self-prescribed variety. This world, for some, is more than they can bear.

Shannon scarfs her food. Internet and smart phones are toys for a modern era. Luxuries. Food, clothing, shelter, these are the building blocks of a life. Most of us will never understand how much existence changes when you don't know where your next meal will come from.

"Good?" the doctor asks.

Shannon nods. He does not ask if she wants seconds before getting up and reheating the remainder of the bharta.

He waits until Shannon is done eating, then brings the dishes to the sink and washes each, setting them on the drying rack. The doctor cannot focus with clutter, which is why his home and office are so immaculate, why the doctor lives alone. Our personal space and surroundings are extensions of our minds. You cannot have disarray in one and expect cohesion in the other.

"Tea?" Dr. Bakshir asks. Shannon shakes him off. He asks her to join him in the living room. He takes the big chair, directing her to the couch. This configuration mirrors a therapy session, which puts the doctor at ease, preparing him for what he must do next.

"How can I help you, Shannon?" the doctor asks.

She looks confused, brings out his business card again, holds it up. "You wanted to talk to me."

"I do." Dr. Bakshir says nothing else. So many techniques he's picked up in his profession. Silence works well because it creates discomfort, forces the patient to fill the empty space with words. Of course, Shannon is a special case. Particular. Perhaps a touch on the spectrum, a mild case of Asperger's. That is not his area of expertise, then or now. Either way, she is honest to a fault. If you ask the right questions.

Dr. Bakshir pushes himself up. "I'm going to make some nice, hot tea." He stands over her, looming. "Sure I can't interest you? Lemon and honey?"

"Okay. I guess."

Waiting in the kitchen for the water to boil, the doctor spies on Shannon, who sits without urgency. The doctor does not consider himself a healer, a shaman, not like that charlatan Uncle Bob, promising imaginary future paydays, subservience yielding untold dividends. The meek will inherit nothing. Only through fierce work and tireless dedication can any lasting happiness be achieved. We are our own best advocates. But even if he were to work one-on-one with Shannon, he fears the damage done is too great. Initial analysis says she has passed the point of no return. He does not like thinking this, and quickly shoves the thought from his mind.

The doctor heats the milk, which is how his mother made it, renders the tea more soothing, reduces the competition between hot and cold, which often results in tepid, tasteless liquid. He adds the special milk to Shannon's cup without asking, a touch of honey. Milk is particularly helpful in aiding the undernourished.

He returns with two cups on tiny plates.

"You don't stay at the church every night?" he asks, taking his seat. "Where else do you sleep?"

"I don't have any one place. I get disability. The first couple weeks of the month I find a cheap motel."

"And what about subsequent weeks?"

Shannon shrugs.

"Must be hard," the doctor says. "Living that way."

Shannon shrugs again.

Dr. Bakshir smiles. "Feels strange, does it? Talking in this capacity after so long?"

"A little."

"This isn't a therapy session, Shannon. I have some questions about our time together at Green Hills, which I will get to. But first I want to catch up. I don't mean to be presumptuous. But you look like you haven't had the easiest time since I saw you last. Is that fair to say?"

"Green Hills was a long time ago, Dr. Bakshir."

"Yes, it was."

Dr. Bakshir tilts his chin toward her cup. "Drink up. Tea is good for your stomach, aids digestion. I use my own special blend. Do you still stay at Uncle Bob's?"

"Sometimes."

"How do you like it there?"

"Okay, I guess. It's hard because of the religious part. I believe in God but I'm not quite as ... I don't know the word."

"Dedicated?"

"Convinced, yeah. Uncle Bob takes in runaways. You hear stories about creepy priests doing stuff, but Uncle Bob isn't like that. He's a good man trying to make a difference in the world."

Dr. Bakshir glances out the window. Flurries drift through the streetlights dotting his cul-de-sac. "It's cold out there. Will you be staying at Uncle Bob's tonight?"

Shannon shakes her head.

"Where will you go?"

"I don't know." Her eyes droop, languid, the effects of the tea calming, making her sedated, sleepy. "I'm sorry. I got so tired all of a sudden."

"Please," the doctor says, "stay here for the night. It's too cold to be out walking the streets."

"That's nice of you, but—"

"We are not doctor and patient anymore. We are just people. The offer isn't entirely selfless. I would like to talk to you, but right now doesn't seem like the best time. You need rest."

Dr. Bakshir points at a room. "That is the guest bedroom." Then he points at a set of stairs. "My room and office are upstairs. Help yourself to anything you need."

The doctor turns and begins to ascend. "If you choose to leave, please lock the door on your way out."

The statement is disingenuous on a couple fronts, which troubles Dr. Bakshir, who does not like to be anything but forthright. One, he seldom locks his door at night; Kensington doesn't warrant it. He seeks to give her agency over a situation she does not control.

And, two, he already knows Shannon O'Connor is not leaving this house tonight.

CHAPTER TWENTY-FIVE

Some days you wake up and tell yourself everything is going to be all right; you are so determined to have a good day, you will it so. Positive attitude makes a difference. From your wake-up coffee, to your morning commute and the part-time job you've just taken at the library/senior center/town hall, to no matter where the day takes you. Lunch, spin class, wine with friends. All works out, everything coming up Milhouse. But if that is true, then, Tracy reasons, there has to be nights like this.

The bad begins after she returns home. Brett will be dropping off Logan soon. Since Tracy started working again, Brett has been taking care of Logan more. Though he lives in another state, distance is deceiving. He's just over the border into Massachusetts. From north central Connecticut, even with traffic, the trip rarely requires more than forty minutes, New England more a cluster of big towns than tiny states. Tracy has heard stories about how it can take an hour to drive nine blocks in the city. New England is not the city. Brett texted, *Accident on 91, running late.* And even though text-to-voice is a real thing, Tracy knows damn well Brett never uses it, which means he's texting and driving with Logan in the car, and this thought produces anxiety, highlights the dangers of this world, accentuates how fortunes can change on a dime.

She's glad Dr. Bakshir has written to say he's ready to resume treatment.

Tracy opens a bottle of wine. She has been appreciative of Brett's extra help. He hasn't made a big deal of it. Even though Brett is Logan's father and asking for help shouldn't be a big deal, Tracy knows divorced couples fight about this stuff, seize such opportunities to poke, be passive-aggressive, exact revenge for past slights. Brett has not done any of these things. He wants to spend more time with his son, and his spring semester promises a lighter load than usual. So Tracy tries to forget about the texting-while-driving, be grateful, and will herself calm.

They never discussed Brett's late-night email, now months old. Tracy considers it a non-issue. Despite it being for the best, Tracy, in some small way, laments he hadn't tried harder. Which she can't reconcile. She doesn't want him back, knows leaving him was the right choice. She is glad it's over, but she also secretly hoped for more pining, pain on his part. This behavior is the exact opposite of what she is lauding Brett for, her pettiness stacked against his navigating their new dynamic with maturity, but she *is* upset about the texting and driving, even if she can't be sure that's what happened, and she will always be hurt by the affairs. This is how it goes sometimes, a good day derailed by a single thought, confirmed or not, the ability the brain has to turn on us. As Dr. Bakshir once told her, "The mind can be a wonderful servant, and a brutal master."

Tracy's mind wanders to Todd. She's seen him a few times since their talk in the car that day. She can't remember who called whom first. It was a week after New Year's, she remembers that.

She's pretty sure she reached out first, but if that's true, how did she get his number? He didn't give it to her when she gave him the weathervane (such a bizarre gift for a house on the water!). Their get togethers, not dates, have always been in public settings, at restaurants where people from Covenant do not go. The dinners and drinks have been as friends, nothing more. No one kisses anyone goodnight. No one tries. They just ... talk. About their lives, hopes, dreams. Regular grown-up conversations. Todd listens. In all the years she was married to Brett, Tracy doesn't think he ever listened, staring past her shoulder, waiting till her mouth stopped moving. Each time she leaves Todd, Tracy feels giddy, like she can't stop smiling, fighting the urge to laugh.

There's that scene in *Unfaithful* with Richard Gere and Diane Lane, who has the affair. Tracy caught it the other night on Netflix. She seldom turns on the TV these days. But Logan was at Brett's, and she wasn't tired or in the mood for reading, which is how she spends most nights before bed. Not the most memorable movie, not a particularly good film. But there's that one scene, where Diane Lane is returning to her home and husband after having spent the afternoon with her lover. She's sitting on the subway, and Lane breaks into this uncontrollable smile. Such a great, impromptu moment. Lane knows what she did was wrong, feels shame, but the act felt so good she can't help it. At first you think the film is trying to make it seem like the sex had been that fantastic, and maybe it was, but that wasn't the way Tracy interpreted it. Diane Lane can't stop smiling because she's broken free, if only for a moment, stepped out of the day-to-day drudgery, the routine, shattered the mold. Not sustainable? So what? She feels alive.

Tracy pours a healthy glass of red and walks to the window, overlooking the lake. Is he down there? She can't see any lights.

Todd brought a generator to the water, running floodlights in order to work later. Snow has started to fall. Overnight is supposed to deliver the first big storm of the season.

The bell rings, nonstop. Logan. He's learned to ring it on his own and finds doing so endlessly amusing. Everything is so new at that age. Logan can listen to the same song seven times, hear the same story a dozen more. Tracy opens the door, and her little boy toddles in her arms, hugging tight. There is no better feeling on Earth than the touch of your child's skin against yours.

Brett waits for an invitation inside. And, for a moment, in the porch light shining down, he is the same boy she fell in love with. Not older, full of deceit, tainted. He's that big-hearted boy who held her hand and tried to write poetry. Moments like this, when she can just look at him, forget what they've been through, she endures the inextricable bond. She'll never be totally out of love with him. How could she? She's known him since they were twelve; he was her first, is the father of her child.

Tracy watches Logan wobble off to find his toys and make a mess of the living room she has just straightened up. "Has he eaten yet?"

Out in the cold, Brett squinches one eye, rubs the back of his neck. "Yes. But you're not going to like it. He wanted french fries." He stops. "McDonald's. I couldn't even get him to eat a hamburger."

"I'm not sure that would've made it any better." Tracy shakes her head. "Do you want to come in?"

Brett slips off his winter coat, hanging it on the hook by the door.

"Can I get you something to drink?" she asks. "Wine? I don't have any hard alcohol. Oh, wait. I think I have that bottle of—"

"I'm not drinking."

"Since when?"

"Few months."

Tracy remembers the email. Timeline adds up. Professing undying late-night love bears all the hallmarks.

"Did a lot of work with my therapist."

"You ... have a therapist?" Tracy studies her ex. A city and regional planning professor, Brett has always been skeptical of psychoanalysis, favoring the quantifiable, measurable, concrete, and tactile.

He doesn't sidestep the jab. "And I realized—and this isn't to make excuses or reassign blame for my behavior—but part of why I ... did those things—" Screw around? Cheat? Act like a randy dog? "—was because I was looking to fill an emptiness, something lacking in me." Her ex-husband takes a seat at the kitchen table. "My father drank till the day he died, and he died a miserable, distant old man. I don't want to be like that."

After kicking Brett out for his many affairs, Tracy has had plenty of conversations with Diana. Her best friend likes to play devil's advocate, asking if there is anything Brett could do to repair the damage, reestablish trust, bring the father of her child home. And Tracy's answer is always the same: no.

But what Brett has just said flirts dangerously close to testing that resolve.

Needing something to do, Tracy calls out to Logan, asking if he's hungry, even though she knows fries will have ruined his appetite. He shouts an abrupt no. Tracy is about to ask Brett if he wants to stay for dinner, a quick bite before the storm gets bad, before the roads get too treacherous to travel and everyone is advised to stay put. Logan grabs the remote control so he can watch

TV. Tracy is saying, "No screens," as she picks up her cell, a text dinging in. Diana.

Turn on Channel 3. Todd.

Ignoring her ex's standing there, Tracy reaches for the remote her son is clutching, which causes unbridled screaming. She flips to Channel 3, where they are running a segment on the Banker Butcher, who has been taken in for questioning about a missing woman. Now they are cutting to reactions from residents, each aghast that a man like Todd Norman is allowed to roam free in the first place. How is he in their town? Tracy can't breathe.

"Oh, yeah," Brett says, walking into the living room, standing behind her. "Heard about this on the news."

A reporter is outside Todd's Covenant apartment, pointing up at his window above the bakery.

"Wait," Brett says. "He's living *here*? In town?" He covers his mouth, a pretentious gesture she remembers hating. "Did you know about this?"

Tracy watches the television, catching a glimpse of his black hair as he is ushered into the Holland precinct, cameras flashing. A news feed scrolls across the bottom of the screen but she can't read what it says.

"I have a headache," Tracy says. "I need to get Logan to bed."

"Of course. Call you tomorrow? So we can set up next week…"

Tracy switches to Logan's cartoon, the balm that soothes, then goes straight for the bottle.

She doesn't hear Brett leave.

CHAPTER TWENTY-SIX

As the report airs on the Covenant precinct television, Sobczak receives a call from Holland detective Stephanie Ronson. He hasn't forgotten Todd Norman lives in his town, building that damned lakehouse of his, but Sobczak's recent reconnection with his daughter Amanda, now expecting a child of her own, has quelled some of the urgency.

"Are you seeing this?" Sobczak asks. "Channel 3." Out the window, the season's first significant snow falls, painting Covenant's fields pastoral, a landscape of bucolic white.

"We leaked the story," Ronson says.

The picture comes into focus. "Would've appreciated a heads-up."

"Would've loved to give you one. We had to move fast."

"What's the rush? The SOB isn't going anywhere."

"Our source at Channel 3 could get it aired. We took our shot."

"Still no leads on Beiko Talo?"

"Nothing solid. Best we can hope is to rattle Norman's cage, pray something shakes loose."

"What makes you so certain he had anything to do with it? Picking up women in nightclubs isn't his MO."

"Are you defending him?"

"No," Sobczak says. "Thinking rationally. I've got a bunch of wannabe rednecks who are gonna see this report. One of them has one too many, decides to take matters into his own hands, and I got a mess to clean up."

"When crimes are committed, the first people you look at are the usual suspects."

"This feels forced. Talo went missing from the Meteorite, a long way from Norman. Plus, Talo is a street kid. Takes drugs, parties, no place to call home. Not uncommon."

"Your disapproval is noted," Ronson says. Her punctuation does not last long. "That's not why I'm calling. I need your help."

Sobczak doesn't want to laugh, a woman is missing, but he has a tough time not scoffing.

"I miss something funny?"

"Yeah. Holland asking Covenant for help. Isn't it supposed to be the other way around? Half my staff is tightening lug nuts or making pastrami grinders."

"There's a weird church on the outskirts of your town."

"Not in Covenant, there isn't." Sobczak knows all the churches. St. Paul's, St. Mark's. Both centrally located. Both Catholic.

"No-man's land. Not exactly Holland County. Not Hartford either. Crossroads Church of God."

"Don't know it."

"Like I said, no-man's land, in the country hills."

"Odd place for a church."

"God is everywhere," Ronson says, voice dripping irony. "Non-denominational."

"I'm Catholic. I don't know what that is."

"Means they aren't affiliated with any sect like Catholic or Protestant. The pastor calls himself Uncle Bob."

"Uncle Bob?"

"The church is a refuge of sorts. Screw-ups trying to detox from drugs. Runaways, prostitutes."

"And you think, what? Beiko Talo's there?"

"We know she stayed there in the past."

Sobczak catches Judi walking in from records. Why is she here so late? He holds up his empty mug, waggling for more coffee. Might as well take advantage.

Judi nods and makes for the pot in the copy room.

"Few months back," Ronson says, "a couple of our guys picked up a young woman. Truck stop. Solicitation. Happens a lot on the Berlin Turnpike. Also caught her with a sizable amount of MDMA. Enough to charge her with distribution."

Judi brings the chief his reheated cup of coffee, prepared how he likes it. He tries to mouth, "Why are you here still?" But she can't understand him. So he points at the clock on the wall, and Judi whispers, "Making copies for the high school bake sale."

"No ID. Let her sit in the cell till morning," Ronson continues, leaving Sobczak to fill in any gaps he may've missed. "Fucked up the processing. She was let go. Bolted. Never showed for her court date."

"Let me guess. Beiko Talo?"

"No. Shannon O'Connor."

"Who's Shannon O'Connor?"

"Remember Green Hills? The girls home where Talo and April Abbott stayed."

"What about it?"

"This is where it gets weird. During her intake, O'Connor mentioned the church and Talo. But that's not where they met. She knew her from a hospital program they'd been in together about ten years earlier."

"Green Hills."

"That's how her name showed up in the system, when we were doing cross checks. That's not the weird part, though. Another name came up as well."

Sobczak waits for the smoking gun. Because there has to be one.

"Our dead girl on the beach. Wendy Mortensen."

"What the..."

"We're looking into it."

"I thought Wendy Mortensen's death was ruled an overdose?"

"At the time."

"Meaning what?"

"Dwayne, she was a junkie. I think we both know nobody performs the most thorough autopsy on junkies. We're pulling her up."

"You need family permission to exhume?"

"Like I said, we're working on it."

Sobczak can't help but feel Ronson is withholding information. A murder happens in his town, he should be privy to all the details. But this is the deal you sign up for when you contract out police work. Sobczak has been relegated to need-to-know.

"O'Connor said a lot of runaways and addicts crash at this Crossroads. It's a refuge for them, a sanctuary. Uncle Bob takes them in, helps them sober up, get straight, find Jesus. I'd like you to talk to Uncle Bob. See what he has to say about Talo and O'Connor. See if Mortensen ever passed through."

"Why me?"

"Because we can't." Ronson groans. "Call it a favor. It's a bureaucratic nightmare. Trust me. Something isn't right with this church."

CHAPTER TWENTY-SEVEN

Dr. Bakshir is open for business, ready to see patients for the first time in over three months, anxious to get back to helping others. Unfortunately, as the doctor is discovering, people aren't always so loyal or understanding.

When Dr. Bakshir contacted his patients, whom he'd been kind enough to refer elsewhere in his absence, most said they preferred to remain with their new practitioner, a decision that surprised the doctor. The patients all had terrific excuses—easier commute, better schedule, how they were in the middle of sensitive subject matter, whatever. Liars. Dr. Bakshir tried not to take it personally. He tried to understand that these decisions are no reflection on his competence. But he let in emotions, and in doing so exposed himself to a litany of feelings with which he did not wish to contend.

He was so angry over the betrayal that he wrote back to the handful of patients who did make appointments, saying he needed more time. A therapist can't do his or her job harboring resentment against those he's pledged to help.

Following his morning jog, the doctor arrives at the office to catch up on billing and paperwork, prepare taxes for the year. Sitting in his office, he has no appointments slated for the day. Knowing no one is coming affects the doctor in profound and personal ways. Mostly by filing him with a pervasive emptiness. He grows so despondent, in fact, he can see, perhaps for the first time, how one might grow so dejected that drugs seem a viable solution.

The front bell dings. Rare for new patients to show up unannounced but not unheard of.

Dr. Bakshir perks up. He hasn't had time to run through all the possibilities waiting for him in the lobby. But had he, Todd Norman would not have made the cut.

"Sorry to show up without an appointment," Norman says. "I'm new in town…" He takes a deep breath, recomposes through the obvious anguish. "I need a therapist."

Several thoughts hit the doctor at once. He's read so much about Todd Norman, from his purported role in the death of his wife, to recent suspicions involving a missing girl. Central to the doctor's thought processes, however, is whether he should treat the man. Ethically, there are too many concerns, of course. The doctor's intimate knowledge fosters a prejudicial bent. Even the slightest cognitive distortion on the doctor's part would impact therapy. The doctor must rebuild his practice. But not at the cost of his integrity. Still, what a fascinating case study…

Norman points at a telephone in the empty office. "I can also call and book an appointment? I wasn't planning on stopping by. I was driving through town, and I saw your sign, and it's … been a rough stretch for me. Without going into too much detail—"

"I'm afraid I cannot treat you, Mr. Norman."

Todd Norman's shoulders slag, and he tilts his head skyward

as if preparing to unleash a primal scream. Instead, he self-regulates his emotions, which impresses the doctor, how cool the man can remain under adversity, part of his own skillset, a practice, no doubt, picked up from previous providers.

"You know who I am."

"It would be difficult for a man with your history to go unnoticed in a town like Covenant."

"I was cleared of the charges."

"That is not for me to comment on."

"No, it was a matter for the courts. And it was decided. Not guilty, on all counts."

Even as Norman says these words, which carry fire and fury, his voice does not rise above the level of normal, genial conversation.

Norman does not hide his disappointment. Like this is some racist soda shop in the 1950s. We reserve the right to refuse service.

"I understand your frustration," Dr. Bakshir says. Despite Norman's reputation, the doctor is not scared of this man, which tells him a lot. The doctor can detect dangerous situations, the skill paramount in avoiding sharing closed quarters with persons capable of violence. The professional side of Dr. Bakshir laments not being able to treat the man; insight into that mind would be mesmerizing.

"Sure. You understand. But you can't help me, right?"

"I'd be more than happy to refer you to other therapists in the area."

"That's okay. I can use the internet too. Have a nice day."

With that, Todd Norman leaves.

After Norman exits the practice, Dr. Bakshir reflects on April

Abbott's time at Green Hills. The facility was residential, and patients couldn't leave the ward, let alone grounds, without administrative permission, which was never granted. Dr. Bakshir was not the only treating psychiatrist on the floor, which included other teens and young adults. That's what made Green Hills so special: the small cluster of young, impressionable patients. Each psychiatrist handled four or five, no more. Of course, Dr. Bakshir didn't live at the hospital. There were guards and night nurses who secured the lockdown facility. Yet, Dr. Bakshir knows April used to sneak out to see her boyfriend. April had turned eighteen toward the end of the program, making her one of the older girls there. Her sneaking out came up in session one day, where the girls—Wendy, April, Beiko, and Shannon—were at each other's throats. Not uncommon when young women are forced to share such a small communal space. An offhanded comment from one of the girls—Beiko he recalls. April denied it. But Dr. Bakshir read the look in her eyes. He saw it was the truth.

Maybe he should've brought it up to the night staff or higher-ups. Except news had already come down that Green Hills would be ending soon. Any disciplinary recourse would've alerted Art Abbott, whom Dr. Bakshir did not trust. April's father was a repressed man, who fretted endlessly over every perceived liberal scourge, from drug use to sexual deviance. Nothing the doctor had seen from April suggested she was guilty of either. A delightful young woman who probably shouldn't have been sent to Green Hills in the first place, April accepted her fate. Unlike other wronged, rebellious teens, she did her time, was an active participant in groups, a genuinely pleasant person to be around. If she was sneaking out to meet Norman, so what? Part of the doctor was impressed, and the other part saw it as re-righting an injustice.

Of course, that was over ten years ago. The doctor was younger then, more idealized. Knowing what happened to April after she left his care, the doctor wishes he could go back and do things differently. Like so many other areas of his life.

He retrieves the business card for the woman investigator who came by a few months earlier.

Dr. Bakshir picks up his cell and punches the phone number for Marjorie Jessup.

***

Sobczak attends church every week. St. Mark's. In his fifty-plus years, he can recall missing only a handful of services. Mostly when he's been sick, which he seldom is. Even the times he and Mary took trips out of town, the chief made sure to find the nearest Catholic church. He appreciates the rituals of Mass, the tokens of ceremony, its tradition. All Catholic churches share similarities. At least the ones in New England, and Sobczak hasn't left the region since being stationed in the R.O.T.C. ages ago. The stained glass windows, the Stations of the Cross, the robes, and pulpit, all bear familiar, comforting qualities. The sight of Jesus dying for his sins, a reminder of the sacrifice made.

Sobczak has never seen a church like this Crossroads Church of God. From the outside, the building more closely resembles a meatpacking plant than it does a place of worship. The large, fading yellow building is situated in the middle of nowhere, off the old highway that has been circumvented, rendered practically obsolete after the addition of the new interstate. The chief has passed this way while driving on I-84, maybe even spying the church, but if he has, it did not register, the building unremarkable in every way. Were it not for the small insignia and cross in the upper right-hand corner, Sobczak might've doubted he'd been given the correct address. He's already spoken with Detective Ronson once this morning, when she confirmed what had previously been established: Wendy Mortensen died of a drug overdose. The second autopsy also reinforced the heroin was laced with fentanyl. It is possible, Ronson speculated, that someone could've deliberately spiked the batch. No way to know.

The Crossroads Church of God displays none of the usual symbols of a church. No marble statues of saints. No steeples or bells, no stone steps. Nothing about the place offers Sobczak any reassurance. In fact, the gargantuan blocky structure produces the opposite effect, instilling a sense of unease. Something that shouldn't be but is.

The chief makes his way across the loose gravel drive. Big windows overlook from high above, and though he sees no one in these windows, Sobczak feels he is being watched.

He hasn't called ahead, opting instead for in-person, arriving in official capacity, his Covenant cop car parked behind him. Given the appearance of the church, coupled with everything Ronson has told him about the place, Sobczak gets the picture of a renegade approach to faith, a rocking of the boat. A new religion. He does not like this. Feels sacrilegious, blasphemous. Non-denominational? What is that? Sounds like something they do out in one of those wacky states like California.

The front door is locked. Another oddity. Since when do churches lock their doors in the middle of the day? No church he knows of would do that. People need access to pray. God never closes His door, so why would a church?

The waifish girl who answers has pockmarked skin and several open sores infecting her lips. Her hair is long, flat, and greasy, unhealthy looking; big, black circles rim her eyes. Against pasty skin, the stark juxtaposition creates the impression of a malnourished raccoon.

"What?" the girl says. She is fifteen if a day, dressed in ill-fitting sweats and oversized tee, as if she's been clothed by a men's big and tall thrift store.

"I'm looking for Pastor Robert Tompkins."

"You mean Uncle Bob?"

"Sure." Sobczak remembers the nickname, another thing he doesn't like.

The girl waves him in. He follows down the long, dim concrete hall, the deep stone locking in the cold. Sobczak can see his breath cloud in front of him. The price to heat a place this big must be astronomical.

At a closed door, the girl raps her knuckles, and a pleasant-sounding voice bellows to come on in.

The man sitting at the desk does not look like a pastor, and when he stands up, loping over with his uneven, gaping strides, he doesn't walk like one either. Dressed in civilian clothes, this man is no shepherd. No collar, no robe. Jeans and a flannel covering a skinny man's potbelly.

Arriving in a squad car, dressed in town blues, Sobczak isn't hiding the fact he's a police officer. Most people, even innocent ones, get tense around police. But Uncle Bob is relaxed, upbeat.

After Sobczak introduces himself, Pastor Uncle Bob dismisses the young girl, who he calls Bean. Sobczak has no way or knowing if that is a first, last, or nickname.

"What can I do you for, hoss?" Pastor Bob points at the seat in front of his desk. "Please, take a load off. Chill. We're all friends here."

"I won't be long," Sobczak says in refusing the invitation. He glances around the room, taking in its less-than-holy design. Several posters of teenage runaways adorn the walls, phone numbers for crisis center hotlines. Addiction concerns, abusive relationships, sex workers. "If You or a Loved One," etc. A few pictures of Jesus hang here and there, but they aren't the traditional Jesus that Sobczak knows, with long hair, holy crown, and piercing blue eyes; these Jesuses are raggedy, modern drawings of a swarthy-skinned man juxtaposed in today's inner-cites, which land a long way from Calvary and Covenant. Familiar Bible verses still appear below the tableaus. In one, Jesus is standing outside what looks like, best Sobczak can tell, a nightclub, flamboyant men holding the hands of other men, several locked in embrace, rainbow flags rippling. Some of the men seem to be bleeding from ... gunshot wounds? Matthew 25:40 stamped beneath: *What you did to the least of my brothers, you were doing it to me.*

Makes no sense to Sobczak. But he isn't here to discuss theology.

"How can I help you, Officer?"

"Pastor Tompkins—"

"Please, all the kids call me Uncle Bob."

"As you can tell, it's been a while since I was a kid. And it's Chief."

Uncle Bob stands up from his chair, walks to the front of the desk, sits on the edge, arm draped over knee, the casual man's position. "Not a kid, eh? You and me both, brother." He hoists a hand. "Sorry. Chief."

Sobczak feels his attention pulled elsewhere in this cold basement, a storage unit in any other facility, certainly not a parish rectory.

"Something wrong, Chief?"

"This is a ... church?"

"It is, sir. Would you like to see our permits?" Uncle Bob cranes his neck, pretending to make for a rolling cart, hardly an efficient record-keeping system. "Then again, we aren't in your jurisdiction, are we?"

"No, you seem to have found a location where you're no one's responsibility. Can't help but wonder if that was intentional."

Uncle Bob smirks. With his big, bushy mustache and long gray hair, he reminds Sobczak of an aging hippy clinging to the dying days of a failed experiment.

"What do you do here?"

"Preach the Word of the Lord."

Sobczak rocks on his heels, unsure how to respond to that one.

"We don't look like any church you ever seen, that it?"

"If I'm being honest? No."

"Good." Uncle Bob hops up, spry for a man his age. He peers out the little windows, slits on basement sills, his back to the chief. "The world is changing. If Christianity is to survive, we need to change with it."

"Christianity has been around for a couple thousand years. I think it's doing just fine."

"Church going man, eh?" Uncle Bob spins around, sizing him up. "Traditional, like your rituals. Catholic?"

Sobczak nods grimly.

"How's attendance at your parish of late?"

"I don't take headcounts." If Sobczak wanted to, he could tell this stranger that, yes, attendance has been declining. But he isn't here to compare flock sizes.

"How about age demographics. More young or old? I'll take a wild stab and say folks tend to be closer to our age." Uncle Bob waves him off because he knows Sobczak isn't interested in answering. "Nothing wrong with that. But we don't live forever. The children *are* our future, and young people aren't going to church as much as they used to. Ritual and tradition are wonderful. But kids today have a whole new set of challenges facing them. School shootings. Unwanted pregnancies. Drugs." Uncle Bob picks up a Bible. "My favorite book. Got a lot of wonderful things in here. Also has dragons, justifies slavery, murder. Heck, Chief, we can't even toss around the ol' pigskin if we take everything in here verbatim."

"I'd think a man of faith would have more reverence for the Good Book."

"Don't get me wrong. It's a terrific guideline to living our lives in Christ. But the rest of it, the implementation of these principles, the application to modern-day issues? That's on us, man."

Sobczak has had enough of this conversation. If he had to guess, he'd say Uncle Bob likes to smoke the occasional jay. But he's not here for that. Sobczak gestures through the brick walls. "Besides reinventing Jesus as a hip cat, what's with all the kids running around?"

"Deeds, brother. The Word put into action. In addition to regular services, which are open to *all* denominations. One God. I am a Christian. But that doesn't mean my Muslim brothers and sisters don't have a home here, too. Ya dig? One God. One Race."

"Yeah. The kids?"

"Runaways. For the most part. The wayward. The lost children."

"Don't you think their parents would like to know where their kids are?"

"Some of them, maybe. Some of them, quite a bit. Like the

fathers who sneak into their rooms late at night, doing things to their children fathers are not meant to do. The mothers who let their babies settle drug debts by offering their little bodies. I'm sure those parents miss those children very much."

"You're telling me every kid I see running around out there is fleeing an abusive home life? If that is true—" and Sobczak has a hard time believing that is the case; this isn't the big city "—there are police to handle these matters."

"You've been in law enforcement a while. Come up against a few domestic violence cases, no? Tell me, when the beaten woman stands in the presence of her abuser, do stories ever change? Bruises become the result of clumsiness? How many black eyes are caused by tripping into a doorknob?" Pastor Uncle Bob shakes his head. "I'm seventy years old. I am not a graceful man. But I can truly say I have never once tripped and landed eye-first into a doorknob."

"So it's a sanctuary. Placed between towns, free of regulation?"

"There's no such thing. We are part of Holland County. Police can visit anytime they'd like to be in God's house."

"That's not what I heard."

"You're here, aren't you?"

It's here Sobczak makes a choice. He could ask for permits, see if Uncle Bob has his paperwork in order, the right to take in minors. He's guessing not. But he also admits the pastor has a point. If what he's saying is true, that these kids are fleeing abusive homelives, then he's doing something good, necessary. And if he's lying? The chief will be taking a good hard look into Uncle Bob's claims. Right now, there's more pressing concerns.

"I'd like to talk about a couple girls who may have passed your way. One a while ago, one more recently."

Uncle Bob waits.

"Beiko Talo and Shannon O'Connor."

Uncle Bob grins.

"Does the name Wendy Mortensen sound familiar?"

"Can I ask what this is about? I try to protect these girls. Sometimes parents, like the type I was telling you about, want their kids back for the wrong reason."

"They aren't kids anymore. A young woman's missing. Beiko Talo and—"

"Yes," Uncle Bob says, "I know Beiko."

"When was the last time you saw her?"

"Mother report her missing?"

"Her mother has spoken with police, yes. Her brother is also concerned."

"That's Hartford County."

Implication: this is none of Sobczak's business.

Uncle Bob turns to his file cart, which turns out to be better organized than Sobczak would've thought. He returns with photographs, spreads them on the desk. "Beiko was fifteen when she came here. This is 'Mom.'" Welts, bruises, deep lacerations. "I also have copies of medical reports from the ER." Uncle Bob begins reading, "...vaginal and anal tearing, most likely due to insertion of a large foreign object—"

"Enough," Sobczak says.

"I would say that's a great response. Enough. Do you know how many times Beiko, at fifteen, reported these crimes? To police?"

Sobczak can't find an adequate response. He knows the system fails from time to time. People, the innocent and the guilty, slip through the cracks.

Uncle Bob winks. "We can agree to disagree."

"If you know where Beiko is, let me see her. I see she's fine, you have my word I will tell her brother, no one else. She is an adult now."

"She's not here."

"After what you told me, about harboring and protecting, how can I believe that?"

"I am still a pastor. I do my best to help those in need. I don't make a habit of lying to officers of the law. As you can see, mostly younger people stay here. When they get to be Beiko's age, they have a harder time with rules. I haven't seen Beiko in close to ... six months?"

"What about Wendy Mortenson? Shannon O'Connor?"

The pastor's bushy old-man brows twitch. "Never met anyone named Wendy, but I saw Shannon a few weeks ago. First time in a while. Popped in and out. Maybe this will help..." The pastor raises a finger, turns to his desk, fishing, scattering loose pages across the blotter. "A man came here a couple months back, asking about Shannon. Wanted me to pass along his contact info. Claimed he was a psychiatrist. I did not like him. Gave me bad vibes. He left his card. I gave it to her."

"You remember his name?"

"I wrote it down." Uncle Bob keeps scrounging around his desk, sifting till he finds what he's looking for, passing along the note.

Sobczak reads the name.

Dr. Meshulum Bakshir.

CHAPTER TWENTY-EIGHT

When Tracy reached out to Amanda Sobczak, the strange part wasn't that the town sheriff's daughter acted like it was totally normal to receive a DM from someone she barely knew; it's the place Amanda suggested meeting for lunch: Secondhand City. Tracy has nothing against thrift shops, and she knows being married to a Covenant cop can't be filling the family coffers with gold. Still, it's not like anyone is poor in Covenant. Even those who rent duplexes by the American Legion would be considered royalty in neighboring boroughs like New Britain or the North End.

"Hey!" Amanda says, going in for the hug, as if these hangouts are a weekly affair. "It's been too long!" Her smile and ease, the embrace, makes Tracy wonder if she remembers high school accurately. Were they better friends? Not like Tracy was a band geek or art room nerd. She was popular, in her own way. She didn't enjoy the social status of the Amandas, Aprils, and Ambers of Covenant High. But who did?

Amanda resumes sifting through a rack of secondhand scarves. "I saw someone post the other day they were thinking about putting together a class reunion." Amanda mimics sticking a finger down her throat. "Can you imagine anything more pathetic? Bunch of bald guys and dumpy housewives." Amanda catches the possible offense. "Let's face it. Not everyone held up as well as we did." Amanda lifts and inspects a scarf, puts it back, moves to the shirt rack, a hideous display of paisley prints and two-toned blouses.

Tracy admits Amanda is as beautiful as she was in high school. Except, either Amanda has been drinking a lot of beer or...

"Yup," Amanda says, noticing Tracy's gawking at her belly. "Almost three months. Starting to show. And hating every minute of it."

"Sorry. I wasn't trying to stare. I had no idea."

Amanda knocks her arm, laughing. "Why would you?" She turns up the aisle.

Tracy follows, fingering fabrics, because that is what Amanda is doing.

"I read online your body changes so fast. You're better off buying throwaways. If you don't have any friends with old maternity clothes lying around."

"I have old maternity clothes lying around." And Tracy does. A whole attic filled with them. She keeps meaning to drop them off at Good Will but never gets around to climbing up there and organizing. But she's surprised by how fast she offers them to Amanda. Even after all these years, still desperate to impress the cool kids.

"You're so sweet." Amanda squeezes her wrist before leaning in. "You wouldn't believe the scores you can find here." She drops her voice to a whisper. "Last week I walked out with a Kate

Spade. Seven bucks. No shit." She looks past Tracy's shoulder. "Ursula Hanbury owns this place. She's about a hundred and eighty-six years old and legally blind. Got her nephew helping out after school. He's ... special."

"Special" is a funny word, so many interpretations. If it follows a name fast, it's a compliment. "Josh is special." But a long delay? Tracy picks up that the Hanbury nephew probably has a developmental impairment.

They peruse the line, Amanda scouring for super deals, Tracy mirroring interest. Mostly she questions why she's here. She has nothing in common with Amanda. Tracy wants to believe this isn't about April Abbott. But her hypocrisy only goes so far.

"I was sorry to hear about Brett," Amanda says, checking labels. "You were always too good for him. Even back in the day, he was a skeezeball. You know we caught him cheating on you at Homecoming?"

"I'm not surprised."

"Casey Lyons. A bunch of us saw them behind the rafters, by the football field. She was on her knees..." Amanda furrows her brow. "We debated whether to tell you. Casey was such a skank. But we didn't think you'd believe us. You were so crazy about him. When did you start dating Brett? Freshman year?"

"Seventh grade."

"It wasn't all bad. You got that beautiful little boy out of the deal. Where is Logan?"

Tracy almost asks how she knows her son's name. Why wouldn't she? Everyone knows everything about everybody in Covenant.

"My friend Diana."

"Diana DelMartino," Amanda says. "Wow. How is *she*? Still a little spitfire? I saw her..." Amanda has to think. "Maybe six months back? She was at the BevMo, sampling wine. Like three in the afternoon. They had a stand with teeny paper cups. She was alone. I was going to say hi but Tom called, and you know how that is. How are your parents? They moved, right?"

"My parents passed away."

"I'm so sorry." Amanda reaches over and squeezes her arm again.

"Thank you. They were older than most parents. It's strange. I miss them. But then I think at least it's over. There's one more heartache I don't have to deal with." Tracy stops herself, laughs.

"What?"

"I don't remember talking with you this much in high school."

"You barely talked to *anyone* in high school. Except Brett Coggins. By the way, kudos on keeping the last name. Somerset sounds *way* better."

Amanda returns to the scarf rack, plucking one she hadn't been looking at earlier, bringing it to the cashier, who honestly does bear a disturbing resemblance to the crypt keeper.

Walking outside into the crisp nip of late January, Amanda leans over, unveils today's haul. "Rathbone. Buck seventy." Amanda points across the street at a tiny eatery. Crusty, dirty snow banks bookend the curbs. "Still have time for a bite?"

"Sure," Tracy says. That was the original plan. So far all they've done is rummage through bargain bins. Tracy hasn't figured out how to ask about April, how to even broach the subject. There is no tactful way to mention you might be dating the man suspected of murdering someone's best friend.

The lunch spot, The One Two Easy, isn't empty. But it isn't bustling either. Then again, what bustles in Covenant? The town has more trees than people.

Ice teas poured, Amanda leans back and smiles, projecting an easygoing countenance that brings Tracy back to eighteen, because even then Amanda Sobczak possessed an exotic, carefree beauty, with those high Eastern European cheekbones. More than that, Amanda carries herself with confidence. Then. And now.

"You remember Judi Drake's party?" Amanda says, stirring the sugar.

Tracy shakes her head.

"Come on! You don't remember Judi's party?" She lowers her gaze. "You and me? Skinny dipping in the pool and drinking Schnapps? We were there till, like, four in the morning, until my *dad* pulled up and flashed the lights?"

Tracy thinks a moment. Wait. "Yeah, I do." It is a vague, washed-out, fuzzy recollection. They'd been drunk. Maybe that's why Tracy had to dig deeper. It was during that partying stretch, another bad Brett breakup, right around the time she got hit in the neck by that rock. A party that ended with, yes, she and Amanda snagging a bottle and skinny dipping in the pool, because there was a pool, they were young, and why not?

Tracy waits for the rest, the reason Amanda is bringing it up. Skinny-dipping in Judi Drake's pool is neither a good nor bad memory, just ... a memory. Amanda keeps smiling. She seems in such a happy mood. Maybe she was always like this. Nice. Were Tracy and her friends jealous because Amanda and the others had been prettier, more popular? Was it still happening now? All the shit-talk at Chili's that day?

"What's on your mind?" Amanda asks. "Looks like you got a secret you're bursting to share."

"I don't want to open up old wounds..."

Amanda laughs. "Just ask."

"April. April Abbott."

Amanda's reaction is curious. It isn't anger and it's not sorrow. Her expression mangles seven different emotions, none strong enough to take command. But if Tracy had to pick one: disappointment.

"I'm sorry," Tracy says. "I don't want to make you relive…"

Amanda turns out the window. The streets seem emptier. Winds whips harder, a world turns colder. Tracy feels horrible, even if she isn't sure why.

"When you reached out, I really thought you wanted to catch up."

"I did," Tracy lies. "I do."

"You know the thing I'm most excited about having a baby?"

She doesn't give Tracy time to answer.

"It'll give me something to do, something to love that'll have to love me back. This is the first time I've had lunch with someone other than my husband in I can't tell you how long." She acts like she aches to laugh. "I am so freaking lonely."

"Amanda, I'm sorry—"

"I should've known better. God, you all hated us."

"No, we didn't … it was high school."

"Right. High school. The last time I had friends. How sad is that?"

A waitress comes and Amanda puts on her happy face, orders a soup and half sandwich. Tracy gets a salad even though she knows she's not going to eat it.

"So, what?" Amanda asks. "You've been tasked with putting together an old high school scrapbook? Why are you asking me about April?"

Tracy considers coming clean, talking about Todd and how

she knows he didn't do it; how better insight into April might help her understand that night and the tragedy that befell. And it might. But her reason is bullshit. Tracy wants to know more about April so she can get a better handle on Todd. These past few weeks, Todd has opened up, sharing his feelings; and he's such an attentive listener, cares what she has to say, is present. Despite all that, there remains a part of him walled off, inaccessible.

Tracy has been lost in her own thoughts so long she hasn't realized Amanda's been speaking this entire time.

"...never changes, does it?" Amanda continues. "The high school drama."

"That's not what—"

"We were such a small school. You don't think we heard everything? Me, April, Amber. The A-holes?"

"It was just a stupid nickname people made up."

"I tried hard to be your friend. You and everyone else. You guys had your own little clique. You kept *us* out. Not the other way around. The shit you'd say..."

"People say stupid stuff when they're that age—"

"Like when Amber moved to town and Lisa Blake started the rumor we were all gay for each other?" Amanda leans in. "Before my mom died, you know I had to sit with her in our living room and tell her that I wasn't a lesbian?" Amanda flashes an okay sign. "Real fun conversation to have, Trace. Sitting with your mother who's going bald from the chemo, ninety pounds and about to die, promising her you'll have a baby someday."

Tracy wishes she could go back ten minutes and never ask about April.

Amanda waves her off. "It wasn't you who started that stupid rumor." She collects her breath, wipes the tears from her eyes, fans her face. "Ugh. Pregnancy. I feel like I'm being held hostage by a billion hormones."

"I remember."

"Tell me it gets better."

"Want me to lie?"

"Oh great." Amanda breaks into laughter.

"It does. The second trimester."

"Yeah?"

"Like a honeymoon period."

"More like the calm before the storm. Everything I've read says the last three months are *brutal*."

"They are," Tracy says, happy to have navigated the minefield, conversation circling back to pleasant. "But in the end, you get—"

"A Logan."

The food arrives and Amanda takes another deep breath, fanning. "Sorry for jumping down your throat."

"I don't know why I brought it up."

"Probably because her killer is living in town?" Amanda doesn't give Tracy a chance to refute anything. "You saw the news the other night? My father already told me he was here. And, surprise! A woman shows up dead on the beach by his house. Now another girl goes missing."

Tracy pokes around her food, nudges a leaf of wilted iceberg.

Amanda grabs the salt, averting eyes. "We hadn't spoken in years. April and me. It's funny. For being ... the A-holes ... I mean, you probably see Lisa Blake and that bunch more than I saw my best friends after graduation."

Tracy doesn't mention having had lunch with Lisa recently.

"What happened? Between you guys. You were inseparable back in the day."

Amanda takes a big bite of her sandwich, waits till she's done swallowing. "I guess it started when Amber's dad died and she went to live with the Abbotts. Toward the end of senior year, Mr. Abbott caught Amber with pot. Got pissed, kicked her out."

"Where'd she go?"

"Church. Got all holy roller. April's dad was such an uptight prick. You remember how she didn't graduate with us? After he kicked out Amber, he put April in a group home. Because Amber was such a bad influence. No shit. April had to take her finals in some nut ward." Amanda rolls her eyes. "Art Abbott, head of the DOT and blah-blah. He was worried about the political fallout. Funny, right?"

None of this sounds familiar to Tracy and she doesn't know where Amanda's story is leading, but she stays silent, hopeful to find out.

"That's when it fell apart. April made a bunch of weirdo friends in the group home, Green Valley or whatever. She was always bringing them around. And *worse*, Amber found Jesus. Then there was the night of Chris Manzaris's party."

Tracy recalls another party she missed.

"Third weekend of November. Was supposed to be, like, this big get together for everyone who'd come home from college. Thanksgiving break. Last chance to see the old gang who stayed local, which was most of us." Amanda gestures out the window, in the direction of Shallow Lake. "Across from where that whackjob is building his lakehouse. What a nightmare."

"The party?"

"Big blowout fight. Me, April, Amber. We'd been drifting apart. It was bound to happen. Add some alcohol to the fire ... never talked after that."

"Sorry," Tracy says, realizing she keeps saying that even though she's not sure what she's apologizing for.

"I miss them both so much." Amanda sounds like she's about to cry. "April especially. I loved her. As much as I've ever loved anyone. April was like the other half of me. Then she met what's-his-name and disappeared to the city." Her attention returns to the cold glass. "Didn't even get an invite to the wedding."

"What happened to Amber?"

"Who knows?"

"I looked for her on social media…"

"Why the hell would you do that? You didn't even know her."

"Thought I'd reach out…"

Amanda fans the tears again. "Ugh," she says, pointing at her face. As if that explains everything. And it sort of does.

"After Brett," Tracy says, "I realized I cut everyone out of my life."

"You won't find Amber on Facebook. After Jesus, she hooked up with some indie rocker guy. Bass player. Followed him across the country. Vanished." Out the window, a long-haul trucker, taking a short cut off the 384, blows past, swirling ice chips and dust. "Texas or some shit. She's never coming back here."

For the remainder of the meal, conversation steers clear of touchy high school subjects. Tracy and Amanda hug goodbye in the parking lot, promising to do this more often, both of them knowing that is not happening. They didn't have anything in common then. Even if they have a couple things in common now—parenthood, loneliness—they mix as well as peanut butter and baked salmon.

Driving home, Tracy thinks about how sad marriage is. She has no idea the interworking of Tom and Amanda's relationship, and maybe Tracy is projecting, but Amanda acts an awful lot like Tracy used to when Brett was screwing around.

Amanda Sobczak needs a friend. But it won't be Tracy Somerset.

CHAPTER TWENTY-NINE

Driving back to the precinct after visiting Dr. Bakshir, a fruit-less trip, Sobczak passes his son-in-law exiting Hollow Point, the town hall access road. Both men slow their cars, hitting the lights, pulling up behind one another and off to the side to keep paths clear for traffic. Though it is doubtful anyone would be heading this way, not with the snow starting to come down. Reports have another storm blowing in. Damage should be limited, with the coast getting six to twelve, inland spared half that. Of course, the country hills are its own beast.

Tom exits his car, coming to his boss's side. Despite the snow, the temperatures aren't unbearable. A couple degrees warmer and this would all be rain. The chief cracks his window.

"Where you coming from?" Tom asks.

"Paying a visit to our town head-shrinker."

"You're ... in therapy?"

"No. Official business."

"We have a psychiatrist?"

"Dr. Bakshir. Lives in Kensington. Practice is here. Edge of town. No one home. Left a message. Waiting for a call back."

"Hold on," Tom says. "What's his name again? We had that crackpot, Chmielewski, who kept getting DUIs. I think the judge sent her there."

"Bakshir."

"Right," Tom says. "Bakshir. Funny first name. Meadowlark or something."

"Meshulum." Saying it leaves a bad taste in Sobczak's mouth.

Tom's face screws up. "Everything okay, Dad?"

Sobczak pulls his cigarettes, holds up the pack. "Remember: not a word to your wife."

Tom crosses himself.

That first inhale of the day always tastes best.

"Holland asked for a favor."

"That's a new one, Holland coming to us."

"That's what I said. Sent me out to a church. Follow up a lead on our missing woman."

"Which church?"

"Loony tunes, new-age place in the cuts."

Tom's teeth chatter. It's like the temperature has suddenly dropped ten degrees, skies charcoaling darker, clouds roiling cinder.

Sobczak waves in his son-in-law.

Tom jogs around the front, sliding in the passenger seat. Sobczak keeps the window unrolled for the smoke, but it's still a lot warmer in the heated car.

"Where you off to?" Sobczak asks.

"The cravings have started. Amanda wants ice cream. Strawberry. With maple syrup. The real stuff, not the kind they sell at Big Y." Tom gestures south. "Have to hit Stew Leonard's."

"I remember when Mary was pregnant with Amanda. Kielbasa and pickles."

Tom checks his cell. "I have time. Tell me about this church."

Sobczak fills in Tom on his meeting with the old hippy pastor at the Crossroads Church of God. "Something about the guy rubbed me wrong."

"You thinking he had something to do with Beiko Talo?"

"No. I don't know. The church is one of those wacko non-denomination types, everyone welcome, it's one God. Whatever. It's fine. Uncle Bob uses the space as a sanctuary for runaways." Sobczak reaches for another cigarette but stops short. Don't need to fall into that trap again. "It's a good thing, right?" Sobczak doesn't know who he's trying to convince. Maybe that's the part that's bugging him: that so many children in town would need help. "Pastor—Uncle Bob said a lot of these kids have been abused. Sexually."

"How old we talking?"

"Young."

"They're probably from the city. Street kids have their own resources and networks. Word gets out. Free shelter, food. Come from miles around." Tom clasps his father-in-law's shoulder. "Covenant's as safe as it's always been."

Sobczak cranes his neck to see out the windshield. The snow is really starting to come down now. Even with the window rolled up and the heat blasted, Sobczak can feel the temps continue to dive. "You should get going before this freezes over."

Tom reaches for the handle, stops. "What's this got to do with that psychiatrist?"

"Don't worry about it." Sobczak shifts into gear. "Right now, you best get that maple syrup and ice cream. A pregnant woman is nothing to mess with."

Tom zippers up, tucks his cap in place. Getting out of the car, he pauses, hanging back.

"Spit it out, Tom."

"Amanda had lunch with Tracy Somerset today."

"And?"

"They haven't spoken since high school. They're not friends. Tracy wrote her out of the blue."

"For lunch?"

"Why is Todd Norman's alibi calling after fifteen years?"

"What are you thinking?"

"I don't know." Tom cinches his coat. "But I'm less worried about creepy pastors and radical churches than I am Todd Norman sending his girlfriend to do recon."

***

The snowfall sequesters Tracy. Oh, who is she kidding? She wasn't going anywhere tonight. Lisa Blake and the rest are at Slider's—a last-minute text inviting her along. After their liquid lunch reunion, Tracy is in no hurry to ever do it again. Even if it wasn't snowing, Tracy's not sitting in a townie bar, over hot wings and lukewarm beers, talking about the ones who got away. Plus, she's not bugging Diana to come out and babysit in a snowstorm.

That's not the truth either. Tracy is waiting on word from Todd, a slow anxiety brewing beneath the surface, keeping her on edge. She hasn't heard from him since he was brought in for questioning. She can't call. Tracy doesn't know if the police confiscated his cell. Then again, depending on how serious authorities are, they might've already subpoenaed phone records. Not that she's done anything wrong. Nor has he.

Logan's in bed for the night. Wine and a fire. Maybe a movie. Sounds about right.

Tracy pours herself a glass and makes for the sofa in the living room. Turning on the television, she searches for an old movie, settling on *Casablanca*, which she's seen a hundred times, and wouldn't mind seeing a hundred more.

The doorbell rings, and Tracy picks up her cell to see if she missed a call because no one drives out and shows up unannounced anymore, not in the middle of a storm.

Carrying her wine to the door, she peels back the curtains and sees him standing there.

Todd doesn't say anything, so she kicks off the conversation with, "Hi." He looks agitated. Not surprising given what he's been through.

"I got stopped by the police."

"I saw on TV."

"No. Just now. Covenant." He points toward the dark side of the lake, spread-out houses hazing soft light. "After Holland PD let me go. Officer Tom Kies. You know him?"

"Not well. I know his wife better. I went to school with them ages ago."

Todd enters but doesn't remove his coat or step further than the front mat.

The house is cozy, fireplace crackling, orange flame flickering, licking old colonial walls, throwing shadows up the red brick. Tracy motions toward the bottle on the table. She wants him to stay. "Can I get you something to drink?" She knows Todd seldom drinks.

He doesn't respond. She can see he wants to say something. Tracy stops halfway, backs up to the kitchen table, bracing, both hands on the back of a chair. She wants him to come closer, kiss her. This desire comes on swift, strong.

"What are you doing?" Todd asks.

"What?" Tracy pops up. "Nothing."

"Having lunch with Amanda Kies? That's the police chief's daughter and my dead wife's best friend. She's married to the town cop. Do you know how much trouble that is going to cause me?"

"I wasn't trying to cause you any trouble."

"I know you didn't intend that. But what did you think was going to happen?" Todd shakes his head. "I *just* got done dealing with Holland over this missing woman bullshit—"

"What's that about?"

"Bullshit," he repeats, his tone steady, inflection calm. The word stands out because Todd rarely swears. "A girl April knew from a hospital program she was in. Twelve years ago. She's missing."

"Hospital program?"

"April's father is high strung and neurotic ... it doesn't matter. This is the rest of my life. Something goes wrong, I'm the first person they talk to." He lifts his hands, which appear on the verge of shaking, but they never do. He runs his hands through his thick black hair, and keeps going till fingertips dig into the back of his skull. "The cops already hate me. I don't need you reminding them how much."

Tracy wants to tell him she's trying to help; that she hoped maybe Amanda might say something, anything, which would let Tracy better advocate for Todd. Running this through her head now, the idea sounds inane. She doesn't know how to say what she wants. Which is him, in her life, and there is no clear path to making that happen, every route fraught with peril, pitfalls, and pains in the ass.

"What are you doing?" Todd repeats. "Here, now, tonight?"

"You came to my house."

"Right," Todd says, making a show of panning around. "Your house. Middle of nowhere." He nods at the ceiling. "Little boy's asleep upstairs?"

Tracy nods.

"You don't seem worried."

"Should I be?"

"What is this about? What are we doing?" Todd comes off the mat, stepping toward the center. "Why are you going around talking to April's friends? Is there something you want to know about me? Ask."

Tracy inches away from the table, stepping to him, then peeling off, grabbing her wine, and staring over the back deck, across the lake, down to the home he is building. "Is the lakehouse that important?"

"Why would you ask me that? Of course it is. I wouldn't be here otherwise."

"There are other places, cities, towns, far from Covenant. Far from here. Fresh-start towns where everyone isn't all up in your business, judging."

"I am going to finish." The way Todd says this carries the defiant weight of a challenge.

Tracy goes to drink her wine, sees a crack in the glass. She sets it down, steps to and then past him, reaching up, over his shoulder, fetching a new one. She is so close she can smell his musk, the burn of sawdust and sweat, hard work on his passion project saturated into the fibers of his coat, his very being. When she pours the wine, he doesn't move, and she brushes against him. A spark of electricity, her heartbeat surges. She had that once with Brett, ages ago. In some ways, Tracy always knew Brett Coggins was bad news, that he would hurt her. Is that what she's feeling now? The allure of danger? Does knowing it's wrong make the mistake more inviting?

Todd breaks the closeness, taking up Tracy's old spot at the window, lost in the blackness of Shallow Lake at night. "Sometimes I don't know why I'm here. Sometimes?" He laughs to himself. "Most times."

"Then why are you?" Tracy retreats from what she was going to say next. Namely, what about her? Does he feel the same? Because if he does, and if he finishes this house, neither will know a moment's peace.

"You think I'm crazy?" he says.

"A little."

Todd turns around, facing her. "But you don't think I had anything to do with it?"

Tracy doesn't have to answer that question. Not anymore.

She looks at the bottle, sees it's half full. Which means Tracy is on her way to polishing off all the wine herself. A glass, two tops, most nights. Why is she drinking so much tonight? Did a part of her know he was coming? Need the courage? The only thing she knows for sure: she wants him.

Tracy steps closer to Todd, staring, eye-level. Maybe that's part of why she isn't afraid. She's almost as tall as he is. No, Trace, that's the wine talking. He's still a man and you're still a woman. He could break you in two if he wanted. Battle of the sexes: no matter how tall you are, you are always coming up short.

She reaches out and takes his hand. She wants to see how it feels, skin on skin. It feels good. He doesn't pull away. A moment later, he moves in. Then his mouth is on hers. Tracy accepts she's wanted this from the moment she met him. Tracy kisses him back, hands sliding to hips as his touch travels, holding her in place, gentle but firm, wanton, insatiable. It has been so long since Tracy was kissed like this.

Neither of them hears the front door open.

CHAPTER THIRTY

"What the hell?" Brett stands at the open front door, snow swirling in, winter gusts punishing with abandon. He drops the roses in his hand, petals scattered on the wings.

"How'd you get in?"

"The door was unlocked." He gestures at Todd. "Who's that?"

"None of your business. You can't just walk into my house."

"I knocked."

"I was busy."

"Obviously. Your house? Used to be *our* house."

"Yeah. *Used* to be. Before you got caught fucking some college girl!"

Todd rubs a hand over his face. Tracy knows this is the last thing he wants, to be stuck in the middle of a divorced couple's fight. She can appreciate how awkward it must be for him—she wouldn't blame him for leaving—but at least Brett doesn't know who Todd is, because that would be a whole new nightmare.

"Maybe I should be going," Todd says.

"Good idea," Brett says.

Todd breezes past Tracy, toward the door. But Brett doesn't move out of the way, making Todd sidestep. Childish and immature. The easy thing to do would be step around, capitulate, let Brett make his stand and acquiesce. Todd isn't doing that.

This moment is more than a macho challenge, more than one man standing in another's way. Tracy feels it. To step around is to surrender, let the bastards win. Todd has done enough of that. Survival has grown contingent on holding ground. Todd isn't going to be bullied by the Brett Cogginses of the world, and he isn't going to let this town define him. Tracy had given Todd an earful that first night over coffee; he's aware of the wringer Brett put her through. Is that why he's staying? She wants to believe that. Then Tracy watches something change in Todd's eyes, the usual warmth has been replaced with something else ... something cold, sinister, dangerous.

The look gives him away.

"I know you. You're that guy! The banker from New York, the one who—"

Todd isn't quite as tall or stout as Brett but now he appears to tower above.

"That's right," Todd says without a trace of emotion. "Makes you wonder why you're dumb enough to stand in my way, doesn't it?"

Brett steps to the side, and Todd grabs the handle. But he doesn't walk into the storm. A chill whispers around Tracy's heart.

Todd closes the door. If this were a Kenny Rogers song, he'd lock it too.

"I think it's you who needs to get going," Todd says.

Tracy has known Brett Coggins a long time. When he was in college, he worked summers with a construction crew, bunch of roughneck-types, misfits, castoffs. He and his co-workers spent a lot of nights after work drinking beer (and now Tracy knows picking up townie girls) in hardscrabble bars. At that age, the alcohol, the line of work resulted in plenty of fights. She remembers meeting up with Brett later, his knuckles bloodied, eye puffy, still drunk, laughing about it. Even though he ended up in academia, Brett isn't soft. He has an edge to him. She's never seen him back down like this.

"And to think I wanted to give it another go." Brett laughs to himself before opening the door and spreading his arms, backing up and out, down the walkway, into the snow and cold, alone. "I drove forty minutes in this crap. I don't know what I was thinking. You are lost, Tracy."

"Fuck you, Brett."

Brett Coggins buttons up. "I'll be talking to my lawyer tomorrow." He motions around the house. "This free ride is over." He gazes toward Todd but never makes eye contact. "You can get a real job and pay your own way for once in your life."

"Get out!"

Brett feigns a tip of a cap, pantomimes some other grand, pretentious gesture. From the driveway, he points at the kitchen table where the half-empty wine bottle sits. "Have another drink. It's going be a long wint—"

Todd slams the door on him.

Then he takes her upstairs.

CHAPTER THIRTY-ONE

SPRING

Sitting outside Capital Lunch, Sobczak checks the dashboard clock. Fifteen minutes early. This is not how he wants to start the day. Revisiting the tumultuous fall and winter of last year.

Holland's attempt to put the heat on Todd Norman misfired in a spectacular way. After they leaked Norman's name to Channel 3, disclosing his plans and divulging current whereabouts, Norman's New York attorney unleashed holy hell. Lawsuits have been filed. Defamation, libel, a bunch of other legal mumbo-jumbo that does not concern Sobczak. He has no idea the validity of these claims. They are Holland's problem. The personal impact it's had on Sobczak: a moratorium on investigating Todd Norman.

With no new news, Sobczak has been able to focus on the best thing in his life: his expected grandchild. Which has come with a most agreeable byproduct: reconciliation with his daughter. It's not like Sobczak and Amanda were ever estranged. They talked, ate together once in a while. But following Mary's passing, their relationship had been, at best, frosty. Now the ice has melted. Being pregnant, Amanda needs her daddy. And it's been wonderful. Sobczak sees his daughter almost every day. He brings her treats from the bakery, jelly donuts and butter tarts, props pillows beneath aching backs and massages barking feet. While on patrol, he'll pop in just to say hello; and whereas previous surprise visits were met with hostility and aggravation, now Amanda's eyes light up, and it reminds Sobczak of the good things in life, how sometimes we get second chances to get it right.

Then Detective Ronson phoned this morning, saying she had new, vital information about their case and Todd Norman. And like that, Sobczak is pulled back in.

Though why she's chosen a hot dog diner several towns over as their meeting spot is anyone's guess. Ronson promised she'd explain everything when he got there. Part of Sobczak doesn't want to know.

When he sees Ronson walk inside the restaurant, he gives her a few. He's gotten the impression this meeting isn't on the up and up.

Sobczak enters the small dinette, bypassing the parade of delicious hot dog combinations. The sweet smells of grilled onions and tangy meats waft as he joins Ronson, who is already sitting at a table, chowing down on a chilidog.

"Not hungry?" she asks. "Best hot dogs in the state."

"My doctor says I have to cut back on ... everything."

"You don't look so bad for a man your age."

"Let me know how you feel when you hit fifty-seven. There's nothing left for me to eat that doesn't taste like a broken promise."

"I'll be there soon enough. Until then…" Ronson sinks her teeth into the plump dog, juicy chili bits dribbling to the plate.

Sobczak has removed his hat, smoothing what's left of his hair. To the casual observer, it might look like he is trying to make himself more attractive. Even though Sobczak's noticed, several times, Stephanie Ronson doesn't wear a ring, he's given up trying to find someone to replace Mary. No one can.

Ronson wipes chili grease from the corner of her mouth, wadding the napkin and dropping it to the tray.

"What happened to Crasnick?"

"Administrative leave. Fallout from the Channel 3 fuck-up in January." The way Ronson says this, Sobczak understands the idea wasn't Crasnick's alone.

Out the long-paned window, a boy on a bicycle peddles past. Fifty degrees and he's wearing nothing but shorts and backward ball cap. Slightest hint of warm weather around here and everyone starts shedding clothes like it's a sweltering day at the beach.

"Why are we sitting at a diner in New Britain?"

"I'll get to that in a minute. Right now," Ronson opens her bag, pulls out four photos, "say hello to the Green Hills girls."

Sobczak recognizes them all. Wendy, April, Beiko, and Shannon.

"They all lived together. Six-month residential program. Farmington."

"We already covered this. Wendy's second autopsy confirmed the OD."

"It did. But now…" Ronson pushes forward the photo of Shannon O'Connor. "Like Beiko Talo, O'Connor has gone missing."

"Two dead, two missing."

"It gets worse. Want to guess who was lead psychiatrist at Green Hills? Give you a hint: last confirmed person to see Shannon O'Connor."

"Bakshir."

When the surveillance of Todd Norman was put on hold, Sobczak never returned to talk to Dr. Bakshir. He was told by Holland County to back off. He backed off. At the time, Shannon O'Connor was a person of interest, not missing. No urgency to follow up. He took advantage of the lull to spend time with his daughter. Sobczak rages inside. Maybe if he'd taken the initiative—been a leader—another young woman's life wouldn't be in jeopardy.

"We've already been by the good doctor's house," Ronson says. "He's in the wind."

"I would've liked to have been involved."

"We had to move fast. And that's why we're here. No one has been at Bakshir's for quite some time. Cupboards, drawers left open, clothes ripped to the floor. Like someone wanted out of there in a hurry. We'll find him. His phone numbers are out of service, but we have his credit card activity being monitored."

"How long's she been missing?"

"We don't know. Maybe as long as three months. Her aunt handles her disability. She finally called it in, said the girl hadn't been by to collect her money since January."

"How's this connect to Norman?"

"The connection to Norman is not as straightforward as I would like."

"Meaning?"

"Do you know anyone in Covenant who is a patient of Bakshir?"

"Until six months ago I didn't even know we had a shrink in Covenant."

"It's the twenty-first century, Dwayne. People see therapists."

"I don't."

"I do. And so do a lot of people I know. That doesn't matter. Tracy Somerset, Norman's frequent alibi, is also a patient."

Sobczak falls back in his plastic chair, running a hand through his thinning hair. "Right," he says. "I talked to her in the parking lot once. When Norman supplied her name as an alibi. That was Bakshir's place." Sobczak says this as if he is just now making the connection. "Guess I shouldn't be too surprised. I don't think she's well. Her ex-husband did a number on her—"

"She's also dating Todd Norman."

Sobczak's slack jaw tells Ronson he did not know that.

"Not keeping up on the latest romantic comedies in your town?"

Sobczak remembers the day Tom was getting Amanda ice cream and maple syrup. He referred to Tracy as Norman's girl-friend. Sobczak thought it was a figure of speech. How did Tom know? How does Ronson? How is everyone kept better abreast than the chief of police?

Ronson starts reading her notes, back to business, attempting to chart causality. "We have several women linked to both Bakshir *and* Norman."

"And two women romantically involved with Todd Norman, same psychiatrist. That's gotta mean something."

"Or not." Ronson separates April Abbott's photo from the others. "We have no proof Norman and Bakshir ever met. Norman is not listed in the visitor's log for Green Hills. Art Abbott and his wife came to visit, of course. No one else. Not even friends."

It's hard for Sobczak to remember the order of these events. Dating drama was Mary's area of expertise. He wishes he'd paid more attention.

"Turns out," Ronson says, "April didn't meet Norman until her second semester at UConn, almost a year later."

"Hold on," Sobczak says. "How do you know this?"

"Because I've been doing my homework."

"I mean, how do you know *any*thing about Green Hills? I thought records were sealed?"

"There's a way around everything. But, no, this information wasn't easy to come by. Which is why we're sitting here, alone, in a hot dog shop." Ronson returns to her detailed research. "We've been through the belongings of Talo and O'Connor, at least what their families hadn't thrown away. We know that after Green Hills ended, the girls kept in contact. We've uncovered correspondence between April, Talo, and O'Connor. We want to check Wendy's room. Get into her hard drive, laptop. Search any possible letters, e-mails."

"What do you need me for?" Sobczak feels his gut churn, intestinal rebellion over having been denied at least one tasty dog.

"Wendy Mortensen's father, Donald, lives here."

"In New Britain?"

Ronson nods, sliding along a scrap of paper.

Sobczak stares at the address. "You want me to talk to Wendy's father?"

"Biological. Parents weren't together. She wasn't raised by him."

"Why can't you do it?" Sobczak knows something isn't on the level. "Your bosses want you to back off? Women are missing."

"Yeah, homeless women, drug addicts. Missing takes on a whole different connotation. I can tell you this, my bosses don't know I'm here, and they sure as hell don't want me wasting any more county resources on what they think is a dead end. Far as they are concerned, Beiko Talo and Shannon O'Connor will pop up again one day. And if they don't? Who gives a shit? I'm cutting corners. But I can't outright defy orders. I work with you, Dwayne. You work with me. Remember back when I wanted to talk to Art Abbott? You asked me to stand down, insisted on taking the lead."

"A lot has happened since January." Sobczak holds up his car keys. "You want to have a run at Art? Let's go. I'll drive you there." Sobczak isn't sure what game she's playing. Just that she's playing *a* game.

Ronson looks down the road of this tiny industrial town, twisting her mouth, like she has to think about whether to share what she says next, whether she trusts Sobczak enough to confide inner-circle knowledge. That she has to think so hard starts to piss him off.

"Wendy didn't know her father," Ronson says. "She went to stay with him before she was eighteen." The Holland detective stops, grows exasperated. "It's complicated, okay? The property is still listed under Donald Mortensen's mother's name. She's dead. Wendy lived with her father. Rented a room. Not yet an adult." Ronson opens her palms, as if to say, "See the problem?" "Split after she turned eighteen. We are in uncharted territory here. I would like to see what's in that room. But so far, Mortensen will not give us access. Since Wendy is too dead to grant permission, we can't get in there without a warrant." Ronson squares Sobczak in the eye. "We don't have enough to get a warrant."

"What do you think I can do that you can't?"

"Start by asking him about Bakshir, see if he recognizes the name." Ronson offers a wry grin. "Use some of your good ol' boy charm."

The address on Sunny Slope Drive showcases a small white house with a tattered, grease-stained American flag, proudly displayed. Beyond that, there isn't much to be proud of. The rest of the residences on the charming block are well maintained on quaint plots. Planter boxes and vegetable gardens, put to bed for the winter, are springing back to life. Donald Mortensen's home is a blight and an eyesore.

Beyond the general lack of upkeep to the property—the overflowing black bags piled on the side of the house; the weather-stripped paint; the grounded car—the house projects a disregard for civility; and, no, Sobczak isn't one for "vibes" or any other new-age nonsense. He's been in law enforcement long enough to tell the difference between a poor man and a bad man.

Sobczak's prejudices are confirmed when he finds Mortensen home at one in the afternoon. There are several reasons why a man might be home at one in the afternoon on a weekday. None of which apply to Donald Mortensen, who is half dressed, unshaven, and reeking of booze.

"What you want?"

Sobczak doesn't have his hat on. With a nip in the April air, he wears his big, blue windbreaker. Mortensen might not recognize him as an officer of the law. Or maybe it doesn't matter. Sobczak isn't in his jurisdiction; this visit holds no sway. He's come as a favor to Ronson, supposed to talk to the man, unsure what he's supposed to gain from doing so. He wants to have an open mind, but within ten seconds of being in Donald Mortensen's presence, Sobczak admits he does not like this man.

"I was hoping to speak with you."

"Yeah, can see that." Mortensen slaps open the screen door with the butt of his palm.

The home's dark interior renders the outside sophisticated, elegant by comparison. The first thing that hits Sobczak is the smell. Not weed or liquor. Human stink, like plugged toilets and clogged drains. Neglected hygiene, rotting teeth, B.O., sweaty clothes, a garbage disposal backed up with glued-together, gristled meats. The blinds are lowered, slated closed, no light allowed in.

Mortensen makes for the refrigerator and snaps free a beer, which he holds up for Sobczak to see. Whether the gesture is meant to seek permission or as an offer to share, Sobczak cannot tell.

"I'm sorry about your daughter."

"Daughter," Mortensen grumbles, his response lost to old pipes groaning underground. "What you need?" He bends to light a butt off the stovetop.

Watching the stooped-over ape-man, who must be around the same age, wheeze and hack lung butter, Sobczak resolves to never again smoke another cigarette.

"Does the name Dr. Bakshir sound familiar?"

Mortensen squints in disbelief. "This a joke?"

"What would be funny about that?"

Mortensen waits, trying to determine if Sobczak is telling the truth. Sobczak isn't sure which part of the question is supposed to be humorous or dishonest.

"Wendy's fuckin' shrink. What about him?"

"For one, he's missing."

"Good. With any luck, the son of a bitch will turn up dead."

Sobczak isn't sure how to respond to that. The man hasn't threatened anyone. He lacks social graces and dignity, neither of which constitutes a crime. Dr. Bakshir is the one wanted for questioning.

"Listen, I already told that other bitch, I registered, okay? Nothing more I need to do. You don't like me? Too fuckin' bad.

And Wendy wasn't so innocent, okay? I put a roof over her head, and her fuckin' mother..." He grumbles and goes for another beer.

"I don't know what you are talking about, Mr. Mortensen."

"That fuckin' out-of-town cop. Come over here this morning."

Ronson?

"You people want me to bleed out my eyes? I didn't know Wendy too good."

"Your daughter."

"Daughter?" he spits. "My cunt ex-wife—"

Sobczak holds up his hand. "Can you watch the language?"

"You're kidding me, right? Cop who don't curse? Where the fuck you from?"

"Not here."

"No shit." Mortensen sniffs back a glob of snot, spits it in the sink. "Rest of my life, any time a cop wants to search me, I have to stop, let them have their way. Want to come in my house? Sure thing, Officer. Bend over and spread 'em? With pleasure, sir! Yeah, I have to comply, but no one said I had to be nice about it."

Sobczak can't figure out why Ronson sent him to this house. He knows she wants access to the room Wendy rented. But Sobczak can't get that far. As soon as he mentioned Bakshir, the man grew hostile, unpredictable bordering on violent.

"When did your daughter start seeing Dr. Bakshir?"

"Are you for real, man? I've had you pricks up my ass for years now. It wasn't my fault, okay? They sent her to live with me, seventeen, looking the way she did, walking around this place half naked. I didn't know her! Not like she was ever mine. I didn't raise her. Her mother kept her secret from me. Then one day she shows up on my doorstep. Eats my food, takes my money. Little bitch. Wendy came on to *me*."

It takes Sobczak a moment, reconciling what Ronson said about Bakshir's area of expertise, sexual abuse survivors, Mortensen's admission of having to register. Combining those things does not arrive naturally in Sobczak's brain.

"Your ... daughter?"

Mortensen sticks a finger in Sobczak's face. "Get out!"

What happens next is pure reflex; no conscious thought goes into the decision. Sobczak will later tell himself it was self-defense. He didn't see a finger; he saw an aggressive action taken. This isn't true. Deep down, Sobczak has wanted to lay out the son of a bitch since they met. He can't remember the last time he's thrown an honest-to-God punch. When he was a kid, maybe? Playground scraps? He doesn't even remember landing the right cross, just Mortensen staring up from the ground, smearing blood across his busted nose with the back of his hand.

They stand outside the house on Sunny Slope, a couple squad cars pulled up on the lawn, Mortensen in handcuffs in the backseat of a cruiser. Stepping outside for air, Sobczak had rung Ronson. Within thirty seconds, she and a pair of New Britain police flew whizzing around the corner. She'd been waiting.

Ronson leads Sobczak off the lawn, across the street, to a vacant lot.

"He has to yield to searches," Ronson says. "Wendy's room is upstairs, and since it's locked, the courts deemed it a private residence. We couldn't search it without Mortensen's permission. A perverted loophole."

"I don't appreciate you setting me up."

"He hit you first. Assaulting a police officer."

"That's not what happened, and you know it."

"A technicality."

"You set me up," Sobczak repeats, less sure this time.

"Let's not get carried away."

"You couldn't involve your people, so you sent me in there."

"I had no idea he'd flash on you."

"What *did* you think would happen?"

Ronson retreats a step, peers around him, at the house, then back to Sobczak. "You're right," she says, lowering her voice. "I wasn't entirely honest with you. Sorry. But we want the same thing here. We don't have time to go through proper channels and do everything by the book. Now we have wiggle room. Mortensen will do anything to avoid prison time."

Sobczak sees her point, even if he's slow to admit it. "I still don't like it."

"Come on," Ronson says. "Admit it. Hitting that asshole felt pretty good."

CHAPTER THIRTY-TWO

Dr. Bakshir sits outside the house on Misty Mountain Drive. Finding the address has not been easy. Like any worthwhile journey, it's been a process. The investigation and bail jumping business had passed through probate, the business card left all but worthless. It was almost as if Marjorie Jessup didn't want to be found. She'd come to him, asking for *his* help. For a man who makes his living dissecting others' minds, sometimes Dr. Bakshir wonders if he'll ever understand how people think.

He hadn't intended to be gone so long. A couple days. He'd find her, do what had to be done. Then the police called, leaving that message about wanting to speak with him. And he couldn't go back. Not yet.

The doctor tossed his cell. Days turned to weeks, months, life on the road, a man living out of a suitcase. It became about more than finding Marjorie Jessup. He needed this time. He was wrong when he said he'd grieved for Wendy. He had not. His time on the road taught him that. Long stretches, nothing to do but think, forced him to incorporate the whole story, accept, learn to live with what he'd done, forgive himself.

Dr. Bakshir knew that he would have to deal with the police. Sooner or later. He had no designs on becoming a fugitive. Everything in due time, order. First, he had to find Jessup, see what she knew, make sure he was in the clear. Usual channels, internet searches, libraries, did little to help him track down the former investigator. But like anything in life, persistence is key. Due to his tenacity, Dr. Bakshir was eventually able to successfully navigate the criminal justice system. An ex-con on parole led him to a fisherman's market in Old Lyme, which is how, in turn, he's found Marjorie Jessup, living on the shores of a gated community in New Fairfield, twenty-five minutes from his home. For as small as Connecticut is, there are countless places to hide.

Evening gloam slides down ragged mountains, moonlight splashing off the water. The doctor exits his car, adjusts his glasses, and climbs the steps to her door. He can see she is home. A large, blocky silhouette sits in a chair, framed by the madness of the nightly news.

When Marjorie Jessup answers, he can tell she does not recognize him. This annoys, irks the doctor. He is a particular man, a well-mannered man. Some might call him stuffy, fussy. He has preferences, yes, but when someone seeks out *your* assistance, gives you *their* card and tells you to contact them, it is in poor taste not to know who they are. Especially after it has taken so long to track them down.

The doctor collects himself. "Hello, Marjorie. Dr. Bakshir? You visited my practice in Covenant. Last fall."

"I'm not working that case anymore."

"May I come in?"

Marjorie pans back at her TV dinner, cooling on a tray, as she takes a moment to consider the request, before grunting, relenting.

"Let me stick this in the oven to keep it warm." She grabs her dinner off a raised lap tray, some kind of browned meat, starch, and fruit gelatin. The implication of an interruption clear, Dr. Bakshir, on better days, might have offered to come back later. These are not better days.

Marjorie returns to the living room, plopping in her recliner, offering the doctor a spot on her paisley couch. The role reversal unnerves him, the shift in power dynamic. This is her home and he has to respect her boundaries, accept this time he is not the one in charge.

Dr. Bakshir sits and waits for offers of tea or coffee, something to drink, standard manners when guests arrive, but Marjorie tenders nothing other than a perturbed look. The doctor tries not to make it personal. Never easy for a man like Dr. Bakshir, personal slights and dereliction of etiquette a pet peeve.

"Marjorie," he starts.

"It's Madge, remember? What can I do for you, Doc?"

"I would like to talk about April Abbott."

Madge nods, chomping on a chunk of lip, a signal she's upset. People work on their own timetable. She was willing to talk when *she* was willing to talk. Months ago. The doctor has taken too long getting back to Madge Jessup, which unnerves her. That is okay. The doctor can wait. Or she can get used to disappointment.

"A little late," she says. Then repeats, slower, as though the doctor is brain addled, "I'm not working the case anymore. I retired. Didn't need the money, and I'd gotten sick of it."

"April was a patient of mine."

"Then what're you asking me about her for?"

"She was one of four girls I took care of, about ten years ago." The doctor reworks the math to exact dates. "Thirteen years ago."

Madge stares at the doctor, scans the wall, searching for a clock.

"You were working for Art Abbott, yes?" Dr. Bakshir says. "I've met him. He is not someone I wish to speak with again."

"Yeah, Art is a real son of a bitch, isn't he?" Madge smirks, hops up. "You want a drink?"

"Tea would be lovely."

"I have whiskey, brandy, and beer."

"I'm okay then."

Madge shakes her head. "If you want to talk to me about this, you want me buzzed. And I don't like to drink alone."

While not a teetotaler, Dr. Bakshir is not a big drinker. A practical man, however, he knows when it is time to take one for the team.

"A beer, I suppose, if I must—"

"Two whiskeys coming right up."

Dr. Bakshir tries to relax. The room is cozy but sterile, antiquated, a time capsule to a forgotten era, décor trapped in the '70s, lots of burnt orange shag carpeting, aquamarine glassware, plastic covering random pieces of tan furniture. He is surprised not to find a lava lamp. The doctor studies the pictures on the wall. Many feature a younger Madge with a man, whom the doctor takes to be her late husband.

Must be hard to lose a lifelong partner. But she'll be joining him soon enough.

Madge returns with two whiskeys. The flushness in her cheeks tells Dr. Bakshir she's pounded a shot or two while in the kitchen.

"You were not easy to find," he says.

"Place belonged to my stepdaddy. Different last name. Wasn't married to my mom." She plops back in the recliner. "Makes tax season easier."

The doctor sips his drink. Far from a connoisseur, he can tell by the acidic burn the whiskey lands a long way from top-shelf. No smooth, oaky finish, the doctor dislikes the hard liquor as much as he expected to.

"So you want to know about April?" Madge says without further prompt. "Or her fucked-up family?" She cackles. "I don't like Art Abbott. I've met enough possessive men in my life. Seen the patterns." Madge's red cheeks plump brighter remembering whom she's talking to. "Sure you seen some assholes in your line of work. Art keeps that house on lockdown, his timid-mouse housewife in check, rules with an iron fist."

"I'm more interested in April and—"

"What got her so fucked up? How bad was she when you knew her?"

"Doctor-patient confidentiality prohibits—"

"Oh, screw that, Doc. I show you mine, you show me yours."

"April had issues. She had a hole that needed to be filled with outside validation."

"If by 'outside validation' you mean a lot of fucking, yes, I guess that would fill the hole."

Dr. Bakshir shifts in his seat.

"Sorry," Madge says, draining the rest of her whiskey. "I forget you're from Covenant. Good Puritan stock."

"I live in—"

"You know you have a swinger's club in Covenant?"

"Excuse me?"

"No shit, Meshulum." She nods in the dark, over those ragged mountains. "Laurel Drive. All your good God-fearing townsfolk assemble there regular to get their freak on." Madge cackles again, the alcohol taking hold.

"I don't understand what that—"

"What's your area of specialty, Doc? Don't play dumb, okay? Fucked-up teens, drugs, sex workers, promiscuity?" She sings these last syllables. "All those girls are sexual abuse survivors. Do you know the percentage of woman working in the sex industry that were sexually abused?"

"Ninety percent."

"I don't know an exact number," Madge says, ignoring his answer. "But I know it's a lot."

"This is all interesting. But it's not what I'm looking for."

"The hell it's not! Most women have been diddled. Use sex to cope with trauma or the general fuckery of life. What's the difference? A paycheck? Ha!" Madge goes for the glass but finds it empty. After licking the rim, she hops up without excusing herself, back into the kitchen, returning with the bottle of Early Times.

For a moment, Madge doesn't say anything, staring ahead, at the pictures on the wall. "Woman lived in New York City, right? April? Before she got killed. Before that, she was a kid. No, these are grown-ups I'm talking about. Don't you listen? I'm telling you everything you need to know. Your lily-white town ain't so lily white. Come on, you're a doctor. Patterns start early. Practice 'em enough, they become habits. We don't get rid of habits, we substitute 'em."

"What did Art Abbott want you to do?"

"Find enough information to bring a civil case against the man he blames for the death of his daughter, the ex-husband, Norman."

"And what did you find out?"

"Nothing to incriminate the husband. He was a cold fish. An odd, pardon the expression, bird. But did he kill her? I don't know. Everything I uncovered was circumstantial. Same as the cops. I can tell you this. If he *did* do it? Man deserves an Oscar. Because he's acting one hell of a part."

"Anything ... else? Perhaps from around the time I worked with her?"

"Art terminated my services. I'm out. I am not helping anyone solve anything. My dinner is getting cold."

"I don't need much more of your time. Anything you can tell me might help."

"Help what? Who? You? Nah, I have confidentiality rules too." Madge sneers. "I came to you asking for help. Remember? We could've talked then. You were too busy. You blew it."

"That was not the case. You asked me if Todd Norman was a patient. He was not. I did not withhold anything."

"You're smarmy. You know that, Doc? Condescending and smug, which comes across as smarmy. You are not a likeable man." Madge takes another slug.

"I am not here to make your friendship."

Madge lolls her tongue inside her mouth. "All right. *Meshulum.* Here's what I'll tell you. Small-town scandals, when they involve families like the Abbotts, get buried, mounds of dirt piled on. April didn't move from Covenant. She was kicked out. She was keeping some bad friends. Dirty friends. She was a seventeen-year-old girl learning about love. Art Abbott found out, didn't like the tarnish on his good, traditional family values. So he sent his baby girl packing."

"You're not implying he had anything to do with her death?" The idea is preposterous. Still, given the direction the conversation has taken, the doctor feels the need to follow up.

"Nah. He loved his daughter. He was just one of those right-leaning, Bible-thumping zealots. Spare the rod. You know the type."

Madge Jessup tries to stand, walk, swaying woozily. She makes it to her dead husband on the wall. But it is not pretty.

"You married, Doc?"

"No."

"Kids?"

"No."

"Yeah. Me either." Madge runs a pudgy finger down the glass, over the face of her dead husband. "All April's problems stemmed from a broken heart. She was in love. High school crush. A girl. Rankled the old man, rubbed him wrong. Sent her away. When she got out of your little program there, I think she tried to go back, make it work. By then that Jesus fella got involved. There was a boy, too. The girl? What's her name? I can't remember. But those two loved each other. I did a lot of poking around. I think something bad happened. But what do I know? Hearts break harder at that age. Who's to say? But I can tell you this. When you punish someone for loving, don't expect a thank you."

***

Sobczak is still upset with the subterfuge, but he has to admit Ronson's ruse worked. Driving away, Sobczak passed Ronson and her crew dissecting Wendy's rented room. The Holland detective said she'd call when they turned up something worthwhile.

Ronson invited Sobczak to stick around, but the chief begged off. He has other plans tonight.

Tom answers the door. For a moment, conflict flows, internal battle waged. Tom will be a better father than Sobczak ever was. This remorse is fast replaced with warmth, reassurance. That's what being a father is all about, giving your children a better future, a better chance, a better life than the one you had.

Sobczak feels his cell buzzing. Ronson. He ignores the call. He's with his family tonight. Sobczak is not letting the job get in the way. Tonight, he doesn't have to be a cop.

A second later, a text dings in:

Found some of Wendy's old journals. Going through now.

And then a few minutes later, another text, Ronson again:

Got a hit on Bakshir. Credit card in New Fairfield, gas station in Waterbury.

Sobczak turns off his cell.

From the foyer, he watches Amanda in the kitchen prepping dinner. Sobczak smells boiling potatoes and frying onions. Sees the large stainless steel bowl she's filling with flour, another ladled with egg yolk, sour cream, butter. The dusted rolling pin. Homemade perogies. A recipe handed down from her mother.

As he stuffs away his cell, Sobczak feels Tom come stand by his side, staring up, studying his expression. Even when the chief thinks he's shutting off, his cop instincts don't power down so easily; he wears the job on his face.

"Everything okay?"

"Work stuff."

"Norman?"

"Maybe. Holland is searching Wendy Mortensen's room right now." Sobczak explains the Green Hills connection. "Hoping to find a common thread. And we got a hit on Bakshir. Waterbury."

"What's the doctor doing there?"

"Who knows?" Sobczak says. "A perfect storm, though." He slaps a hand on his son-in-law's back. "Work can take a backseat for one night." He motions toward his daughter, now almost seven months pregnant. Has there ever been a more beautiful sight?

"You gonna find out the sex of the baby?"

"No. Amanda wants it to be a surprise."

"Take my advice, son. Find out now so you can start painting the room pink or blue. Life will deal you plenty of surprises.

CHAPTER THIRTY-THREE

Tracy wakes in the new-dawn light, warm, safe, and for the first time in a long time she doesn't feel alone. She reaches over for Todd, but finds the spot where he should be cold. Dragging herself out of bed, she plucks a tee shirt from the floor, and goes to the window. She does not see Todd's truck. Maybe he's gone into town to get them breakfast, even though there is plenty of food in the small, temporary refrigerator.

With the thaw of spring, the lakehouse has become habitable. It's not done yet. But close. The plumbing and electricity work, home insulated. Appliances still need to be installed, washer and dryer, permanent fridge, stovetop. The exterior requires painting. Details, such as wainscoting and trim, must be addressed. Then there are the amenities—rainshower heads for the walk-in, granite countertop, racks for the wine cellar. Considering Tracy has never seen Todd drink more than the occasional glass of pinot with steak, she feels this last one might be for her. The upstairs bathroom isn't complete. He's ordered the tile, which he needs before wiring the heated floor; and there is still work to do in the basement, which right now serves mostly as storage. It's a house, if not quite a home.

Logan is with Brett. After the New Year's blow-up, her ex did speak to a lawyer. Todd spoke to his attorney, David Deal, any and all inquiry directed through the New York City law offices. Brett's threats ended as soon as they began. He might not like it, the chastising of his manhood, but so far Brett seems willing to work with Tracy and this new dynamic. She knows, ego aside, he wants what's best for their son. And Brett recognizes a losing battle when he sees one.

They could have stayed at Tracy's house. Last night, for the first time, Todd suggested they go to the lakehouse. Their houses are separated by half a mile and a large body of water. Which bed they made love on wasn't what was at stake. The invitation boasted much more. Todd wasn't just inviting her into his house; he was asking her into his life.

On the brown branches along the ridge of Shallow Lake, flowers have begun to sprout, small yellow and creamy pink buds. Big black crows sit, framed in the gray light.

Tires spin on gravel, and the truck pulls up. Todd hops out with two coffees on a tray, holding a grease-smeared white paper bag. She can smell the buttery egg and cheese croissants. As he gets closer, Tracy notices the cut on his forehead, fresh and raised, pink swelling around it, as if he's been struck by a rock or worse.

"What happened?"

Todd points to the trees around them. "I was trying to sneak off and get breakfast before you woke up. Couldn't see and got thwacked by a branch."

Tracy reaches out to touch his face. He flinches.

They stand in silence. Still feels awkward. Last night they'd made love by the moonlight of his lakehouse, his touch pure, strong, tender, perfect. In the morning light, it's never so easy. Not that Tracy has a lot of comparison to go by. But in between the breakups, there were others. Rebounds, revenge one-night stands, more obligatory than wanted. Each time was different, unique. Except this part, vulnerability exposed by the morning light.

"What time do you have to get Logan?"

"What time is it?"

Todd pretends to check a clock in the sky. "I think my watch stopped."

"Then I suppose we have a little longer." She takes him by the hand, and they return to the lakehouse.

Tracy lies in the crook of Todd's arm. Last night had been wonderful; this morning was better. Without darkness to hide behind, they were forced to both be present, aware of now. Every thrust, every inch, how he'd remain still for what felt like minutes at a time, two bodies fused as one. Tracy orgasmed more this morning than at any point with Brett.

Now she is spent, exhausted, blissed out, the quadrant of large thrumming heaters warming the house to toasty.

There's no right or wrong. Not when it feels this good, the way he fits inside her. An odd pair of flawed pieces that perfectly fill the other, fragmented and ostracized alone, together whole.

As satisfying as that picture is when it comes into focus, the process is never quick or easy. And the dismantling of something so beautiful always arrives fast, ugly, and unforgiving.

The squad car lights register ahead of the sound, which lags reaction time. One second you have your head on his chest, nestled in the crook of his arm, feeling like things might work out in this crazy life after all. Then they come in, a pair of uniforms barking, ordering, a woman in plain clothes overseeing it all. There is shouting to put hands where they can be seen, the unnecessary embarrassment of having to shield nakedness with sheets, before you're separated, commanded to get dressed. Questions about what's happening go unanswered. You hear the reading of rights, something about a missing woman, missing women. And then you are standing outside, freezing, jeans and tee hastily thrown on, as the police lead him to their squad car. A pair of hands holds you back, manhandling, before you break free and scream, loud enough for everyone to stop what they are doing and stare at you like you're mad.

"He was with me last night! We were here all night long!"

One of the cops breaks off, pushes you back, while the other fastens the handcuffs on him, clasping them extra tight, as if to prove a point, before he's shoved into the back of a squad car, a common thug.

From the rear window, he turns around, those vibrant blue eyes now dead, defeated.

Then the car speeds off, leaving you standing in the cold.

***

Back in his house for the first time in several weeks, Dr. Bakshir removes his shoes at the door, sliding into his slippers, and heads for the kitchen to make tea. Something isn't right. The house is in disarray. Opened drawers and cupboards, rifled papers. Dr. Bakshir's decision to find Madge Jessup may've been rash, the loss of Wendy, Beiko, Shannon gripping him hard. Leaving, he'd been in a hurry, but he didn't create and abandon this mess. He despises clutter. Someone has been here. He can smell their scent, like an animal, a predator invading nesting grounds, sniffing around his eggs.

Tea poured, cup in hand, Dr. Bakshir enters the living room, where he encounters more evidence of an intruder. Magazines off the coffee table, books from shelves toppled to the floor, split open. This is a violation. He switches on the television, something he does not often do. Right now, he longs for the mindless distraction.

When the news comes on, he knows that distraction will not last.

The doctor accepts his life will never again be the same.

CHAPTER THIRTY-FOUR

Sobczak enters the station to a celebration. The whole volunteer force cheers when they see him. Judi Drake and Ron Lamontagne are handing out cupcakes. Town reporter Eric Serafin and photographer Marcus DeMata have stopped by, swilling Dunkin' Donuts from a takeout cardboard box. Brad the janitor tries to high-five someone.

"What's going on?"

Tom shoos everyone away as he fills in the chief.

"Been trying to call you all morning."

"Turned off my cell last night at your place." Sobczak feels for his phone. Not in his pockets. "Must've forgot to turn it on." He cranes back toward the front door and his car.

"We got the bastard," Tom says, swelling with pride.

"Who?"

"Norman."

"What—how?"

"Wendy Mortensen's room. They found journals. Letters from April Abbott to Wendy where she talks about being afraid for her life."

"Holland call?"

"When they couldn't reach you, yeah. Detective Ronson says these letters paint Norman as a sociopath, a controlling madman with violent tendencies."

"That's not enough to get an arrest warrant."

"No," Tom agrees. "But an anonymous call came in last night on the tip line. Someone spotted our green truck at the lakehouse."

"When?" Sobczak has watched Norman enough to know the color is wrong. "Norman's truck is red."

"Whose side are you on?" Tom laughs. "They searched the lakehouse." He stops, pausing to let the news sink in. "They found bloody clothes in the basement. Woman's shirt. Urine, underwear. They're testing for DNA."

Something doesn't feel right. "Anonymous tip? When?"

"Last night."

"After they searched Mortensen's room?"

"I thought you'd be happier."

"What did Ronson say about Bakshir?"

The front door flies open. Everyone stops and turns toward Tracy Somerset, hair wild, a rat's nest, eyes crazy, bugging like she's taken a narcotic, something bad and dangerous, like cocaine. There's no nice way to put it: she looks deranged.

"He was with me last night," Tracy shouts, loud enough for the whole department to hear. "Todd. We spent the night together at his lakehouse." Like she's proud of this fact. "The police arrested him this morning. They said he kidnapped someone. But he couldn't have. Because he was with me."

As eyes lock on Tracy, the chief observes her shifting, growing self-conscious, a bug under the magnifying glass disturbed by prolonged accusations.

Sobczak comes to her side, goes to take her arm, escort her from the judgment zone. "Let's talk in my office."

She shakes him off. "I am not ashamed."

"No one said you were." Sobczak notes the prying eyes. "More privacy," he whispers.

She relents, allowing him to guide her into his office, where he shuts the door.

"Sit down," he says. "Please."

"No. I'm not sitting down. And I'm not letting you arrest Todd for something he did not do."

Sobczak sighs. But not to catch his breath or punctuate a moment. No, the deep breath encapsulates much more than that. It is the act of a man desperate to have his life return to the one he knows.

"Are you sure you want to do this?"

"It's the truth."

"This has been in the works a long time, ongoing investigation. Six months' worth. These crimes could've been committed any time in that span."

"I've been with him ... for a while."

"But you can't account for every minute of every day and night, can you? I'll be honest with you, Tracy. Even if you wanted to provide an alibi—your word isn't good enough. A judge would want proof of that. In writing. Documents, receipts, eyewitness corroboration. You know what happens if they decide you aren't telling the truth? Perjury. Contempt of court." He lets that sink in. "You could lose custody of Logan."

"Don't you ever use my son to threaten me." She seethes. "Where is Todd?"

"Holland Police have him."

"I want to make a statement."

"It won't do any good. The charges against Todd go beyond last night. Two women are missing. Women with ties to Todd." And Dr. Bakshir, Sobczak thinks. "Go home. I promise I'll call when I—"

"No. I want to make a statement."

Sobczak stands from his chair, exasperated. He's trying to help this woman.

"Now!"

The chief doesn't have time for this. He calls Tom into his office over the intercom, a needlessly officious gesture since he could just open the door, but he's frustrated, fed up.

"Yeah, boss?"

"Take Miss Somerset to Holland PD. She wants to make a statement."

Tracy heads off with a triumphant air. Let her waste her time.

Sobczak calls Holland but Ronson isn't in. He leaves a message. The ordeal is over. This is not his problem anymore. They nabbed Norman. Why doesn't Sobczak feel better? Never the most technologically savvy, Sobczak powers up his old desktop. He knows his way around the internet fine, just prefers old school, physical newspapers. He searches Todd Norman's name, expecting an avalanche of articles—even the big New York papers are sure to pick this up. But there's nothing. Just old stories about the original murder, which suck Sobczak down the rabbit hole. He's more than familiar with the murder. He keeps hoping something will jump out, a timeline error or detail missed. Then he realizes he's wasting his time. The best prosecutors and detectives built the case, researched and interviewed persons of interest ad nauseum, vigilant in crosschecking inconsistencies.

The chief reclines, tries to make sense of this morning's arrest, process it, pushing doubt from his mind. He can't. Timing. On their own, those old letters between April and Wendy are hearsay. Inadmissible. Without that tip about the bloody shirt and underpants in the basement, same with the clothes. Why would Todd Norman keep a shirt in his basement? So meticulous and thorough to this point, only to be undone by a serial trophy?

A knock on the door. Joe Campbell has stopped in from the Getty station with a box of donuts. Good news travels fast in a tiny town. Even though Sobczak's physician has warned him to lay off saturated fats, Sobczak snags a powdered custard.

"Somethin' wrong, Chief?"

"Not enough sleep."

"I heard the good news."

"Yup. We got him."

"I'mma leave this with you." Joe Campbell passes along the donut box. "I just come by to grab this quarter's tickets."

"We've had a good run of late," Sobczak says. "Tom likes to sit out on Deming with the gun. Perfect spot to nab speeders."

Joe screws up his face. "Haven't had one from Tom in ages." He laughs. "Tom's too nice a guy. He don't want no one mad at him." Joe hoists a few crinkled yellow receipts. "These are all yours," he says, tucking them in his back pocket. "Anyway, I best get to the impound yard."

Sobczak's never thought of the local Getty like that, the impound yard, but that's what it is. One of the perks working for both the gas station and town police force, Joe gets to keep some of the vehicles. Kickbacks. Though it isn't called that. Whenever cars or trucks get towed—failures to appear, unpaid parking tickets, DUIs—they bring them to Joe. If no one picks them up, Joe gets to vulture for parts. The back of Getty is essentially a used car lot.

Judi pops in her head. "You did it, Chief! What finally nailed him?"

Sobczak ignores her questions, calls after Joe.

"Yeah, Chief?"

"You gonna be at the Getty station later?"

"You bet."

"I'll stop by. Something I want to discuss."

Joe Campbell grins, salutes, and scampers off.

Sobczak realizes Judi is still standing there, waiting for an answer. He explains about the letters, the bloody shirt. He does not mention the anonymous tip or green truck. Whatever he says suffices because Judi rejoins the rest of the cheering staff.

The chief looks over his rag-tag crew, at Joe Campbell, who hasn't made it out the door, cornered by Eric and Mark. There's Judi and Ron, even the janitor Brad, who is missing a thumb. They aren't perfect. But they're family. Everyone is happy. Sobczak longs to tap into some of that same pride they feel.

Maybe in a bigger town this would've been handled differently, no big deal. But when the body of Wendy Mortensen washed up on the shores of Shallow Lake, death had come to Covenant; and when those women went missing, the entire region became ensconced in a mystery. Never mind that scumbag drug addicts dumped an overdosed junkie. Never mind that the missing women weren't from town or that no bodies have been recovered. Covenant at large had zeroed in on Todd Norman. His attempt to infiltrate their community had been met with swift and decisive action.

Sobczak counted himself among the man's biggest detractors. Through the glut of glad-hands and congratulations, the chief is besieged by doubts.

Bakshir's still out there. Sobczak's going to drive to the doctor's house. Ronson said they'd gotten a hit on a credit card in Waterbury. New Fairfield to Waterbury tells Sobczak the doctor is headed back this way. Why now? Sobczak grabs his hat and car keys, locks up his office. He excuses himself from the thrum, ignoring his staff's pestering questions, moving toward the door. He can't shake the timing. Bloody clothes suddenly show up just as they are checking Wendy's room? Like that, Dr. Bakshir is off the hook? Too much coincidence rumbling in the old chief's belly. Too many questions.

When he opens the precinct doors, he sees he doesn't have to go far for answers.

Dr. Bakshir waits on the welcome mat.

"I'd like to confess," the doctor says.

CHAPTER THIRTY-FIVE

By the time Deputy Tom Kies delivers Tracy to the Holland precinct, Todd's NYC lawyer David Deal is already there. He is a short, stout man with silver hair and round belly, which his jacket can't fasten around. Tracy has spoken with him before on the phone regarding the custody case, but he introduces himself anyway. Genial but curt, pleasant but officious, and above all—despite his diminutive stature—imposing. She waits for him to throw an arm around her waist, say, "Take a walk with me." Some men were born to be lawyers. Before he can give an update, however, a woman pushes through the bullpen, face twisted in rage.

"Detective Ronson," she says, hands on hips, aggressive, confrontational. "So you're the girlfriend?"

Deal inserts himself between the two, says anything the detective needs to say to Tracy can go through him.

"Oh, I know all about Ms. Somerset." Ronson cranes back to where Todd is being processed. A sea of blue uniforms swarms him. How humiliating. Four officers, handcuffs dangling from belts, guns on display. Total power play designed to make you feel small, weak, helpless. You are property. You have no rights, not anymore. A grown adult reduced to asking permission to use the bathroom. Todd belongs to the state. He shows no emotion.

They're all the same, cops, this Ronson no different. The detective has Tracy by at least ten years, trying to bully her with confidence that borders on brassiness. Tracy didn't come all this way to get pushed around, shamed for following her heart.

"It's okay," she says to Deal. "I'd love to answer the detective's questions." Then to Ronson: "I want to give a statement. I am Todd's girlfriend, and I can account for his whereabouts. What night do you need an alibi for?" She says this without regret, projecting pride best she can, ready to fight for what she believes in.

As soon as the words drop, Tracy sees her bravado is unnecessary. The cops are returning Todd's possessions. Meek heads hang subservient. Tracy knew Deal was good, but the expediency with which he's been able to pull this off transcends impressive. Whatever the New York attorney has said or done, Todd is walking out a free man. Or as free as his life will ever be. Tracy watches the reversal of fortune unfold real-time, as the higher-ups of Holland PD approach Todd, one by one, extending the department's most sincere apologies.

Detective Ronson glowers, glares, ready to wail. Of course she can't. She has bosses, protocol, orders to follow.

Instead, she leans close to Tracy, whispers, "A mom should be more careful who she lets around her kid."

Todd comes their way. David Deal peels off to greet his client. Tracy rushes to his side to gain separation from the nasty lady detective.

In the pit, cops swarm, answering phones, barking commands, giving updates. This place isn't like Covenant's mom-and-pop shop; this is a real police station. Rows of desks and coffee pots and vending machines and tall gray filing cabinets, conversations and codes, ongoing chatter about never-ending cases, telephones that don't stop ringing.

The same higher-ups in suits retreat to the perimeters to discuss aspects of the case. Tracy overhears the words "DNA" and "no match." She doesn't care about their reasons. They've admitted their mistake. They are letting Todd go.

He looks exhausted. Tracy wants to say something comforting to console, convey that the worst is over. But she doesn't want to lie. Tracy doesn't know what happens next; and no matter how bad it seems, it can always get worse. She wants him to know he is not alone. She needs him to know that. She takes his hand, squeezes it; she isn't going anywhere.

When the time comes to clear out, Detective Ronson does not shake Todd's hand. But she will say, "Sorry for the misunderstanding," a mea culpa no doubt demanded by superiors, however disingenuous.

Her eyes lock on Tracy's, before Ronson breaks off, says, "Officer Kies, tell your boss a statement will not be necessary." Ronson stares them all down. "For now."

"No problem," Tom replies.

Covenant's deputy has been standing there, so quiet this entire time, Tracy had forgotten he was still here.

CHAPTER THIRTY-SIX

Back in his office, Sobczak shuts the door. The chief is not reading rights or putting on cuffs, which is not how he envisioned his next meeting with Dr. Meshulum Bakshir.

"You've been a hard man to pin down," Sobczak says.

"I closed my practice. Personal time."

"Where have you been for the past two months?"

"Looking for someone."

"Who?"

"A private investigator named Marjorie Jessup. She was working for Art Abbott, trying to bring a civil case against Todd Norman. But she closed her business. She moved away and was difficult to find."

Sobczak takes out his little pad. "You have an address for this Jessup?"

Bakshir supplies the requested information.

"And this took you over two months?"

238

"That and other things."

Sobczak spreads his hands, a gesture that says, "Such as?" The short day has already started to grate on the old chief.

"Wendy's death has been hard on me." The doctor takes off his glasses, polishes them, a stalling technique. Sobczak has seen this before, the guilty who are aware of—but not yet ready to admit—their transgressions, a sinner in the confessional. Takes time to work up the nerve. "I needed to process."

"Process?" Sobczak repeats. Sounds like head-shrinking nonsense.

Dr. Bakshir does not respond, either with words or expression.

"And why did you want to speak with this Jessup so bad?"

"Because if she was thorough in her investigation of April's life, she would've uncovered information about my time at Green Hills."

"And what about Green Hills had you so worried?"

"My affair with Wendy Mortensen."

Sobczak knows the ages of these women, most of whom were minors. Bakshir picks up on this.

"We didn't begin our relationship until after the program concluded, when Wendy was of legal age."

"This is all because you didn't want people knowing you were sleeping with a patient?"

"Among other things."

"What do you want to confess, Dr. Bakshir? Is this about Shannon O'Connor?"

"Shannon?" The doctor's face betrays authentic surprise.

Sobczak withholds knowing that Bakshir was the last person to see Shannon O'Connor, holding the card close to the vest, willing to see how the game plays out.

"It's my fault," Dr. Bakshir says, "why Wendy was using heroin, why she overdosed."

"You were with her when she overdosed?"

"No. I hadn't seen her in several years." Dr. Bakshir closes his eyes, tight, pained, working up the resolve to share his shame. "After they closed the Green Hills program, I continued treating Wendy. She was special. Of all the girls, I wanted to help her most. A doctor isn't supposed to do that. Have favorites. April, she was going to be fine. She had money and means. Her ultimate fate was a fluke. Beiko and Shannon were too hard to access. The damage done to these girls, I couldn't address. Not without more time and commitment. But Wendy? Wendy I could save. Except they cut the program's funding." He turns to face the wall. "If I had more time..."

"If you had more time." Sobczak does not pose this as a question. Nor does he ask whether insurance factored into his decision of who he could save. Or if that decision was based purely on sexual attraction. Instead, Sobczak says, "She was a girl."

"When I met her, yes. But when ... our relationship ... began she was older." The doctor clings to this point. And, if true, despicable, yes—the doctor is old enough to be her father; a gross violation of ethics, you bet—but there is no crime.

"We were making great progress..." Dr. Bakshir stops his story here.

Sobczak can tell by the pregnant pause this is what the doctor has come for. This will be his confession.

"I arrived at my office late one day." The doctor takes off his eyeglasses, breathes on the lenses. "Wendy was already inside. I don't know how. The practice should've been locked. I'd later conclude she'd stolen a key." With a shirt cuff, he polishes, refits, adjusts. The doctor stares off to the side. The riddle of how Wendy got in his office that day is not the point of this story, and they both know it. "When I opened the door, she stood naked, her long black hair falling off her shoulders in a way that said every inch of the presentation had been planned, down to the grooming of the pubic region. The way the light reflected off her soft skin, showcasing her perfect eighteen-year-old body. She did not say a word. I closed the door. At first, I thought I did this in case someone walked in the lobby, so no one would see or misconstrue, though later, that too, I realized was a lie. I wanted her.

"Afterward, when I had time to reflect—all these years to reflect—I've come to realize what Wendy's gesture meant. On the surface, to the untrained eye, the act was simple. But human sexuality is both simple and robustly complex. I keep returning to what happened in that room." The doctor rubs a hand over his unshaven face. "It had been a test. For years, Wendy's worth had been determined by men's reaction to her body. She was sexually abused as a child, teenage years spent promiscuous. Which is not uncommon for survivors of sexual trauma. She offered herself to me that day to see if I would resist temptation, not be like other men, if I could be trusted."

Dr. Bakshir looks the chief dead-on.

"It had been a test. And I failed."

"Right now," Sobczak says, "the Holland police are holding Todd Norman for the kidnapping and possible murders of Beiko Talo and Shannon O'Connor."

"My God…"

"While I appreciate your confession, I need to know, based on your work at Green Hills, if can you think of any reason Norman would want to harm either Beiko or Shannon. Perhaps something

April said in therapy? A secret the girls may've shared?"

"I don't know what I can tell you about Beiko. I did look for her several months ago, wanting to discuss what I spoke of. I called her brother but he hadn't seen her and couldn't tell me where to look. When I heard the news she was missing, I assumed she'd run away and would turn up somewhere else in New England. She never liked it here. But…" The doctor's face waxes puzzled. "How long has Shannon been declared missing?"

"Three months. Maybe longer."

"I spoke to Shannon yesterday afternoon."

"Yesterday?"

"I told her I'd touch base when I got back to town. Before I left, she'd spent the night at my house. On the couch. She was exhausted, famished, needed rest. The next morning, we spoke, and then I dropped her at an apartment in North Hartford."

"Where is she?"

"Same apartment where I found her yesterday afternoon."

"Where?"

"In North Hartford."

"I'll need a number and address."

"This is not a place police are invited," Dr. Bakshir says. "Can I arrange for her to meet you?"

Sobczak bristles at being asked a favor from a man in no position for ask for one. His cop gut also tells him Bakshir is telling the truth. The North End has too many gangs, drugs, firearms, is too unpredictable. He doesn't want to scare off Shannon. Using her doctor as liaison might be the smart move.

"Let me contact her," Dr. Bakshir says. "In the meantime, put me in a cell. Until you can see with your own two eyes she is okay. I will have her meet you at a church she frequents. It's a shelter of sorts, in the country—"

"Crossroads Church of God."

"You know it?"

"Okay," Sobczak says, willing to play along. "If you don't mind waiting behind bars while I check out your story."

"It's the least I can do." And Dr. Bakshir seems to mean that.

The doctor makes his call. Shannon O'Connor, very much alive, agrees to meet Sobczak at the Crossroads Church of God. There is still the disappearance of Beiko Talo to contend with. What will the DNA test show? Will Norman be willing to cooperate in exchange for leniency? Though these crimes involve Covenant, Sobczak accepts so much of the situation is beyond his control. There must be something he can do.

Before Sobczak has a chance to ponder these questions, Ronson rings back.

There is no urgency. DNA test from the bloody shirt and urine-soaked underpants have come in. No match.

Todd Norman has already been released.

Damn.

CHAPTER THIRTY-SEVEN

Todd and Tracy arrive back at her house late in the day. Diana is there with Logan. Despite the fact that Tracy has, for all intents and purposes, been dating Todd a few months, this is the first time she has introduced him to her best friend. There's an unspoken understanding. There is a new man in Tracy's life.

Tracy makes dinner while Todd and Diana occupy Logan in the living room.

For the first time in a long time Tracy feels like she's part of a family again.

With little time to prepare, Tracy whips up pork chops and mixed greens. Despite minor protests, Diana joins them. Delicious, Todd says. Wonderful as always, Diana says. Logan is extra chatty, and seems to gravitate toward Todd, even more than he does his own mother or Auntie Diana.

After dinner, Tracy makes coffee, and they all adjourn to the living room to watch Logan run around and play and be silly. Then it's time for Tracy to put Logan to bed, a painless task these days. When she returns to the kitchen, she finds Todd, coat on, preparing to leave.

"Where are you going?"

"Back to the lakehouse."

"This late?"

"I need to be there. I am so close to being done." He smiles, comforted, content. "Thank you for believing in me."

"So that's it?" Tracy says. "You've moved into the neighborhood?"

"Looks that way."

He kisses her good night, says they'll talk tomorrow.

As he drives away, she stands at the window, watching him go.

Diana comes up beside her. "You know, I don't have any plans tonight. If you have somewhere else you need to be." She winks. "Go. We'll be fine." Diana hugs her best friend. "You deserve to be happy."

Tracy hesitates. She hasn't seen her boy all day, but he is already asleep, and Diana is right: she does deserve to be happy.

The drive around the lake is not a long one.

Tracy smells the smoke before she sees the fire, which comes into view, a spectacular orange burst, shooting flames high into the dark sky, tantalizing stars.

When she pulls up Svea Road, the fire roars full force, heat radiating in waves, so strong she can feel it through the vents, like it might melt the upholstery even this far away. She sees Todd standing there, statue-still, watching the flames flicker.

Tracy punches the car in park and runs from the vehicle.

"We've got to do something."

"It's too late."

He's right. The fire is fast-acting, raging, refuting all that hard work. The blaze consumes.

Soon the fire department arrives, Sobczak not long afterward.

"What happened?"

"The house was burning when I got here."

"You've got to catch who did this," Tracy demands. "This is arson."

"Hold on," Sobczak says. "We don't know that."

"The hell we don't!"

"Tracy, please," Todd says.

"What?" She turns to the chief, to Todd, back to the chief. "He—" Tracy stabs a finger at Sobczak "—told you this would happen."

"He never said that. Not in so many words."

"No, just that news might leak to locals, who'd take matters into their own hands."

"We don't know that's what happened," Todd says. "Maybe it's faulty wiring."

"You don't believe that."

"No, I don't." Todd walks toward the fire.

Tracy lingers behind with Sobczak.

"You know this was deliberate."

"We don't know anything right now. But," he adds, "*if* it was arson, we will catch who did it."

"I'm sure. With all the prejudice against Todd, no one in this town is lifting a finger to help him."

"How well do you know this man?"

"Excuse me?" Tracy answers, appalled by the audacity. Then something pulls her back, makes her think a moment, consider the actual question. How well *does* she know this man?

Fire department trucks take aim with their high-powered hoses, volunteer manpower streaming hundreds of gallons of water to contain the inferno. More cars and trucks arrive, townsfolk watching the lakehouse go up in smoke, like a fireworks show on the 4th of July.

***

As he drives to the Crossroads, Sobczak rings Ronson.

"Somebody burned down Norman's lakehouse."

"Probably Norman. Check the insurance policy."

"It's not funny."

"Wasn't trying to be."

"You really think Norman torched his own place?"

"Maybe. Won't catch him for this either. He's too slick."

The background clatters like a barroom. Ronson's speech sounds slurred. The chief knows how disappointed she must be. Sometimes it seems she wants to catch Norman more than he does.

"We didn't have a warrant to search the place," she says. "The shirt wasn't in plain view. Would've been tossed regardless." She exhales defeat. "Doesn't matter. DNA's not a match. Not enough blood, and urine is a lousy source. Too old, corroded."

"If it wasn't Talo's blood, whose was it?"

"Who knows?"

"Maybe someone is setting him up?"

"Frame jobs are from bad TV shows, Dwayne."

"The man gets away with murder, beats a high-profile case, only to kidnap and murder another woman? That anonymous tip was too convenient."

"We have two missing women."

"One," Sobczak says. He fills in Ronson on Bakshir and going to meet Shannon O'Connor at the Crossroads, which was where he'd been headed before being sidetracked by the fire.

"I would've liked to speak with Bakshir," she says.

"He's not going anywhere. He's cooling in a cell till I get back." Sobczak turns up an old, familiar road.

"Who would want to set up Norman?"

"Old business partner? Client whose money he lost?"

"NYCPD investigated that angle. Every real estate deal and transaction, stock sale and merger. They uncovered nothing. That was the spin at the trial. How utterly dull the man was. Squeaky clean."

"Maybe he is clean." Sobczak turns in the church parking lot, switching suspects. "What about Art Abbott? He hired the PI, Jessup. Maybe she found out something. Information he didn't want leaked. The man was in politics at one point. Our kids were friends. Art was far from father of the year."

"You're getting desperate. Lots of men are bad fathers who fuck up their kids. Doesn't make them murderers."

"Maybe Norman's story about an intruder is the truth. Maybe his wife's death was random. Maybe a junkie overdosed. Maybe a couple homeless women aren't at home because they don't have one." Sobczak punches it in park. "Maybe you best talk to Art."

"You sure? Last time you were scared I'd be too hard on the man, ruffle precious feathers."

"Things change."

"Not sure I want to get any more involved," Ronson says. "I got enough of a mess on my hands."

"This is why you are contracted, Holland. And you owe me."

"Owe you?"

"Mortensen. You sent me in there under false pretense. We'll call it even."

Chief Sobczak waits inside Uncle Bob's Crossroads Church of God, helping drain a second pot of bad coffee. Sobczak's patience is fraying thin.

When Sobczak arrived, Uncle Bob said he'd just missed Shannon. She left to see a friend, would be right back. Sobczak doesn't care what pills Shannon O'Connor is popping, or whatever else she is doing with her "friend." He wants to see, with his own two eyes, she's okay.

That was two hours ago. Sobczak isn't ready to accuse a man of the cloth, however strange the fabric, of lying. Not yet at least.

When it becomes clear she isn't coming back any time soon, Sobczak bites the bullet, decides to wait at the church till she shows. Sleep gets the best of him. The pastor offers the rectory, which is what Uncle Bob calls it, although the space more closely resembles a college dormitory. Alongside a spattering of holy texts and multiple versions of the Bible, numerous new-age tomes adorn the shelves, a self-help guide called *The Power of Now* and another book, *Zen and the Art of Motorcycle Maintenance*. Sobczak doesn't know what religion these books espouse, and he doesn't care to find out.

Sobczak wakes at dawn and still no sign of O'Connor. Uncle Bob's unrelenting cheerfulness begins to irritate the old cop. The pastor's been up a while, third pot of coffee well past burnt.

Every time Sobczak presses him about where Shannon O'Connor is, Uncle Bob says, "Have faith, brother."

Sobczak excuses himself, steps out the back door, into the cool spring air, and punches his cell.

"Never showed," Sobczak says after Ronson picks up.

"What's the pastor say?" Her voice tells him he's woken her up. At this hour, he probably has.

"Uncle Hippy here? He's too busy tripping the light fantastic to know what planet he's on." Sobczak lights a smoke, spits on the ground, grinding his back teeth, furious over having fallen for Bakshir's fakery. Though he still can't see what the doctor has to gain, or why Uncle Bob would play along.

"Think he's jerking our chain?"

"I don't know what to think," Sobczak says. Fat raindrops plop from the dark sky.

The backdoor swings open. Uncle Bob, all smiles, hollers, "Shannon's back, Chief."

"Sit tight."

"Let's make sure she's there this time. I'll hold the line."

Sobczak walks through the catacombs of the old church, down dark and musty corridors, Uncle Bob leading the way, passage closing. He loses signal.

Something doesn't feel right, the route unfamiliar.

Then the light pours in, and they are in another room, on a different side of the church. And sitting on a sofa, Shannon O'Connor. Her eyes say she is under the influence of something. She appears sedated, and Sobczak wonders how long she's been here. He never heard a car. Whatever she's taken was powerful. Uncle Bob must've been letting her sleep it off.

Sobczak checks the bars on his cell, enough signal to shoot off a quick text to Ronson.

She's here.

Ronson texts back:

Art Abbott in Miami w/ wife. Cruise. Trying to get message.

Sobczak tucks away his cell. Uncle Bob has an arm slung around O'Connor, whose languid eyes project the weight of the broken. Funny how sometimes those painkillers can make the pain even worse.

"You want I should leave?" Uncle Bob says.

Sobczak figures the girl will be more comfortable if she sees a friendly face. He tells the pastor to stick around.

Then to O'Connor: "A lot of people have been looking for you."

"Sorry." Her head droops severely, like it's in danger of slipping off her neck. "Did I do something wrong?"

Sobczak considers playing the heavy, using whatever she is on as leverage to get her to talk. That won't be necessary. Anyone can see that Shannon O'Connor, despite pushing thirty, is just a scared kid.

"No," he says. "Nothing like that. Need your help. Do you know Dr. Bakshir?"

She nods.

"You see him recently?"

"Couple days ago. He stopped by this house I'm staying at." Her eyelids flutter. "We met at Green Hills."

"How long ago was that? The program."

Through an opiate-laced nod, she fills in Sobczak on the particulars of the group home, time frame, issues they dealt with. She glances up, uncomfortable.

"It's okay," Uncle Bob says. "This is a judgment-free zone. I may be a pastor, but I was younger at one point too. Grew up in an era where sex wasn't a bad word."

Hearing the old pastor say the word "sex" makes Sobczak cringe.

"When I was younger," she says, "I was promin—promis—I slept with a lot of people. Compulsive behavior."

"Like an addict?"

Shannon O'Connor shifts uneasy. "I don't know. I was—I liked the attention. But it got bad. Drinking and stuff, waking up with strange men, women, people. I needed help. My family wanted me to get help."

"And this was the hospital group?"

"Yeah. But Green Hills wasn't like a hospital. We had rooms and stuff. In a house. A different kind of house."

With every question, she confirms Dr. Bakshir's story. Maybe it is the drugs that make her so forthcoming. She is truthful, open, almost to a fault. There is a simple quality to her, a naivety, child-like and trusting. Shannon O'Connor does not lack for intelligence. Her answers are articulate, straightforward but strangely divorced from reality. Of course, she is also under the influence. Or maybe she answers his questions this honestly because she has no reason not to. There is nothing anyone can do to Shannon O'Connor to make her life any worse.

They've been talking for an hour, and Sobczak has learned lit-tle he didn't already know. Bakshir's story checks out, and with Shannon O'Connor not missing, Sobczak has no reason to hold the doctor.

Sobczak thanks Uncle Bob, who has sat chaperone-silent for most of the inquiry. O'Connor is already closing her eyes, drifting back to dreamland.

"One last thing, Shannon," Sobczak says before she goes. "When you saw Dr. Bakshir that first night, what did he want to talk to you about?"

"Wendy."

"Do you remember anything said that would've led him to skip town? He's been gone almost two months."

"All I told him was the truth. That Wendy loved him. And she never stopped."

CHAPTER THIRTY-EIGHT

The cruel April sun punctures the gray sky, shafts of silver light splitting the blinds, across the headboard. Tracy fears she is losing him. Todd hadn't wanted to talk last night. Or maybe he'd wanted to but was unable. For five years, the man has been living a nightmare, spurred on by a single, solitary yet attainable goal: a promise he'd made to his dead wife. He'd almost fulfilled it too. Despite the constant attacks, the hurled insults, harassment, accusation of certain guilt, he never surrendered, never gave up. Now this. So close to the finish line.

"Morning," he says, opening his eyes.

Tracy realizes she's been staring at him for a while, a creepy sensation, being stared at, which everyone feels, even in their sleep.

She waits, sees his eyes gather force as if he has something to say. But no words come. Logan will be awake shortly, any hope of conversation gone. The needs of a toddler, diaper changes, breakfast, snuggles, take precedent. So she stares at Todd, willing him to speak.

It works.

"Why?" he asks.

She assumes he is talking about the fire, the bad breaks, the hardships.

"People can't see past what they can't see past."

"No—why did you believe in me? From day one. That first night. You saw something in me I wasn't sure I saw in myself."

Tracy doesn't tell him she, too, had doubts. Who wouldn't? Or maybe he'd seen something in her that she couldn't see in herself, an inverse reflection. Maybe this is why a million-in-one shot might work; why two people, brought together by horrific circumstance, have a fighting chance. Because even when he speaks, like in her car that day on the shore, knowing he is innocent, a part of him seems to question it, as if it were all a dream.

"April had affairs."

Tracy keeps still, holding her breath. He hasn't spoken much about his dead wife. The opportunity feels fleeting.

"Coming back here was an attempt to save the marriage. We were going to try to have a baby." He laughs to himself. "Last refuge of a scoundrel. Having a baby to save a marriage. Jesus." Todd checks with her, making sure she gets the joke. Tracy understands, all too well.

"It started before we were married," Todd continues. "The infidelity. I'm not trying to speak bad about her. I loved my wife very much. There was an insatiable quality to her. And secrets. Always secrets." He slides up in bed. "Why do we think we can be the ones to save them?"

Tracy likes that he's said "we." He's right. You can't pull anyone out of the mess and drag them to safety. Stand on a chair, try to pull them up, let them try to pull you down. See who wins. Be the good girlfriend, the good fiancée, the good wife. All she ended up being: the sucker. People do not change. Not without serious, dedicated effort. Almost unheard of, an anomaly. We are who we are.

"I think the sleeping around gave her identity," Todd says. "I don't know if you know her family, her father—"

"Art Abbott was in the public eye a while. Most people thought he'd go further than he did."

"He's not a bad man. I know how much he hates me, the things he says, but if what he believes were true, why shouldn't he hate me?"

Todd turns toward the plain white wall, which used to showcase pictures of Tracy and Brett, Brett's family, her ex-in-laws, her ex-family. The wall is bare now. She's never gotten around to adding new photos, faded outlines evidencing the life she once had.

"The last civil conversation we had," Todd says. "Art and I, before the lawsuits and court battles, before everything went to hell—Art was not the warmest of men—but we were at a tavern, catching a ballgame on TV, one of those times April and I came back to Covenant to work on the house. She never wanted to visit her family. We came at my insistence. April told them we were trying to have a baby, which put everyone in a good mood. We were sitting at the bar. I said something like, 'Can you pass the peanuts, Art?' He goes, 'Call me Dad.'" Todd pinches his eyes. "Stupid, right? I'd never been close to my own father. It's just a word. But it meant a lot."

Tracy's landline rings, and she snatches it off the end table, hoping it won't wake Logan, but knowing it already has. She can hear him crying from the next room before she picks up.

After hello, she listens, quiet. "Okay," she says, "I'll tell him."

She hangs up. "Fire inspector determined it was arson."

Todd doesn't say anything. Why would he? They both knew it was arson. The question is: who will the police blame? Logan screeches louder.

Tracy tells Todd she'll be right back.

Logan is extra fussy this morning, and changing him takes longer than usual. He fights her every step of the way. Even when he is in these moods, Logan makes it hard to stay angry with him. Tracy remembers that anecdote about toddlers: it's why God makes them so cute at this age. The only way the human race survives. Tracy tickles him and soon her baby boy is giggling, and there's her little man. His PJ bottoms are wet, soaked through, and there are no clean pants for some reason, so she has to fish out a pair from the dirty clothes, thinking about all the laundry she needs to catch up on.

By the time Tracy makes it to the kitchen, she finds a note waiting for her. It is not a long note. Just one line. No sign-off or salutation.

Going to the city.

Tracy tells herself he has some business to take care of, loose ends to tie up. Logan starts to cry.

Tracy calls and it goes straight to voicemail. She wonders if his cell was burned in the fire, even though she knows that's not true. Service can be spotty out here. She reassures herself he'll be back, emotions vacillating, ebbing between angry that he hadn't said goodbye, and feeling like her heart is breaking. Or maybe he needs the time to process what has happened. She searches for faith. All their time together? This is what she gets? One generic line? Tantamount to a break-up via text. There's something between them. Isn't there? More than just the sex. Is that all she's been to him? She feeds, soothes Logan, her mind racing. Has she misread the situation? So badly? Again?

Trying to shove these thoughts out of her head, Tracy bundles Logan in a heavy jacket, even though temps are pushing a balmy sixty degrees, warm for this time of year, and heads to Diana's. She needs a friend.

Diana brings a bottle of water to the kitchen table, Tracy's face plastered with abject shellshock. Tracy hands Logan her cell, cued to a cartoon to keep him occupied while she has a breakdown. She hates passing off parenting to a screen but she feels like she can't breathe. Logan sits at their feet on the floor, watching talking dogs that serve as the sole police force for a small waterside town.

"What is going on?"

Tracy shows her the note.

"Maybe he had to pick up some things? All his stuff was lost in the fire."

"Why not say that? Why not wait till I'm back from changing Logan? He bolts while I'm preoccupied being a mom?"

"He's confident enough in your relationship he can go without a big production?"

Tracy wants to believe that. "You think so?"

"I don't know," Diana says. "But I saw the way that man looks at you." She takes Tracy's hand. "He cares about you."

"Oh my God. Have I turned into one of those weirdo clingy women?"

"Don't be too hard on yourself. Wait," Diana says. "He doesn't have any rabbits, does he?"

"Hilarious."

"Dating a man like Todd is unchartered territory."

"Do you think he did it?"

"What? Murdered April?" Diana laughs. "Little late to ask that, no? Your basket is already overflowing with those eggs."

"The police called this morning. Arson."

"Who do they think started it?"

"They didn't say."

"Todd?"

"Maybe that's why he left." Tracy starts crying, soft at first. Then she's sobbing, the quiet cries of a mother who has mastered the emotion soundless so she doesn't scare her son. How many nights did she spend like this after finding out about Brett? Locked in a bathroom, sobbing, screaming into a towel? Managing to cradle and care for her baby while all the delicate parts inside her cracked. It feels like her whole world is falling apart, like she's being pulled left, right, six ways to Sunday, and every direction between here and hell. Is this even about Todd, a man she's known barely half a year? Or has this all been a way to escape the drudgery, the day-to-day? Are they both guilty of using the other? Her attempts at stealth fail. Logan reaches up, concerned, hugging her, like any boy would when his mommy cries. Diana leans over and holds them both. What is Tracy doing with her life? Skirting a custody battle with her ex, in a relationship, if that's what it even is, with a man who is what? Emotionally unavailable, at best? And at worst...?

Where has he gone? Of all mornings, why did he pick this one to talk about April? Affairs, sleeping around, Art Abbott, and lost identities? Was he warning her? Himself? The dangers of opening your heart after getting burned so goddamn bad the first time?

She needs to talk to the one person who can answer these questions best.

Tracy asks if she can leave Logan there. Of course. Diana DelMartino is nothing if not a rock, and Tracy shudders to think of life without her.

Across town, Tracy pulls into Amanda Sobczak's driveway. She reminds herself that isn't her last name anymore; it's Kies. But her cop husband's patrol car isn't there; it's an easy detail to overlook.

Amanda answers the door, neither surprised nor pleased. "Great. It's you."

Tracy realizes the obvious: since last time they met, Amanda has learned she is dating Todd. Tracy hadn't considered that on the drive over, and thinking about it now makes her feel like an idiot.

"I can't believe you have the balls to show up here."

Hands clasped around a coffee mug, Amanda abandons Tracy at the door. But at least she doesn't slam it in her face.

Tracy steps inside the home, a typical, modest Covenant dwelling with sailor stitching and plenty of odd New England trinkets, signs with rules for lodging tinkers. So much of the town was built in the 1700s. A large part of Covenant's charm manifests itself through retaining the nomenclature of the era.

Nowhere near as pleasant as the day they met for lunch, Amanda is really showing now, big baby bump left with nowhere to hide. Tracy wants to ask questions, how is she holding up, feeling, is she sleeping well, eating okay, and she means it, because pregnancy is a bond all mothers share, but judging by Amanda's white-knuckled grip and death stare, Tracy decides to forgo any sisterhood-of-woman sentiment.

Beyond her shoulder, out the sliding glass door, fruitless stalks stake the vast Covenant forest, a barren hillside on the verge of blooming verdant.

"I hate this town," Amanda says. "I wish I'd left like April."

Of all the A-holes, Amanda had the best head on her shoulders, the one with the most potential, their leader, and she is the one who got left behind. That must sting, to be forgotten.

"What do you want, Tracy?" The question comes with no warmth, no patience, which should be expected. For the best. Now Tracy can drop any pretense of civility.

"I want to talk about April."

"Did your boyfriend send you here?"

"Todd isn't my boyfriend." This is true. Sort of. She's not sure what Todd is to her. Are they seeing each other, exclusive? She assumes they are exclusive. But she's never asked. At times, he can be so present, nurturing, caring, and concerned. Other times? A million light years from home.

"My father is the town sheriff. My husband is pretty much his only employee. You think they're not talking to me?"

"It's not like that."

"What's it like, then? Friends with benefits? Casually fucking the man who killed my best friend?"

"Todd didn't kill April."

"What is wrong with you? You're like one of those psychos who marry their convict pen pal." Amanda's quick, even-keel dismissal is what makes it so cold. Her words cut to Tracy's biggest fear. "Are you *that* desperate? Jesus, you have a kid. What kind of mother…? Christ, you are screwed up. When you wrote and suggested lunch that day, I was, like, 'Okay, she was weird in high school, boy crazy and clingy, but that was high school. People grow up.' Except you're just as weird and clingy now. Who in their right mind starts dating a man *accused of murder*? I can't even…"

Tracy entertains no illusion of changing Amanda's mind. She simply wants as many answers as she can get before Amanda throws her out.

"What happened between you and April?"

"Excuse me?"

"That day at the One Two Easy, you said you had a falling out with April and Amber."

"Those two left me! Didn't give me another thought!" She

wraps two fingers around one another. "We were like *that*. Then they get better offers, a pair of fuck buddies, and I'm stuck here for the rest of my life in this shitburg."

Tracy fixates on the two fingers, aware of the odd girl out.

"But April was moving back here."

"Yeah. Until your new boyfriend killed her."

"Did you guys reconnect? Talk?"

"None of your goddamn business."

"What happened to Amber?"

"Amber?" Amanda's eyes unveil murder. "I haven't talked to Amber Coit in twelve fucking years." Amanda pinches the top of her nose, so hard the color drains pale, a swell of hurt and rage filling, consuming, taking charge. "How the hell should I know? And why would you care? Not like you were friends with any of us. You all ostracized us, talked shit, like *we* were the assholes. But it was *you*, Tracy. You and Lisa Blake and the rest of them."

"The poor popular girls. Everyone wanted to be you, Amanda."

"That's coveting. That's not friendship." Amanda sneers before vacillating to the precipice of tears. "April and Amber were the only friends I ever had."

"Why don't you talk to Amber anymore?"

Amanda pulls a jug of vodka from the freezer and pours a tall glass. Tracy can hear the subzero liquid crack the glass. Before she can suggest taking a shot maybe isn't the best thing for the baby, Amanda pounds it. "Amber was gone before she left."

"What's that supposed to mean?"

"She found Jesus, became a church rat, cut out me and April."

"Church rat?"

"That Crossroads Church of Bullshit, out in the sticks. Brainwashed her. Made her turn her back on the people who loved her.

What the fuck do you care? You have no idea what my life is like, how lonely I am."

"At least you're married."

"You don't have a clue."

"I was married. I understand what it's like. I understand the disappointment, the dull routines, the months where it feels like you don't exchange a meaningful word."

Tracy's statement doesn't deserve a response. But Amanda gives one anyway. "Can you please get the fuck out of my house? Tom is going to be home soon and I have to get dinner ready. Thanks for stopping by."

Tracy isn't getting through the door again. "What happened the night of Chris Manzaris's party?"

"Huh?"

"The big party at the lake. You said you guys had a fight—"

Amanda hurls the bottle past Tracy's head. The glass bounces off the wall intact, waiting to shatter till it hits the floor.

"Get out!"

CHAPTER THIRTY-NINE

At the Covenant precinct, Dr. Bakshir sits with Sobczak, case studies, open files fanned across the big, round table in the center of the room. They've been here for hours. When Sobczak let the doctor go earlier, Bakshir promised to return, to do what he is doing now: share everything he has from those Green Hills sessions twelve years ago.

Bakshir doesn't hide behind confidentiality laws. He is a shamed man who, now unshackled, exudes the desire—the need—to help. Sobczak isn't interested in being anyone's absolution, and he's reluctant to conspire with a man like Bakshir, what he did to Wendy Mortensen unconscionable, but he's not turning down the offer either.

"April was sent to Green Hills by her father. Art was concerned about her wild tendencies. Sex, drugs, drinking. A teenager."

"She had sex at a young age," Sobczak says. "And?"

"I think it was more than that."

"There's no point being shy now, Doc."

"It's not a matter of modesty." Dr. Bakshir taps the reports. "Adolescence is a time of secrecy. None of these girls were terribly forthright."

Sobczak wants to ask how forthright Wendy had been. But he bites his tongue. He needs the doctor's cooperation.

"I can tell you what I deduced," Dr. Bakshir says. "This is conjecture, based on our sessions, what I, as a therapist, was able to piece together."

"I'm not asking you to solve a case. Tell me what you know. I'll take it from there."

"I believe April was caught questioning her sexuality."

"What's that supposed to mean?"

"She was involved in a same-sex relationship."

"In high school?"

"Seventeen is a powerful age for emotions. I'm not sure at that age she would've been able to put a label on it. But, yes, I believe she felt she was in love."

"Was there anyone in particular she was ... close to?"

The doctor pores over his notes. "I don't have a name," says Dr. Bakshir, and Sobczak feels relieved he didn't say his daughter's name, though why that should matter, he does not know. "She was very protective. And I can't recall. This is over ten years ago. But there was also a boy she was seeing, whom she developed strong feelings for. April was co-dependent. Because her father withheld his love, placed conditions upon it, she *needed* to be in love with someone. When she arrived at Green Hills, she switched gears, became obsessed with this boy. A form of transference."

"Who?"

"Todd Norman, I assume. Since they left for the city shortly after she was released from Green Hills."

Sobczak doesn't mention the doctor's timeline may be off.

"Her father was not happy with our work. I urged April to take her time, slow down, explore these feelings. She wanted to please her father. This created conflict. Art Abbott didn't see desired results fast enough." The doctor takes off his glasses. "The relationship April ended up in was an abusive one, emotionally, the boy controlling."

That part sounds like Norman, all right.

"This is not uncommon. A girl picks a romantic partner who mirrors her father. Classic Electra Complex. April was terrified of her father, I can tell you that. He had a temper, was capable of outbursts."

When the doctor stops his story, the chief winds his hand to speed up the process, but Dr. Bakshir is a precise, particular man who will not be rushed.

"You must understand," the doctor continues, "the tenets of confidentiality transcend legality. Trust is central to what I do."

"Privacy, sacred, I get it."

"I'm not sure you do. I'm not sure anyone can appreciate the magnitude. Therapy is a life-long process. It never ends." Dr. Bakshir stops, tents his hands as though he's praying. Maybe in some ways he is. "I can never practice psychiatry again. I failed my patients. What I am about to tell you now is a resignation letter to the profession I love, a profession I dedicated my life to. You may not believe me after what I told you, but I was very good at my job." The doctor oozes anguish, attempting to broach authenticity. It is painful to watch. "I helped a lot of people."

"I'm sure you did." Sobczak doesn't know what good, if any, the doctor has done. Doesn't care. He wants Bakshir to keep talking.

"Wendy and I were having lunch one day, not far from my office. This was many months after the program closed. November, perhaps. There's a café near where I work."

Bakshir's insistence to keep repeating he and Wendy were

near his office cements Sobczak's view that the doctor still, despite his pleas for forgiveness, doesn't grasp the magnitude of what he's done, the harm he's caused.

"April came by the practice. I wasn't there. She found me at the café and wanted to talk." Dr. Bakshir stalls, reassembles the narrative to paint himself in the best possible light. "April and Wendy had problems getting along."

Jealousy? Judgment? Ronson said there were letters between Wendy and April after April married Norman. Intimate letters of confidence. Reconciliation? Or is the doctor skewing details to protect his role in all of this?

"I wasn't April's doctor anymore. But I wanted to help. I excused myself from Wendy, who was not pleased. April and I went outside, into the small parking lot. The day brisk, blustery. She said she was worried."

"About what?"

"Someone hurting her. Physically."

"Someone?"

"She didn't say whom, but insisted it was serious. I said if she was worried, she should talk to the police." The doctor catches Sobczak's eye. "At the time, like you, I thought it was overreaction. Teenage drama."

"I never said that—"

"April wanted me to go somewhere with her. Wendy came out of the restaurant. I couldn't have a scene. I told her no. April left."

The doctor reaches in his folder, pulls out a handwritten note, and slides it across the chief's desk. Sobczak reads the note, looks at the doctor. "Who wrote this?"

"The handwriting is April's."

"Where did you find this?"

"Slipped under my door, about a week later."

"Who are 'they'?"

"Norman. Her father. I don't know."

"You've had this note how many years? And you are coming to the police now?"

"Why would I come before?"

"There was a trial for her murder."

"I did not follow that. And even if I had ... it is unsigned. She gives no name. This is not my fault!"

"You couldn't risk anyone finding out about you and Wendy."

Dr. Bakshir stabs at the scrap of paper. "What does that note really say?"

"Based on what you've told me? That April is accusing some-one, in all likelihood Norman, or perhaps her father, of threaten-ing to kill her. This is withholding information, Meshulum."

"I am here now. Context, Chief Sobczak. And we don't know that. At the time? It was just a letter from a disturbed high school girl. I did not take it literally."

Sobczak has to talk to Norman. He needs to get Abbott off that boat. Once Art reaches international waters, he'll be gone for-ever, free from extradition.

He reads the note again.

They're going to kill me.

Shadows dance on the wall, passing car headlights fanning, the grind of brakes on ground-down gravel.

A few moments later, a woman enters with a small child. Sob-czak recognizes little Logan Coggins. But Tracy Somerset is not with him.

"Chief," Diana DelMartino says. "Tracy is missing."

CHAPTER FORTY

Tracy Somerset wakes in the dark, the back of her head throbbing, temples pounding to an out-of-time beat. She doesn't know where she is, can't remember how she got here.

What is the last thing she remembers? Leaving Amanda's house, driving back home. Then she had an idea. That's right. She pulled up the address for the Crossroads Church of God, texted Diana she'd be a little longer.

The Crossroads Church of God was a long haul, in the middle of nowhere. Tracy tried to recall changes senior year. Flashes started to return. Snippets, snapshots, peripheral remnants of fragmented teenage years. Even though they were two grades below, the A-holes were must-see TV. Hate them, mock them, secretly want to be them. Amanda was right: coveted. The three, Amanda, April, Amber. Little stylized peas in designer-labeled pods. If you saw one, you saw all three. But that last year...

Tracy was dating Brett, he was her everything, and she eschewed the pack mentality of seventeen-year-old celebrity. But being at such a small school, Tracy also couldn't escape it. Might as well have been one big class. Telling herself she avoided the affliction is a lie. And now these details return. April and Amanda. No Amber. Amanda and Amber. No April. April and… Did Tracy recall anything about religion, Jesus? No. Nothing comes up. But Amber Coit *did* begin acting different, she remembers that.

Tracy should be asking different questions, like how she got here, but, disoriented, she never completes a thought, trapped in a never-ending time loop, a bargain matinée production of *Our Town*. Little things like Amber not being a total bitch, holding doors open for others, smiling, asking how someone else was feeling. Common decency. Which had never been part of the A-hole's credo. But, no, this wasn't high school; this was afterward. A few weeks' span following graduation. Bumping into Amber at the market, gas station, Main Street Deli. Maybe once, twice?

Her head aches, a dull, throbbing pain. Not a migraine. She was driving. A crash. All these thoughts flood, separate and apart, at once isolated and together, recollection non-linear.

Tracy had passed the large, square, yellow building several times, spied it from the highway. Warehouse. Not a warehouse, a church. Had to be it. No other buildings anywhere in sight. She pulled into the parking lot. Way up in the corner, the lettering: Crossroads Church of God and a tiny cross.

From the lightless room she's in now, Tracy rouses, almost snaps out of the fugue state, but then she is dragged back under the black waters of blunt head trauma, unable to articulate, not cognizant, reason muted.

What happened at the church?

Some lights were on, spring dusk descending, sun arguing to stay up later. Out front, a couple young girls, teenagers, the wild kind with too much eye make-up, smoking cigarettes by the front door.

"Is this the Crossroads?" Tracy asked, even though she'd read the writing on the wall.

One of the girls brushed her off, not condescending to respond to Tracy's lame adult question. But the other nodded.

"Is there someone in charge? A priest or…?"

"Uncle Bob is inside."

"Uncle Bob?"

"He's the pastor. But he likes us to call him Uncle Bob."

A bunch of teenage girls hanging around a priest who calls himself Uncle Bob. No, this isn't creepy at all.

The nicer of the two pointed at the front door. "He's in his office."

Tracy hesitated.

Yes, she remembers thinking: don't go inside.

"He's nice," the girl had said, "go on," before shutting out the intruder.

Down the long hall, lights grew dim, felt like the walls of this hall were closing in. Like this wasn't a parish but a catacomb, a crypt, a tomb. Dark, damp, the absence of light rendering the space extra claustrophobic.

Like this basement she is in now.

He greeted her in the hallway, backlit by interior light, face concealed, a silhouette.

"I help you?" the man said.

No question.

Tracy had stopped, blood icing her veins. It was so cold. The man stepped closer.

"I'm Pastor Tompkins. But my friends call me Uncle Bob." He

extended a hand. His grip was limp, the flesh of his palm clammy, lifeless.

"How can I help you?" the pastor asked again, rephrasing the question. And when Tracy didn't answer, he added, "Are you okay, Miss?"

They were still in the dark hallway, a realization that made the pastor embarrassed, but not by the surroundings; rather, he was disappointed in himself for lacking manners.

"I'm sorry," he said, "please, come in."

The conversation is coming back to her now. She's remembering. He didn't scare her. His smile came into view. A kind, non-threatening, grandpa smile. She was safe here.

The office didn't look like a place a priest or pastor would spend his free time. There were plenty of religious pictures and books, but there were also secular decorations. Posters of bands kids today might like. Tracy didn't recognize these groups but they didn't appear Christian, more hip-hop, pop. Strange.

The pastor noticed her looking at the walls. "You have to meet kids where they are coming from. Religion is a tougher sell these days. To preach the Word, to help, we—those in the service of the Lord—must change too. Please." He gestured at a seat in front of his desk. "How can I help you, Miss…?"

Tracy told him her name.

He beamed, bushy mustache stretching. "Okay, Miss Tracy. But please call me Uncle Bob. All the kids here do."

"Kids?"

He explained how the church took in runaways, damaged youths, the wayward.

"Like the Salvation Army?" she asked.

"No, not like the Salvation Army. We don't treat our guests like slaves." Uncle Bob shook himself off. "I apologize. I take umbrage with the Salvation Army. I think they misrepresent themselves to the public, and they are bigoted." Then he added, "Discriminatory. Homophobic."

This had taken Tracy aback, a shock that must have reflected on her face.

"The Bible is a wonderful book with a lot of good things to say. But it's also got some pretty wonky stuff in there too. I can't believe in a God who would grant me intelligence and then punish me for using it."

She recalls liking that phrase: *Can't believe in a God who would grant me intelligence and then punish me for using it.*

After that it gets fuzzy. But she wasn't afraid. She felt peace, love, acceptance.

The next part of the conversation comes back clearly: "I think this person would've been a member of the congregation?" Her voice. "Maybe a youth group?"

"What was her name?"

"Amber Coit."

The pastor's face beamed. "Oh, yes, Amber. A sweet, sweet girl. Beautiful soul."

"Do you know where she is?"

"I haven't heard from Amber in, well, it would be about twelve years. She came here, like so many, seeking shelter from the storm."

"Drugs?"

"No. Broken heart. A bad breakup had left her devastated."

Tracy laughed. "That's high school." She recalled her many bad breakups with Brett, how each one felt like the end of the world.

"She was in love with a friend whose family had taken her in."

"The Abbotts?"

Tracy's head throbs. She can feel a lump on her head. But not with her hands. Why can't she move her hands? She is drifting in and out of consciousness, trying to recall what happened at the church, trying to will herself awake, make her body stir, but the scene is disintegrating, like the shoddy pixilation of an old video game, weak reception, another gap, dead zone.

"Did she ever mention someone named Todd Norman?"

Tracy felt guilty asking about Todd, telling herself she didn't believe for one moment he had anything to do with this. She doesn't. Does she? Did he? She doesn't. He couldn't have...

"I don't recognize the name. But I *do* remember she was worried about the girl's father, thought he might harm her."

Is he suggesting Art Abbott hurt Amber?

"I think they planned on running away together." His kind eyes crinkled again. "I'd like to believe maybe they did."

"I don't think so."

Uncle Bob stopped smiling.

"What if something happened to her first?"

"Dear, I'm repeating a story told by a frightened, heartbroken teenager many years ago." He paused, face grave, concerned. "But if you really think something happened to Amber, I suggest talking to the police."

Tracy had driven out of the parking lot, down the dark, winding roads of the Covenant cuts, thinking about what the pastor had told her. April's father hurting Amber? Did he say that? Not exactly. He said they planned to run away together. Who? The boy and girl? Or the two girls? April and Amber? The timeline not right, uneven, inexact.

The blow came from behind. Revved engine, no headlights, tires squealing. Rammed off the road, she was sent careening down the steep embankment. She tried to regain control but it was too late, vehicle slipping sideways, tumbling, rolling on its back, until the car righted onto four wheels just in time to smack the tree trunk head on and for Tracy's skull to smash against the steering wheel, neck snapping, whiplashed.

Then she woke up here.

Now her other senses return. She still can't see. But she can hear the lapping waves and smell remains of the fire.

CHAPTER FORTY-ONE

As Sobczak is talking to Diana DelMartino, Tom walks into the precinct, and seeing little Logan, he drops to a knee. The boy runs to him. A short while ago, Tom had spent the morning playing with the boy while Tracy was here, acting crazy, making threats, inconsolable. Sobczak is surprised a child as young as Logan would remember. But kids that age are like animals, in a good way, using sense over intellect; they trust their instincts. You can tell a good person versus a bad person by how animals and small children respond to them. Tom will make a wonderful father.

This thought is immediately followed by: what in the hell is happening to this quiet, wholesome town? Dead women, missing persons? Families move here to get away from the city, because it is safe, and in the span of six months Covenant has transmogrified into a cityscape nightmare.

"Tell me again why you think Tracy is missing."

"Tracy is missing?" Tom says, coming over.

"Because she sent me a text eight hours ago. Said she'd be home in two hours."

"So she's six hours late?" Sobczak says.

"It takes forty-eight until a person can be considered missing," Tom adds.

"Six hours is a long time when you have a little boy."

"Did she say where she was going? Do you have the text?"

Diana shares the text, which relays what she said it would.

"No destination," Sobczak repeats, for his own benefit. "Where's Todd?"

"Tracy said he went back to New York. Had to sort out some stuff."

"What does that mean?"

"I don't know."

"What did Tracy think it meant?"

"She didn't know either."

"Oh boy."

"Oh boy what?"

"What do you think of Todd Norman?"

Diana acts as surrogate, defending his innocence. "You think Todd had a three-month relationship with Tracy, then decided to kidnapped her?"

"Tom," Sobczak says. "Take a drive around the lake. Make sure Tracy's car didn't break down. Maybe her cell died."

"You got it, boss." Tom attempts to tousle little Logan's hair, but the boy runs to Diana's side, hiding behind her leg. Sobczak doesn't like this. Something feels off. The way the boy clings to Diana, Sobczak can see he's scared, that he, too, senses the danger his mother is in.

After everyone leaves, Sobczak picks up the phone and rings Stephanie Ronson.

"Good evening, Dwayne." She sounds almost perky. "This is a surprise."

Sobczak waits, trying to pin her mood, which feels foreign. He's dealt with Ronson plenty. "Perky" is not a word he'd use to describe the hard-nosed Holland County detective.

"Sorry," she says. "I have a couple friends over. Long week. Letting loose. On my third glass of *very* good wine." Laughter in the background. "Please tell me this is personal and not a professional call." More laughter bleeding through, and then someone being told to shut up in the background.

"Tracy Somerset, Todd Norman's girlfriend, is missing."

"Where's Norman?" Ronson says, sobering up fast, the noise behind her gone as if she's been jettisoned, sequestered in another, more private room.

"New York. That's what he said to Tracy this morning."

"Now Tracy is gone." Statement, not question.

"I don't like it either."

"Why can't people understand the obvious answer is usually the correct one?"

Sobczak fills her in on his conversation with Dr. Bakshir, what he said about Art Abbott, the parts about April, the girlfriend, the break-up, the fast-moving rebound infatuation with the new boyfriend, Norman, the note.

"You're taking the word of Bakshir?" Ronson scoffs. "*That* man should be in prison."

"A lot of this info comes from a private investigator in New Fairfield."

"Talk to him?"

"It's a her. And no. Not yet."

"Okay, let's say Bakshir's account is accurate. They met before college. All it does is confirm April and Norman were head over heels too soon. Infatuation rarely ends well."

"What about the first part? The girlfriend. Forbidden love. Art Abbott being incensed? We need to get him off that cruise ship."

"How am I supposed to do that?"

"Call Miami PD? Port Authority?"

"I doubt he's fleeing. No one has accused him of anything. He's had these tickets for nine months. I checked. I want to talk to him as well. But what you are suggesting? Art Abbott, former commissioner of the DOT, murdered his own child? Several years later? Because she fooled around with a girlfriend in high school? Kids that age experiment."

Sobczak takes a deep breath. She's right. He's overreacting, jamming together pieces that don't fit, his picture distorted.

"I sent my deputy out looking for her," Sobczak says. "Covenant's got a lot of places to get lost."

"What is that woman's story? Why would anyone date a man like Norman?"

"Tracy? Always considered her smart, put together. Married young, waited to start a family. Her ex screwed her over, and…" Sobczak stops. "I have no idea. Last time I saw her, she was acting irrational, emotional." He takes another deep, reassuring breath. Takes time to root out the insanity putting funny thoughts in his head. "Let's hope she took a corner too quick, blew a tire, and is just stranded. I'll let you know when we find her."

After he ends the call, Sobczak hops in his squad car, drives from the precinct into the small town center, mapping possible routes Tracy may've taken. Up the hill, around the corner, to the market, and back toward her house. Nothing. He circles the cul-de-sac, stops, gets out, past the portable basketball hoop, peers over the banks of burbling streams that drain into the lake. He tries to call Tom but can't get through.

Several blocks over, Sobczak finds himself on Amanda's street,

Crooked Brook. He needs to see her face, the pieces of Mary that are in there, the reminder that he is more than the ineffectual figurehead of a crumbling town. A husband, a father, a good man.

Amanda looks exasperated. Sobczak remembers she is pregnant, hormonal. Her lack of enthusiasm isn't necessarily a return to hostility and distance.

"What do you want, Dad?"

Why can't his daughter be happy to see him? These past few months have been heavenly—has reconciliation been wishful thinking? Deep down he knows she holds him accountable for Mary's death. It is unfair for Amanda to blame her father. And yet, he understands the primitive parts of people, the illogical responses that are gut-based, reactionary. Amanda will always be that little girl, watching helplessly as her mother fades away, the life drained from her face, puckered and sallow, orbital sockets sucked deep in the skull, hair falling out in clumps, a mangy old doll. A dad is supposed to be strong, be able to fix things, make them right. Sobczak could not. Life's disappointments do not always follow a logical arc. He needs to be compassionate, understanding, see it from his daughter's point of view. But he is hurt, too, and the words just come out.

"What did I do wrong?"

"Huh?"

"Sometimes you look at me like you hate me."

"I don't hate you." Amanda cocks her head, forcing a grin. "I'm tired." She gazes, forlorn, at her large belly. "You'd be tired too if you were carting around this cannonball. Come in."

Sobczak enters his daughter's home. Tonight feels different than it has recently, and he's not sure why. He feels ostracized, a stranger to his own child.

"Can I get you something to drink? Dad?"

Sobczak snaps out of his reflection, embarrassed. After spending so much time with Dr. Bakshir, he feels like he's turning into one of those whackadoodles who needs that sort of thing, therapy, talking about feelings, whining about the past. Get over it. Pull it together, big guy.

"I'm fine," he says. "Have you talked to Tom?"

"Not in a few hours." Amanda checks the clock on the stove. "Why?"

"A woman is missing." He's careful not to say "another woman." Sobczak knows Tom doesn't share the intimate, dirty details of the job with his wife. He wouldn't want to scare her. "Tracy Somerset."

Amanda opens her mouth like she has something pertinent to say. But she doesn't say anything, just folds her arms, clamps up.

"Do you know her?"

"We went to school together."

"Friends?"

"I wouldn't say that. Why are you asking me if I was friends with Tracy Somerset?" Amanda pours some water from her bottle.

Dr. Bakshir's conversation rolls around his head. He doesn't want to interrogate his own daughter, but she must have known about her friends' relationships, the fallout. She'd been at the Abbotts. Was Art capable of that level of violence? What did she think of Todd Norman when April started dating him?

"Amanda, I have to ask you something."

"Please don't make it about Mom. I've been thinking about her so much. I'm not sure I could take it."

"It's not about your mother. It's about April and Amber."

Amanda's reconciliatory patience disappears, replaced by ire. "You've *got* to be kidding me."

Sobczak is not sure how to broach what he wants to say, so he just comes out and says it. "Did they have ... a sexual relationship?"

Amanda responds like this is the most preposterous thing her father has ever said. "Jesus Christ. You too?" She spits out a laugh. It sounds mean, cruel. "Sorry. But you are so uptight about this stuff. Now you want to ask me questions about the three weeks my two best friends thought they were lesbians?" She is laughing at him. "Want to ask me about the time I made out with Shelby Stevens in tenth grade on a dare? How about when I caught Tom fingering April in the pool shed? Sixteen-year-olds are oversexed. We fuck."

"Stop," Sobczak says, holding up a hand.

"You are such a prig. That's what people do in Covenant. There's nothing else *to* do. Kids get fucked up, they screw. I know you think this place is a swell, all-American slice of apple pie. But news flash, Dad: every kid lies to their parents." She shakes her head. "Except maybe you. You probably really *were* at the library. Jesus."

"Do not take the Lord's name in—"

"Jesus! Jesus! Jesus fucking Christ!"

"You are acting like a child."

"I am? Listen to yourself, pretending you're a real cop. You hand out speeding tickets. Anything *really* goes wrong, you have *actual* police fix it." Amanda turns toward the general direction of an appliance displaying the time. "It's late. I have to go to bed. Tracy ran off with her serial killer boyfriend. Mystery solved. Let the police handle it, Dad."

"What did you think of Todd when April started dating him?"

"Nothing. I never met the guy. April dated Tom in high school. I didn't start dating Tom till *after* graduation in the fall, after they broke up. I went to prom with Corey Talbot. *Mom* took the pictures. You were too busy at the bar while I was fucking him in the back of the limo. Now get out!"

Walking into the dark, country air, Sobczak feels the gut punch. So certain, so proud his entire life, dreaming up an idyllic world that does not exist.

His cell buzzes. Joe Campbell.

"Got a car crash out here, Chief. Childer's Ravine." Sobczak doesn't want to hear what Joe says next. "Tracy Somerset."

"How is she?"

"Don't know," Joe says. "She's not here."

"What do you mean?"

"She ain't here. Timmy Alkas called me at the Getty. Him and Mangiafico were driving back from Ledyard, said there's a car in the ravine. I called but you didn't answer. Brought out the tow. Checked the registration. Back fender is crumped to hell."

"Hit and run?"

"Rolled over, hit a tree. There's blood on the wheel."

Sobczak snatches his cigarettes. "You miss any calls from Tom?"

"Nope. Nothing."

Sobczak gets the exact location of the crash, tells Joe to keep looking for Tracy. If she's injured, she can't be far.

Hanging up the phone, Sobczak tries Tom. Voicemail. He kills the motor and flicks the cigarette, huffing to his daughter's door.

"What is it now?" Amanda sniffs. "Have you been smoking?"

"We found Tracy's car. There's been an accident. Childer's Ravine. I need to get ahold of Tom. You have any idea where he could be?"

Amanda grabs her iPhone. "I can tell you exactly where he is."

"How?"

Amanda laughs as she pulls up the app, a locator that uses satellites to find people's cells. Sobczak watches as though it's magic.

Then his daughter's face grows pained, and she heads back inside, walks to the kitchen windows overlooking Shallow Lake.

"I thought you said the crash was by Childer's?"

"It was."

"That's the other side of the lake…"

Sobczak joins her at the window, water glinting in the moonlight. She points straight ahead. "He's over there."

Tom's cell signal bleeps at the site of Todd Norman's burned-down lakehouse.

CHAPTER FORTY-TWO

When their eyes meet and Tracy sees Todd, truly takes him in, she's forced to admit something she's known for a long time: she loves him. The way this realization washes over her cascades like a waterfall, envelopes, consumes her. And, by the way he returns her gaze, she can tell he feels the same. Tracy is certain that if the gags weren't in their mouths, pulled taut against dry lips, hands tied behind their backs, they'd shout it clear to the mountaintops.

Tracy smells the smoke, stronger now. Eyes adjusting to the darkness, she spies the collapsed structure, charred wood and chunks of cement block. The lakehouse basement, still standing after the fire.

How did they get here? Who did this?

Art Abbott.

The way the building has caved in on itself, the remaining space suffocates like a tomb. Tracy's heart rate spikes, as if her important organs have been vacuumed into her throat, sealed in space-saver plastic.

She meets Todd's eyes again. They do not show fear. Even without words, he conveys security. He wants her to know he will get them out of this.

Wood and timber are ripped, wrenched, cleared away. It takes a while for all the debris to be removed and a path to be cleared. Footsteps descend, into the darkness; hands grip dislodged pipes that now serve as handrails.

When Tracy sees Tom Kies, the kind deputy who was playing with her little boy the other day, her heartbeat slows, returning to normal, or at least a manageable pace. The good guys are here.

The relief does not last long.

Tom does not resemble the kind man from other day. This evening, he looks angry, wild, old, unstable.

For a long time he gesticulates between her and Todd, rabid snarl chewing his face ragged, a hungry junkyard dog. Where is the decent man stacking blocks, giggling with her son? The town cop everyone likes? Tom is supposed to be the nice one.

Tracy realizes he has no intention of cutting them free. Glimpses and snippets return, flashes of her barely conscious body dragged from the wreckage. Stars and treetops and mean eyes staring down.

Tom's sleeves are rolled up. His gun is out. He scrapes the barrel against his side, digging tip into thigh, eyes like a bus station hobo left too long in the cold, bugging, forever scanning the peripheral for signs of infiltration.

Tracy's shakes in her chair, toppling to the point of tipping over. She settles down, takes stock of the situation. Her hands are bound with string, twine, not tape or plastic. Secure, but not too tight. With a little more effort, minimal skin loss, she can slip this knot. What then?

"I never asked for any of this," Tom says, but he is not talking to either Todd or Tracy.

Tom paces the burnt basement of the lakehouse, mumbling to himself, cursing under his breath, a seething ball of crazy.

The strong antiseptic scent of a chilled New England night leaks through the collapsed remains.

She's almost slipped the knot, hands closer to free.

Tracy spies the praying mantis weathervane, the housewarming gift she brought Todd a few months ago, that afternoon she made the first move. Not far away, in the rubble. Its sharp point refracts the spring moonlight. It is time to make a move again.

Her hands have slithered out. Rope burned, chafed. She does not acknowledge the pain.

"I would never hurt anyone."

Shadows drip from above, a light source sweeping grounds.

Headlights. Another car is here. Tracy wants to believe this time it is good news. But she doesn't have faith. She and Todd are buried underground with a maniac cop talking to himself and swinging a gun. No one knows where they are. She can't shout for help. She has no way of knowing if the person, or persons, up above are on their side. It is up to her.

Tracy turns to Todd. His eyes never leave her face.

He wants her to know: everything will be all right.

Yes, she thinks. I know.

Tracy breaks free from the chair and scrambles for the weather-vane.

Chief Sobczak stops the car when he sees Tom's patrol vehicle, the front end mangled from the accident on Childer's Ridge. Amanda, who insisted on coming to find her husband, the father of her child, has no idea what Sobczak suspects.

"Stay here," he tells his daughter. "Do not get out of this car."

"Dad, what's going on?"

"Please, trust me. Okay?" It is too late to turn around and bring her home. "I am leaving the keys in the ignition. If something feels wrong, sounds wrong, you drive away, okay?"

"Dad, you're scaring me."

"Listen to me. Do what I say. This one time. Please. Slide into the driver seat. Any sign of trouble, drive away. Got it?"

She nods.

Climbing out of the car, Sobczak calls Ronson, tells her to bring cavalry. He creeps toward the collapsed structure.

A gunshot rings below, reverberating from the caverns and scattering the crows perched in tall trees.

CHAPTER FORTY-THREE

Sobczak spins and waves his arms, shouting for Amanda to go. Then he races around the blackened aftermath of the lakehouse until he sees an opening. Sig Sauer drawn, he yanks back the scorched wood, descending a set of decrepit stairs.

He pulls his flashlight, aghast by the scene.

Todd Norman is bound to a chair, gagged. His son-in-law Tom—his daughter's husband, the father of his soon-to-be grandchild—sits on the ground, a weathervane staked clear through his foot. A gun lies limply in his hand. He makes no effort to remove the stake, his vacant gaze staring at nothing. Tracy Somerset's back is pressed to a wall. She stands stone still, as though apprehensive to breathe. Above her head, a chunk of wood taken out by a bullet. Missed its mark by at least two feet.

Tracy starts shaking back and forth. Sobczak holds up his hand, urging her to stay calm. Blood pools beneath Tom's sole. He appears to be in shock.

"He kidnapped us!" Tracy shouts, pointing. "He ran my car off the road and tied me up." A chair lays toppled; twine restraints snake the dusty floor.

"Tom?" Sobczak steps tentatively, but his son-in-law will not look at him. He's sobbing, crying, chest-deflating heaves.

"He was going to kill us!" Tracy screams. "Todd and me. He's crazy!"

Sobczak holds his hand higher, pleads for Tracy to please, please, please be quiet and let him figure this out. Turning his attention to Todd, Sobczak has his pocketknife pulled, prepared to slice him free. He sees the handcuffs. Covenant issued. Sobczak fumbles for his belt, one eye on Tom, whose head slumps in shame. Sobczak sorts the keys, slips the lock, frees Norman. The metal cuffs clank to the ground.

Sobczak watches as the two lovers run to one another.

"Get out of here," he tells them. "Wait upstairs."

They crawl through the ruins, into the bright moonlight, until it is just Sobczak and Tom, whose fingers curl around the grip, muzzle scraping thigh, pistol tip gouging flesh.

Sobczak approaches, hand on handle, cautious but alert, like one does a wounded wild animal, a bobcat or a wolf caught in a trap. Except Tom isn't dangerous. Tom is a kind, good man.

"Tom?" Sobczak removes his hand from his gun, holsters it, makes a show of trust. "Just you and me. Son. Dad. Talk to me."

Sobczak backs up, places a flashlight on the old workbench. Tom turns. The face, serrated from spotlight, mirrors something sick, unholy. This isn't Tom.

Sobczak maintains a safe distance. "Talk to me."

"I love her. So much. I'll never stop."

"Amanda loves you too. That's why you have to put down the gun."

"I'm not going to hurt her!" Tom's whole head whips around, a violent, unnatural motion, skull rotating more than Sobczak would think humanly possible. Then again, this whole situation is surreal.

"You think I'd hurt her? She is carrying our child!" Tom begs for understanding, red eyes rimmed with tears; he has been crying a while. And longer than just tonight. This is the face of man at war with demons. How had Sobczak not seen it?

"Of course you won't hurt her."

"I ... knew. Tracy, she knew. Norman. Talo. That investigator, Jessup. You—you'd have figured it out soon enough. I thought if I fixed it..." Tom throws back his head. "Why would she want to come here?"

"Who?"

"April! This is all her fault!"

"What does April Abbott have to do with this?"

"Don't!" Tom points a finger, crimson rage choking his complexion. "Don't play me!"

"No one is playing anyone."

"You know about Amber!"

"Yes, I know. April and Amber had a relationship. No big deal. High school."

"A relationship? Ha! Maybe you really are as dumb as Amanda says you are." Tom's hand, the one holding the gun, starts to shake. Then stops. He starts to whine. "She cut herself in the truck. But it wasn't enough blood. She peed her pants..."

"Huh?"

"The shirt ... never mind. It's all wrong."

Tom is cracking, talking nonsense. Sobczak needs to contain the situation, not let it escalate. Don't let emotion in; do not make it personal. Clean, detached. "What happened tonight? Can you tell me that? Why were Tracy and Norman tied up?"

Tom starts convulsing again.

"Careful," Sobczak says, one hand out, the other back on his grip.

"We can still get you out of this. Don't do anything foolish. Your baby is going to need her father."

Tom stops crying long enough to attempt a smile.

"Where is Beiko Talo?"

Calm and peace wash over Tom.

Sobczak freezes. Time stands still.

"The woods behind the farm. By the playground on Cider Mill." Tom lifts the gun, sticks the muzzle beneath his chin. "That's where I buried her."

Sobczak takes a step to run, tries to lift his hands, scream, "Stop!"

He isn't quick enough.

Tom pulls the trigger.

CHAPTER FORTY-FOUR

Above ground, Holland police canvas the area. Only a few hundred yards from where they found Wendy Mortensen's lifeless body last year. Today, the property is flush again in a sea of blue canopied by the lush, green forest coming back to life. Unlike Sobczak's herky-jerk, makeshift team, Holland PD operates like a well-oiled machine. Dozens of police cordon off, wrap up, extract, isolate, coordinate, the precision with which they execute daunting.

Despite instructions, Sobczak's daughter, Amanda, never left. She stands off to the side, teary-eyed but brave-faced. She knows what happened in the basement. Sobczak told her first. Like everyone else, she has no answers. She observes the repercussions in shock, emotionless, stoic. How can one process this information?

Statements are given. Sobczak gets the story from Todd Norman and Tracy Somerset. These details do little to shine light on motivation, the big question of why. But the particulars will form the basis of the official report.

As Todd was leaving to pick up belongings in New York, before returning to start his new life with Tracy, Tom pulled him over, said he was taking him in for more questioning. Todd did not put up a fight when Tom slapped on the cuffs. He was then led to the lakehouse, where he was kept hostage alone in the burned-out basement. Until Tom ran Tracy off the road and locked her underground too.

Why? This is the question Sobczak keeps hammering, the one nobody can answer. Neither Tracy nor Todd offer more than speculation of prejudice, fruition of the promise that someone eventually would try to run Norman out of town. Sobczak is guilty of feeding this fear too. Some hotheaded local out for vengeance. It never once crossed his mind that lunatic would be Tom.

But when they pop the trunk to Tom's patrol car, police discover gasoline-soaked rags and accelerant used to start the fire. And when Sobczak contacts the impound yard, Joe Campbell confirms Tom signed out trucks on three separate occasions. One of which was, yes, a newer green Ford with a dented fender. Even as these details cement Tom's guilt, reason remains elusive. Only one man knows for sure what happened and why, and he, Tom Kies, son-in-law, husband, town deputy, soon-to-be father, just blew his fucking brains out.

Sobczak does not get to beg off because this is too personal. There is no one else to represent the interests of the town, the family. It is up to Sobczak. He owes it to Amanda and his unborn grandchild. He speaks with Ronson and her team, which again includes Detective Crasnick, reinstated. Sobczak repeats what he's learned, listens to their findings. He hopes hearing these discoveries aloud will shine light on the situation. It does not. Come morning sun, they will search the fields behind the barn on Cider Mill to recover Beiko Talo's remains.

No one will sleep much before then. Sobczak can't imagine Todd and Tracy getting any real rest. He knows Amanda won't. He wants to be there for her. But he has to drive with Ronson and Crasnick down to New Fairfield, where they wake a drowsy Marjorie Jessup, who reiterates everything Dr. Bakshir said. A father worried about his teenage daughter, drugs, sex, wild tendencies, a civil suit called off for fear it would sully reputations. End of story.

Back in Covenant, Sobczak does not go home. He drives by his daughter's house, but, seeing no lights on, returns to the precinct where he sits in his big office chair, unable to turn off his brain as he questions everything he thought he was sure of.

In the morning, before sunrise, before the dogs can be sent to canvas the fields behind the barn on Cider Mill, Ronson phones. The search has been called off. There is no need. They have found Beiko Talo.

She is alive.

CHAPTER FORTY-FIVE

Driving to the bus station in Springfield, Massachusetts, Sobczak and Ronson find conversation difficult on this stuffy, overcast spring day. The big question of motive has been replaced by a bigger one: why did Tom confess to killing a woman who isn't dead?

At the Peter Pan station, Beiko Talo steps off the bus. She carries herself much the same way Shannon O'Connor did, beaten down by the world, tattered backpack in tow. Beiko is skinny, skittish, in desperate need of affection, like a feral kitten found behind a gas station dumpster in the rain.

The three of them drive to the nearest restaurant, Denny's, where the two cops tell Beiko to order anything she wants. She is not shy about taking them up on their offer. Before asking pressing questions, they wait for her food to arrive, which Beiko pounces on, inhaling bacon and biscuits, sausage links and rubbery eggs that look like they've been sitting under a heat lamp for an hour.

Not until she's finished the last morsel does she begin her story.

It starts one cold, rainy night many months ago at the Meteorite, where a handsome man bought her a drink, paid her compliments, picked her up. Sobczak and Ronson show photos. Beiko instantly points to Tom Kies. Once they were in his truck, he restrained, blindfolded her. No, he didn't hurt her but she did cut her arm on some loose metal bracing. They drove to a house in the country. The Savage Hill home where Sobczak gave chase through the woods. He left her like that, tied up. The man never told Beiko who he was, or why he'd chosen her, but when he returned, she feared what he planned to do. He'd stalk around, pacing, muttering. She could hear him grumbling, talking to himself, asking questions, like he was arguing with a second person but there was no one else there. She says she was so scared she peed her pants. He left again. When he came back this time, he had a change of clothes. He told her not to scream. He removed the gag and blindfold but left her hands bound, said if she made a sound, he'd kill her. Then he told her to get in the truck.

Beiko expected to be driven somewhere even more remote, where the man would murder her, perhaps after raping her first. But he didn't. He drove to the bus station. He handed her five twenties, one hundred dollars, and a one-way bus ticket to Rutland, Vermont.

The last thing he said: "Don't come back to Connecticut or talk to anyone here. If I find out you have, I will shoot you. Your brother too."

"And you've been in Rutland this whole time?" Ronson asks.

"Yes." Until the Vermont state trooper showed up at her squat, Beiko had no idea she was missing.

"You never called your family?" Sobczak says.

"I didn't want him to hurt my brother. He made it clear to disappear. So I did. I made friends up there. It's easy, living the way I do."

Sobczak doesn't need clarification. Street kids have their own resources and networks.

For the rest of the morning, over more stacks of pancakes, mounds of fried potatoes, and thick, round hams, Beiko talks about Green Hills, Dr. Bakshir, April Abbott, Shannon O'Connor, and Wendy Mortensen. Some of it they already know. Wendy and the doctor. April and her love life. Some they wish they didn't. Beiko talks about herself, shares the harsh realities of her existence, the day-to-day hell of being homeless and unwanted, the times she frequented truck stops, turning tricks for quick cash, the arrests, the litany of fake identities used to evade prosecution. It's a sad story that tugs at the fabric of Sobczak's reality.

But it's her confirmation that Tom Kies, a man he thought of as son, did, in fact, commit these heinous crimes that rocks Sobczak's faith hardest.

When she is done, they offer to drive Beiko back to Hartford or Wellington to see her brother. But she says no. She will call and let Scott know she is okay. Maybe she'll phone her mother too. But she is never coming back to Connecticut.

The two cops walk her inside the Peter Pan depot, purchase the one-way ticket. She doesn't ask for more than that. They wait till she boards the bus. Then Beiko Talo is disappeared again.

CHAPTER FORTY-SIX

SUMMER

In the weeks that follow, Covenant buzzes with the news, and the once tranquil New England town is, again, headlining the major papers. *The Courant. The Herald. The Journal Inquirer.* Even makes the *Post.* Local Cop Suffers Psychotic Break, Kidnaps Woman, More Questions Than Answers.

Still, what caused Tom Kies, a man with no history of mental illness, to do the things he did remains elusive. There is speculation about the pressure of becoming a dad, reopening wounds of the fractured relationship he had with his own father. Cop fatigue, another popular theory. Some have Tom exacting revenge for the murder of his wife's best friend. Chief Sobczak does not buy any of this revisionist retelling, but without other theories to swap in their place, what can he do?

After the suicide, Sobczak re-visits Bakshir, brings him in, grills the doctor, foot to throat. No mercy. Uncle Bob too. He re-interviews Madge Jessup, presses harder. He would like to talk to Shannon O'Connor but, like Beiko Talo, she is gone again, living among the shadows. Still, the answers do not come.

Of course, as soon as Art Abbott returns from his thirteen-day Caribbean cruise, Sobczak hauls in the former DOT commissioner, interrogates him and his wife, their lawyer always present. These interviews are contentious, Art livid over the affront, the invasion and implications, Beverley sobbing at the mere mention of their dead daughter's name, Sobczak relentless. Art repeats his disdain for Todd Norman, who he rails against, reiterating certain guilt, and anyone who believes otherwise is a fool. He doesn't care about Tom Kies or the morons gullible enough to buy the BS. Norman killed April, and nothing anyone says will change his mind. Art does not talk about the past, his daughter's wild years, Amber Coit, any of it. He will speak of one subject: Todd Norman and the cops too stupid to catch him. Lawsuits are threatened. They are not carried out.

Sobczak does not stop investigating. Sobczak interviews old schoolmates of Tom, April, and Amber. These people, from Lisa Blake to Dave Mancini, are easy to get in touch with. Few leave Covenant, and all are willing to share what they know. A handful admits hearing rumors of a sexual relationship between April and Amber. The majority denies knowing anything. Neither response sheds light.

This forces Sobczak into a position he does not want to be in: having to interrogate his own daughter. As a father, he can only get so close. As an officer of the law, he has a job to do. Sobczak tries his best to remain impartial, ask the tough questions. Did she notice a change in Tom? ("Yes.") Did she start to suspect something was wrong? ("He was keeping odd hours. I thought it was because of the baby, panic about being a dad. I had no idea. I feel so stupid.") He records witness response, same as with the others. But watching his daughter, so close to giving birth, break down, cry and sob, proves more than the old cop can bear.

Despite a less than satisfying conclusion, Chief Sobczak is forced to agree with Holland County's official findings: the kidnappings of Beiko Talo, Todd Norman, and Tracy Somerset are the work of one man: Tom Kies.

Then the news dies down. There are worse crimes in other towns, far from Covenant, far from here. Slowly, things return to normal. Or as normal as they can ever be after something like this.

Following the investigation, Sobczak invites Amanda to come live with him. He is surprised when she says yes. Second chances in life are rare, and Sobczak is not going to make the same mistakes twice.

Todd, Tracy, and little Logan Coggins pack up and leave town, moving to New York, all lingering correspondence handled through Norman's attorney. As with Holland's rulings about the kidnappings, Sobczak has no choice but to live with the jury's decision. He may not like it. But he will not be another Art Abbott, stubbornly clinging to prejudice after the fact. Todd Norman, strange as it sounds, was just a man trying to honor his dead wife's memory. Sobczak feels uncomfortable when he tells himself this; doing so makes his insides churn, like egg salad left too long in the hot sun. But as Detective Ronson once said: the most logical conclusion is usually correct.

Sobczak wants to believe he wishes both Todd and Tracy well. This is hard to do.

Sobczak works through these lingering issues in his therapy sessions. To see a doctor, he must drive several towns over, to Farmington. There is no psychologist in Covenant, not since Dr. Bakshir, stripped of his license, moved away; and it's not like Sobczak would've seen him anyway.

In his work with Dr. Walker, Sobczak opens up in ways he didn't believe possible. It doesn't happen overnight. Sobczak is a guarded man. Fifty-seven years of living one way are not changed by a single event, however traumatic. But therapy is good for him. He likes Dr. Walker, who eventually breaks through the self-erected façades and walls. Sobczak sees with every ending there is a new beginning. Dr. Walker tells him it is okay to use hardships and defeats to grow; to use them as lessons; to become a better man. Sobczak, for the first time since Mary's death, truly grieves the loss of his wife. He accepts he hasn't allowed himself to experience the entire spectrum of emotions. Some nights, when no one is around, he lets himself cry.

Spring days creep into summer, that glorious time in southern New England where wet, dewy April gives way to the incubated temperatures of May; the sweet smells of newly mowed grass and ripe pollen drenching the air. During this time, Amanda and her father grow closer, the death of her husband the tragedy that unites them. Sobczak would've preferred other avenues, of course. But in losing her husband, Amanda gains a father. She finally understands the broader ramifications of Mary's death: she didn't just lose a mother; her dad lost his wife.

Watching his daughter blossom, belly full of life, is the most wondrous spectacle Sobczak has ever seen. Amanda, his baby girl who turned into the woman he never knew, has become accessible in ways he never thought possible. They talk. They plan for a future that, with each passing day, starts to seem real, hopeful, good again. He does not talk to Amanda about Tom, except in brief moments where pleasant memories are shared. A trip to Rocky Neck. An autumn afternoon spent picking apples. Memorable Christmases. Any attempts to dig deeper are met with abject hostility. The subject is the one area where Amanda remains inaccessible.

Then, in late May, hometown newspaper reporter Eric Serafin discovers the missing piece: a hotel clerk confirms that during early construction of the lakehouse, on those trips where Todd Norman did not join his wife, Tom and April spent several afternoons at the Coronet Motor Inn, a hotel on the edge of a neighboring town. Credit card statements confirm this. The reporter brings this to Sobczak, who asks him to sit on it while he talks to his daughter. Of course, Serafin agrees. Covenant takes care of its own.

These are the hardest conversations Sobczak has ever had to have with his daughter, ones in which he is forced to confront the grim reality that her dead husband had been carrying on an affair with her dead best friend. With all the Green Hills girls staying in touch, Sobczak now has his motive. Tom wanted to keep the affair quiet. He didn't have the heart to kill, though. He let Beiko go. He surely would've done the same with Todd and Tracy. The man was not a murderer.

Teary-eyed, Amanda shares what, to now, she has been reluctant to divulge: files from Tom's computer, love letters to April. Amanda says she discovered them after Tom's suicide, when she was boxing his belongings, but she didn't see the point in making these letters public, unwilling to smear her dead husband's memory any more. Amanda admits the two were in love in high school, and now the math adds up. It wasn't Todd Norman whom April began dating after Amber Coit; it was Tom, the boy she was infatuated with. Until Tom met Amanda. Sobczak doesn't have to wonder why he never knew this. The cancer consumed him too.

Sobczak can't understand how his instincts could be so off, how, as a police officer, he could be wrong about so much. But as difficult as it is for Sobczak, he can only imagine how horrible it must be for Amanda, knowing her husband had been living a secret double life.

Except the news produces the opposite effect. Whereas many in town had previously viewed Amanda in prickly terms, envious of her beauty and charms, she is now a sympathetic figure, that poor woman married to a monster.

Of course, Art Abbott refutes claims of an affair, calls allegations slander, threatens more lawsuits, demands the police bring Todd Norman to justice. Nothing comes of these threats.

Then news of Edgar Mace reaches town, and puts it all to rest.

Late one night, Sobczak receives the call.

"Long time no hear, Stephanie."

After perfunctory small talk, catching up on the weather and what it feels like to almost be a grandpa, Ronson gets to the real reason for reaching out.

"We have a confession on April Abbott's murder."

"Hold on."

It's ten o'clock, Amanda long asleep. The Covenant summer skies clear to Shallow Lake, stars shimmering off the water. Sobczak opens the glass slider and slips out to the back porch for a quick smoke. He strikes a match. Crickets chirp, frogs croak.

"Who?" he asks.

"Edgar Mace."

"Is that name supposed to sound familiar?"

"Doubt it. Originally from NYC. Lifelong crook and drifter drug addict. Cops picked up Mace one night at a single occupancy hotel on the Berlin Turnpike. The Coronet. Been living there the past five years. A rattrap. Last August, B and E at a pharmacy, before all this began. When the police ran him through the system, warrants from his days in New York popped up, connection to a possible homicide years ago. Mace was transferred, processed, stuck in Ricker's."

"When did he confess to killing April?"

"Not sure. Could've been as long as a year ago. I just learned about it. He'd been locked up for months and months. Case bumped, delayed, put on the back burner while the city dealt with worse people. DA struck a deal with Mace's public defender. In exchange for confessing to his assorted crimes—bank robbery, rape, murders—"

"Sounds like a delightful guy."

"—Edgar Mace will be spared the death penalty. One of these crimes: the killing of April Abbott. Mace says he broke in looking for money. Didn't think anyone was home. Saw April, panicked. Second-degree charge tacked on to the litany of transgressions. Not like it's going to matter."

"How's that?"

"A life sentence lasts only as long as you live. He was already never getting out. There's always pressure to solve cold cases, clear the books. Stick little gold stars on poster board, cross off another job well done."

The implication Mace may've been railroaded doesn't sit well with Sobczak but he wants to be done with this, almost wishes Ronson hadn't called. The wound was beginning to heal, and this latest news teases the scab.

"Thought you'd want to know," she says, waiting for a response. And when he has nothing to add: "Well, take care of yourself, Dwayne…"

"Wait," he says. "What was the name of the motel? On the Berlin Turnpike, where they picked up Mace?"

"The Coronet Motor Inn."

Hanging up, Sobczak digs through his files. He doesn't have to dig deep. The police arrested Edgar Mace at the same SRO hotel where Tom and April had their liaisons.

If Sobczak can't swallow the gin-joint location where Wendy Mortensen's body was found, he has a harder time dismissing the coincidence of Mace's living at the Coronet Motor Inn.

Sobczak declines to pursue this further. Tom is dead. April Abbott is dead. Who's left to ask? Moreover, Sobczak realizes he doesn't want to know the answer.

For Todd Norman, however, Mace's admission delivers a magic pill. In the newspapers, he goes from pariah to victim, his story of an intruder validated. Todd Norman, who'd maintained his innocence from day one, is welcomed back to the fold. He gets it all back. His old life. The job. The money. The respect. All of it. Like none of it ever happened.

Except it did.

Some days Sobczak considers reaching out to Norman to apologize. But he decides the kindest thing he can do is leave Todd and Tracy alone.

In June, Amanda gives birth to a baby girl.

A YEAR AND A HALF LATER

On a crisp late-October morning, Chief Sobczak is on his way to meet his daughter. He plans to take Doreen to the orchard to pick apples. Though his granddaughter isn't quite eighteen months old, she is Sobczak's world, a healing balm. Sobczak makes time for moments like this, something he didn't do enough of the first time around. Since the craziness of two winters ago, the biggest crime Covenant has seen was a hit and run outside the Dairy Queen. The victim suffered a broken ankle, the culprit, a retired schoolteacher/ wrestling coach, Jim Day, easily apprehended.

Most days are quiet, uneventful but not uninteresting. With the scent of autumn in the air, Sobczak can reflect, move forward. There's nothing to be gained from wallowing in the past. The future is now, and living in it is the only possibility for growth. He is making great progress with Dr. Walker.

After Doreen was born, Amanda sold her house, too many memories. She moved back in with her father. Amanda has started working, part time, for the town library. She likes to get out of the house a couple days a week. Sobczak is happy to babysit. He cherishes the time with his grandbaby. Ramon, the cop hired to replace Tom, proves more than capable during these absences.

Sitting in the Sunnyside Café, a cheap eats dinette, Sobczak is leafing through his mixed green salad, when sees a woman at the counter. Something about her is familiar. He can't quite place what. After several minutes, the name comes to him: Shannon O'Connor.

Part of him wants to forget, ignore, eat his uninspiring salad in peace; the other part of him, the police officer, knows he cannot do that.

"Hello, Shannon," Sobczak says, sidling up on the stool next to her.

The woman looks over. She does not seem well. The last time Sobczak talked to Shannon was at the old church. She didn't look well then. She appears far worse now. Though not even two years have passed, Shannon seems to have aged ten. Her hair is brittle and she smells like she hasn't showered in a while. She wears padded layers of hobo wool, and one of her shoes is held together with Duct tape. On the counter lies a few crinkled bills, evidence to the wait staff that the vagabond, indeed, has the funds to pay for her supper. It is clear she is still homeless, wandering, addicted.

To his surprise, Shannon recognizes him. A smile comes to her face. It is a sad smile all the same.

"Hello, Chief." Shannon is drinking a Coke and eating a grilled cheese sandwich. She puts down the sandwich, excited to talk, as if they are dear, old friends. "How have you been?"

Beside Shannon sits a ratty backpack. If Sobczak were to search that backpack, he would find contraband. But he does not ask to search, does not invent probable cause to justify doing so. He could not care less how Shannon O'Connor is killing herself.

He has questions about Dr. Bakshir's group and the Green Hills girls; about all the loose ends that did not tie off neatly with the revelation of Tom and April's affair or the confession of Edgar Mace.

This is a sign, Shannon's passing through town. She might pass through again. She might not. She might die before she gets the chance. This could be the final opportunity to track down Amber Coit, who, despite numerous attempts, has remained unreachable.

"I'm doing well," Sobczak says. He does not ask her the same.

Shannon attempts a smile, but aborts the effort, covering her mouth, as if just now aware of the shabby state of her custard-stained teeth.

"I was looking for you," he says. "Couple years back. We never got to follow up. Had questions for you. Still do."

Shannon shrugs. Her lifestyle doesn't afford time for these sorts of regrets. Sobczak sees the woman sitting beside him, used up, worn down; a woman who supports her habit the only way she can. This thought makes him sad. But he can't save the world. And he cannot save Shannon O'Connor.

"Can we talk about your time in Dr. Bakshir's group? At Green Hills—"

Before Sobczak can say more, she cuts him off. "I think about that time a lot. Everyone was so fucked up." She stops. "Sorry."

"It's okay." Let her curse all she wants. "How well did you know April Abbott?"

"I knew them all. We were good friends. April, Wendy, Beiko."

"Do you remember when April first got there? How did she interact with the others? Dr. Bakshir?"

Shannon ignores the question. "I remember more *after* Green Hills. We stayed friends. Not Wendy so much. But me, Beiko,

April." Shannon takes a bite of her sandwich, melted cheese sticking to chapped lips. "Mostly, I remember the night of the party."

"What party?"

Shannon shares a story. The story of a story, details of violence raining down from heaven, thunder and lightning, evil portals yawning in the earth. Her story is incoherent. There are devils and demons and lakes with rings of fire. Sobczak sits there and listens to the crazy lady ramble. Sometimes she makes sense. The time of year (November); the reason for the party (friends home from college). Most of the time she does not ("The devil is real, Chief Sobczak, I've met him."). This is what happens, Sobczak thinks, when someone surrenders to the wickedness of this world.

"Have you talked Uncle Bob?" he says. "Maybe you should go back to the church."

Shannon stares at a big, round clock on the wall, the hollow sound of her voice reverberating throughout the dull chamber. But she does not stop talking, about discovering secret messages written for her in books and on billboards, the battle waged for her soul, the tale she tells, bedlam fantasy. And Sobczak's about had enough. Until she mentions a barn, Cider Mill, and the old playground.

"What did you say?"

"I saw it all. It was late. Everyone else had gone home. They kept calling me Beiko." She laughs. "They didn't even know my name."

"Hold on, Shannon. When you saw what?"

"When the girl hit the other girl in the head with a rock."

"What girl?"

"I think she was jealous."

"Who? Which girl?"

"April's friend. I watched behind the barn. The boy helped bury the body." She stops, polishing off her grilled cheese and swiping away the crumbs. "They put her in the box."

"What box?"

"The one by the water. The fishing shed."

"What are you talking about?"

"I think she was still alive. Until the girl hit her again. She kept hitting her. There was a lot of blood."

Out the window, Sobczak sees Amanda pushing little Doreen in a stroller. Shannon shifts the dirty dollar bills to the center.

Amanda sees her father, waves, stuck in the cold, unable to get the stroller up the stairs alone.

Shannon turns to leave. Sobczak takes her arm. She shrieks at being touched, and the old chief jumps back. Out the window, Sobczak watches Amanda trying to pull the stroller up the stairs on her own, Doreen's little hands bright pink without mittens.

Instinctively, Sobczak wants to help his daughter, who has almost made it up the steps, one hand on the stroller, the other reaching to wedge open the door, wheels tipping back with the wind. Sobczak instructs Shannon not to move. He rushes to help his daughter, stroller wheels getting stuck on the bottom of the door. He pulls, starts to get frustrated, but seeing the fear in Amanda's eyes, retreats. Sobczak catches his breath, collects himself to try again. Deep breath. The wheel is caught. Dislodge, backtrack, redo. This time he is able to free the wheel. With delicate precision he assists in hoisting the stroller inside. Doreen is cooing. She is always so happy to see her grandpa.

When Sobczak turns around, Shannon O'Connor is gone.

The day in the orchard is wonderful. Doreen smiles, giggles, plays peek-a-boo. When Sobczak touches her little baby hands, she closes her plump fist around his fingers, so warm, so trusting. No better feeling on Earth.

They pick apples. Honeycrisp and Ginger Gold, Paula Reds and McIntosh. Amanda will press them later, mashing them into homemade baby food.

After Sobczak drops off his granddaughter at the library, he makes for the station, but finds himself detoured, driving through the cuts, into the deep, dark wood. The next thing he knows he is in the swamps of Covenant, at the far end of Shallow Lake, on Cider Mill Road.

Around the bend is the old playground, where he used to take Amanda when she was little. Access is gated now, road washed out. The water has saturated the ground, pulling down old structures, sucking them back inside the salted earth, what is left of the playground, cast-off metal parts floating in a sea of junkyard flotsam, corroded swing set legs and splintered teeter-totter seats.

He parks his car, slogs to the edge of the marsh, boots sucked, stuck in the mud. The sun is going down. Sobczak pulls his flashlight and scans ahead.

Getting around this part of the lake takes a long time. Sobczak frequently tells himself to forget about it, walk away. Get in the warm car. Time for dinner, visit with the family, catch a ballgame. Nightly beer, comfort, stability. Then to bed, get up, and do it all over again.

But he doesn't turn back. He keeps walking, forging ahead across these sinking fields.

The crumbling barn comes into view, and his beam settles on the box.

Like a shed but smaller. It too is falling down, wood rotted by the elements. People used to ice fish on this side of Shallow Lake. No one comes here anymore.

Sobczak steps around the sloppy reeds and rusted beer cans bobbing in low-tide silt, the earth slurping his soles with each uncertain step.

At the shed, he holds his breath and opens the door.

Empty.

Sobczak can turn around now. Go home, back to his little house, see his daughter, his grandbaby. It is a good life.

A harvest moon rises high on the crest, shining through the cracks. An open door dangles off its hinges.

Sobczak steps inside, stoops over. Nothing covers the ground but filth and sludge, algae scum that's risen to the top. He pauses a moment before falling to his knees. Sobczak sticks his hands in the soft sands. The ground gives, does not resist, and soon he is elbow deep in the mud.

He starts digging.

And he keeps digging.

And he doesn't stop until he works his fingers to the bone.

Acknowledgements

Thanks (as always) to my lovely wife, Justine, and my two boys, Holden and Jackson Kerouac (I know Daddy is a little strange; writing will do that to you). (Justine, someday I swear I will learn to be present and not living in a fantasy world twenty-three hours a day. Hell, as long as I'm promising the impossible, I'll be less moody too.)

And then the rest: Jason Pinter; James McGowan; Pam Stack and Liam Sweeny (without your big pats on the back I'm not sure I get through that stretch); all my terrific and supportive friends in the crime writing community; and last a HUGE SHOUT-OUT to those who let me borrow, tweak, and totally warp your identities—Duane Sobczak; Diana DelMartino; Lisa Blake; Tom Kies; and company.

ABOUT THE AUTHOR

Joe Clifford is the author of five novels in his bestselling, Anthony Award-nominated Jay Porter series, as well as the acclaimed addiction memoir *Junkie Love*.

He lives in the Bay Area with his wife and two sons. Visit him at www.joeclifford.com and follow him at @joeclifford23.